Oh!

Oh!

Twenty-seven Stories

LEON ROOKE

TORONTO

Exile Editions
1997

This edition is published by Exile Editions Limited,
20 Dale Avenue, Toronto, Ontario, Canada   M4W 1K4

Sales Distribution:
General Distribution Services
30 Lesmill Road
Don Mills, ON
M3B 2T6
1-800-387-0172

Layout and Design by *MICHAEL P. CALLAGHAN*
Composed and Typeset at *MOONS OF JUPITER, TORONTO*
Printed and Bound by *AMPERSAND PRINTING, GUELPH*
Cover Photograph by *GREGORY DRU*
Author's Photograph by *JOHN REEVES*

The publisher wishes to acknowledge the assis-
tance toward publication of the Canada Council
and the Ontario Arts Council.

The Canada Council
Conseil des Arts du Canada

Some of these stories appeared, often in different form, in *The
Antioch Review, TriQuarterly, American Voice, Ploughshares,
Fiction International, StoryQuarterly, Third Coast, The North
Carolina Review, Exile, Quarry, This Magazine, Prairie Fire, The
New Quarterly, The Malahat Review,* and in the anthologies
Writing Home, Stag Line, Paper Guitar, and *The American Story:
The Best of Story Quarterly.*

Several appear in the author's book, *Arte,* Edizioni del Bradipo,
Lugo, Italy, 1997.

Thanks to editors, all.

ISBN 1-55096-178-0

This book
is for Branko Gorjup and Francesca Valente

Stories

GYPSY ART

Young Fazzini was apprenticed to an artist who made incredible boxes that were like airy castles, each with a thousand rooms and baffling appendages. One day the master said to Fazzini, "You don't understand art, or boxes, or castles. You need to run with gypsies and lose yourself in amazing adventures." At home Fazzini's parents were ever bickering at him. "Grow up," they said. "Avail yourself of every opportunity. Let not the smallest blade of grass go unnoticed." In other words, hit the road. So Fazzini struck off on the road, eager for any adventure. On the road Fazzini met a gypsy woman, big-boned and unruly. The woman took Fazzini to her encampment. He was the love of her life, she said, and requested the other gypsies refrain from spitting at him. Within the hour they were married. Fazzini could not believe his luck. He had been in love before, though never so deliriously. His wife tired herself out, proclaiming her love. They fell asleep entwined. All the gypsies were entwined one with another, Fazzini and his own gypsy somewhere in the middle. Then the gypsies hit the road. Fazzini had a headache. He wondered why it was he had awakened under the sour apple trees and where the gypsies had gone. Later on he realized his toe must be broken, since walking was such a difficulty. The sun was unbearable and the only shade in the vicinity was taken up with wild animals which hissed at him when he neared. Fazzini fashioned crude crutches from the branches of the apple tree. The crutches hurt, his underarms were raw, but at least he could walk. Fazzini had been warned as a youth to avoid gypsies, but hadn't paid attention. He had felt contempt in those days for anyone so arrogant as to believe their calling in life was to issue advice. How many the times his mother had slapped his face? He did not want to go home again, but now he was going home because this adventure on the road had not worked out as planned. He had taken the wrong road. Next time he met a gypsy

woman on the road he would know better. He wouldn't
be so easy to fool. From time to time he rested by the
road under the shade of more sour apple trees. Life
would be all right, God, he thought, if you will deliver
me a little food. A nice prosciutto would be divine. A
bottle of vino, dear God, as well. Lately Fazzini had been
talking to God as though God was a sweet woman. It
paid to compliment Her, although in his personal opinion a good cattolico should not advertise the fact.
Deeply religious people should keep their feelings to
themselves. The crutches felt fine now; such an ungrate-
ful fellow he had been, complaining endlessly of every
triviality. His toe had miraculously healed. It was a
magic toe. People he passed on the road were of two
sorts, civil or uncivil. They spat at him, or sought to set
him off in opposing directions. More than one person
offered the opinion that he appeared able-bodied. Why
did he not secure meaningful employment? Fazzini
trudged on; he had many a mile to traverse, and ambi-
tion was his guide. He was a mature fellow now — no
longer the crass fool. If his family saw him they would
be amazed. On a high meadow Fazzini discerned an
encampment of gypsies. He hid behind bushes, throwing rocks into their camp. When they ran at him he also
ran. Fazzini and gypsies just did not get along. "You
gypsies," he said to them, "are the dregs of the earth."
The maddened gypsies threw Fazzini in the river. This
was round about the Spesso Fumo lowlands where the
Spesso Fumo River finally allows itself to be seen. The
gypsies jumped into the river themselves. They washed
themselves, they sang. A gypsy with an ugly bruise on
his forehead embraced Fazzini constantly. "Your stones
have knocked sense into my head," this man said. "You
shall henceforth be known as the King of the Gypsies."
But once Fazzini was in their camp the gypsy women
swore at him. They spat. They made him cook their
gypsy food and wash their gypsy clothes. Even their
gypsy feet. They made him tend the horses and dogs.
They were at him every minute. The gypsies not bad-
gering him were singing gypsy songs. Fazzini, in all his
life, had never heard such ugly, uninspiring songs. One

night when all the gypsies were asleep Fazzini crawled away from the gypsy camp on his hands and knees. He crawled until his knees bled. All along the escape route he was pursued by an insane crew of black flies. After a time he no longer bothered with the ticks pricking at his scalp. He was hungry and cold. He talked sweetly to his sweetheart God, complimenting Her at length on Her fine dress, but God wasn't fooled. She knew he was speaking only to hear his own voice. He changed his voice, which did not fool Her either. She wore fine jewels, though, and was quite radiant. She looked to him like She was on Her way to a party. His hands burned. All that lye soap that the gypsies had made him boil. So many boiling pots, so many pots that Fazzini was made to stir. Gooey stuff, hard on the limbs. His very elbows ached. The gypsies simply did not know how to live. They knew no other life. The refineries of life were unknown to them. Plus, babies everywhere, always crying, and only Fazzini to care for them. Crawling babies that went about on all fours until on their own accord they uprighted themselves and pranced about as mature gypsies yodeling senseless gypsy songs. It was sickening, if you wanted to know the truth. But what did Fazzini care? He was free of their lot now. He'd learned a thing or two. He had experience under his belt which he meant to put to good use. He wished his family could see him now. They would be amazed. Finally Fazzini decided he would stand up. Why all that crawling anyway? He guessed he'd crawled a million miles. Now it was raining; the heavens pouring down. What's that? Oh my God, yes, there's a road! Now, Fazzini thought, I know where I am. No more of this bush life for me. Immediately upon taking to the road, Fazzini found himself intercepted by an unruly gang of men who appeared out of nowhere. They wore slickers, carried umbrellas, did not heed the ferocious heavens, the pelting rain. This gang wanted right out to know whether Fazzini had seen anywhere in the vicinity a dirty band of roving gypsies. "Speak up," they said, "and we'll go easy on you." They slapped Fazzini around. They punched him one way and another. This gang, truly they were enraged.

You trust a gypsy at your peril, they told him. They were on foot, they said, because the gypsies had stolen their wagons. Oh, and their horses too. And the womenfolk. The gypsies had set fire to their haystacks. They'd raided every hen coop and carried away good God-fearing children, to raise these children as mangy gypsies. The gang had been on the gypsies' trail for weeks. Now they were close. They could smell gypsies nearby. Come to that, Fazzini smelt like a gypsy himself. "If you want to know why we are swatting you, that is why." Fazzini objected. "I hate gypsies more than you," he said. "Those gypsies just have no respect for the common decencies. They are godless creatures. You would not believe the bizarre acts they had me perform. Chickens? Who was made to pluck those chickens? Your womenfolk? Forget your womenfolk. Already they are more the gypsy than the gypsies are themselves." Fazzini felt proud of himself. His tale of woe worked this gang of roughcuts into a frenzied state. They proclaimed their own virtues endlessly, firing off muskets right and left. Fazzini raised one finger in the air, and pointed the way the wind was blowing. Go that way, he said. You'll find those scurvy gypsies before the sun goes down. The gang was so enlivened by this news they decided then and there to have a party. To celebrate this turn in their fate, why not? Unloosen the jugs. Everybody have a good drink to make us mean, then it's onward to sweet revenge. One jug led to another and soon all were so wildly drunk not one of them, including Fazzini, could stand up. Fazzini did not know how it happened: one second he was by the river, his pee grandly arching, and the next second he was in the drink. He was in the Spesso Fumo River, which had finally showed itself. Fazzini had to swim like a rat. Agony, you want to know the truth. So many times he nearly perished. Glub-glub, Fazzini the drowned rodent. The river at flood stage, current sweeping him along. Debris flowing by him: rooftops, pigs, cows, fowl. The whole of the once dry earth flowing with him. He clutched at mud and wet grass, ferns, katydids, sprig of daffodil; not so easy was it getting ashore. He drifted miles and miles and no longer knew where he was. Finally the heavens relented, the rain softened, he was at eddy in a swirling pool. Fazzini cried out; the object he had been clinging to over the past hours, clinging to for dear life, was a swollen dead man. Oh, dear God, Fazzini said. Oh, my Lord, I love Your shoes. What pretty feet! Bella! Bella! He tried pushing the dead man away — *go! go!* — but the eddy repeatedly floated the dead body back at him. The arms of the dead man flung themselves over his shoulders, the face time and time again tried kissing him. It tried crawling itself up over him. Rape! Fazzini thought. That dead man means raping me. What a come-down. May I never know tranquillity? All I wanted from this world was a dignified life. A little something to eat now and then. A warm bed. Flotsam, foam, and the dead man encircled him. Fazzini's legs dangled uselessly in the river's depths. "What's that?" Fazzini asked. "There, swimming by?" A giant turtle. Well, dear God. Fazzini threw himself at the turtle, catching its shell on either side. Astonished, the turtle whipped back its head. Its jaws clamped entirely through one of Fazzini's hands. The turtle dived and twisted in a frenzy of disbelief. Its feet clawed; it dived, it surfaced, it flipped over and over and over. It was a turtle thoroughly deranged. Fazzini's head reposed on the shell's muck. The turtle was now away from the eddy. Fazzini had courage; he was fighting for his life; he held on. He must have slept. When he opened his eyes the sun was bright, he felt warmth. He was akimbo upon the silent earth. Don't just lie there. Show your mettle, Fazzini told himself. You've endured the worst patch. Trudge, Trudge. A thicket? A thicket, yes, so many vines and trees. So many squirrels jumping tree to tree. So many snakes. "And who," Fazzini asked of the black flies, "invited you?" Eventually Fazzini, trudging, saw a campfire at blaze within a clearing; he trudged towards it. He looked first for wagons but saw no wagons. The campers were not gypsies, then; his luck was looking up. In fact, the campfire was deserted, despite the flaring fire, cinders volleying to the heavens. I'll just warm myself, Fazzini thought. Yoo-hoo! I wonder if they have any grub. Fazzini warmed himself. He felt so much better now. Someone had been even nice enough to leave a nice green tent, neatly propped. My lucky day, Fazzini thought. He lifted the tent flap, and immediately felt faint. In a swoon, hot all over. Oh, God, he said, I love Your ears, Your nose, Your beautiful lips. Have I spoken of Your most incredible knees, Your ankles, Your fine, firm buttocks? "Grr and crunch," the beast in front of him said. Yikes! A giant black, grunting, creature stared back at him. Fazzini smelt it. It had a terrible smell reminiscent of smelly feet. The creature was busy eating something. It looked him over closely, but went on eating. A small fold-up desk had been set up inside the tent. On the desk was spread a large map. An explorer's jacket hung from a nail on the centre pole. Fazzini took the jacket; he took the map, which felt oily. Oh, my God, English biscuits! He quickly took these; he filled his mouth with biscuits. "Just go on," he told the beast, "with what you are doing." The creature nodded sagely. He and the beast were pals. The beast seemed not to mind what Fazzini took. It went on eating. It slurped and chomped, blood and gore dribbling from its chin and paws; the beast flung out one arm, offering Fazzini a long, dripping bone. Want some? Fazzini wasn't tempted. The biscuits had filled him. The beast watched him steadily, ever with a benign air. Afterwards, when the beast endeavored to embrace him, Fazzini ran. That beast is worse than the gypsies, Fazzini thought. I'm not coupling with bears. Oh, Mother in heaven, how many pedestals must I set You upon? Never mind, my Darling. I will scour the land, mend each broken toe, or nose, or thumb. Each eyelid. He blundered through the thicket. He felt brave. Renewed. He wished his family could see him now; they'd take back more than one of their previous harsh words. Soon Fazzini realized he was hearing music. He turned one direction and another. He whipped his head about. He dropped down and lay first one ear and then another against the cold earth. Music wafted his way from every direction. It was all the same music, gypsy music. By my life, Fazzini thought, those gypsies are everywhere! Well, he'd avoid them. A person could only accept gypsy company for so long.

Gypsies are entirely too demanding. One desires one's own kind, Fazzini thought. That is how God has made the earth. Let the gypsies stay to their domain and I will cling to mine. Fazzini went on talking to himself like that. After his ordeals, why not? Plus, black flies were after him again. Ticks burrowing. Big fat pussy ticks in his scalp, mean black flat buggers everywhere else. His hand numb from the turtle's snapping jaws. His hand ugly, throbbing, heated up big as a drum. I'll get that tended to, Fazzini thought. You need not worry on my account. "I like Your hat, God," Fazzini said. "That's a splendid hat. Let no one tell You different. Create Your own fashion, I say. Pay no attention to what the rabble say. Your hair looks wonderful too. And such lovely skin. I'll grant You the rouge is heavy, someone would say overdone, but I like it. Please Yourself, that's what Fazzini says." He fell silent. No need to get carried away; no need to laver on the compliments with a spoon. There was something to be said for straight talk. But why run the risk? When had straight-talking got him anywhere? It had landed him with gypsies, that's what straight talk had done. Onwards now. Trudge, trudge. In his new jacket. You'd think just once God would compliment him. *Say, now, Fazzini, lad! That's a spiffy jacket! Aren't you the cheeky one! Brava, brava!* Indeed, Fazzini's view was that he cut a fine figure. Who wouldn't think so? Anyone with a fair gaze would be bound to be impressed. When he reached society, the quality people would see at a glance the kind of man he was. Style would carry the day. A soldier of fortune, yes! Tides betide. Before the moon set, without a doubt he would meet and marry a beautiful woman, marry and settle down. High time too, Fazzini thought. Time to shy away from this rover life, this existence without meat or merit. Yes, high time. It had taken him a long time to recognize the flaws in his character; now he was determined to set himself to mending these flaws. Youth, what did youth know? Sooner or later a person had to grow up. You had to work your way through it, didn't you? "Well, mother dear," Fazzini said, "that's my advice." Black flies coated his face; why flit here and there when already they'd found hospitable lodging for the night? First order of business, when he reached the city, was to do something about those flies. Then to the vineyard to slacken his thirst. To the Music Hall. All those high kicks, those heaving bosoms, all those naked legs! Yes, yes, if you would be so kind! *Cacciucco alla livornese,* why not? He'd want a good song to cheer him up. Not this crude gypsy zing-a-ling. Then to the studio of his artist friend, to re-apprentice himself. He too could build incredible boxes now, boxes each with a thousand rooms and anterooms, catacombs and towers, cat walks connecting one tower to another, and a thousand secret chambers holding incredible adventure behind every door. But, wait, here he was limping again. Those old war wounds, his broken toe, the bloated arm, each aching like the very devil. And beasts of the wild over there under sour apple trees consuming every inch of shade. Plus here came a caravan of unruly gypsies — gypsies astride mules, riding creaking wagons, herding along an endless sweep of ponies, lambs, swine, acrobatic goats, caged monkeys, plumed birds that hopped on one leg. Up there, putting bite to the lead reins, a fine, slinky-eyed woman, bare-breasted, under a wilderness of hair, one and then another luscious eye winking wickedly at him.

"Tell your fortune, good-looking. Read your future? Today only, special price!"

"Why, hello there," Fazzini said. "Gypsies, are you? Oh, I've known a gypsy or two in my life. Salt of the earth. My heavens, I even married one. Big-boned and unruly, brimming over with love. Are you by chance going my way?"

"Sure, sure," the gypsies said. "Going here, going there! Today only, we are on our way to our airy castle in the sky. Much gold there, pig roasts, love eternal, wine that flows as from a waterfall."

The gypsies saw he was a nervy deluded fellow, the innocent romantic. His face encrusted, possibly suffering a fracture of the larynx; just a plain pasty-faced boy too long adrift from home.

They placed him inside a cage filled with chickens, outfitting him with a long blade, a sack to catch the feathers.

Art, Fazzini thought. Art is my life.

I love Your smile, he said to God. I love the rustle of Your skirts, the sun in Your hair, Your gay laughter, the fragrance of Your lilac-scented skin.

He would pluck feathers from the confused hysterical birds; he would go at this task feather by feather. The simple life is not to be disavowed.

Save me, my Darling. I lick the very sweat of Thy hand.

SIDEBAR TO THE JUDICIARY PROCEEDINGS, THE NURNBERG WAR TRIALS, NOVEMBER, 1945

[The Speaker, in black judicial robes, reclines in an easy chair, occasionally sipping from a cognac glass. Behind him can be seen the flags of the victorious nations. Lights throw shadows from the cutout figures who comprise his audience.]

The craniologist who came to measure Heidegger's brain was made to stand in the rain by the front step while Elfride went to ask the famous philosopher would he be willing.

Heidegger was in his study, surrounded by a pile of open books. He told Elfride not to be absurd. He was not to be disturbed.

Elfride told her husband that the craniologist had said the task would only take a minute. At this Heidegger laughed a scornful laugh. "We shall see about that," he said. Elfride had to jump aside, so quickly did he exit the room.

The craniologist, no fool, had found partial protection from the rain under the roof's overhang. Heidegger, striding fast, was outside in the rain himself before he knew it — whipping his head about in search of the visitor.

He did not see the craniologist until the man spoke. "Over here."

Already they were both drenched.

What the craniologist saw was a short, thick-waisted man with a heavy face, a large, squarish brow, jet black hair, and an untended moustache patterned after the Fuhrer's.

The philosopher saw a stringbean mortician, astoundingly advanced in years, possessing an overlarge head.

Elfride had taken up a stance in the doorway, which Heidegger, as often was the case, had left open. The great man could not be bothered with closing doors. She looked at the two of them standing under the overhang, and at the rain splattering their shoes and the cuffs of their pants, and did not say to them what it occurred to her to say — that even dogs knew enough to come in out of the rain.

The craniologist was explaining his intentions.

Heidegger took the visitor to be a man of bureaucratic dullness, inflated with a sense of his own importance. This made the philosopher impatient and rude.

As for the craniologist, Goebbels's office had told him the Magus likely would be difficult — aloof, brusque, opinionated — and that he should persevere and endeavor not to offend, as Heidegger was under consideration for an exalted position within the Party. He had not expected a man of such small stature.

Elfride remained in the doorway, biting at a hangnail, but with an air that suggested she thought herself every bit as important as them.

"If you want anything," she said, "you will let me know. But I am not bringing my good china out here in the rain."

The craniologist stood up straighter. He told her that he had not come here to eat.

Heidegger told Elfride to stop bothering them with her trivialities.

After showing both of them — by a look that flooded her face — how horrified their comments made her feel, Elfride disappeared behind the slammed door.

"Women," the craniologist said, "have small brains."

Heidegger did not leap to his wife's defense.

He was thinking that the craniologist had by far the privileged spot under the roof's overhang. Hardly any rain was falling on him. He was thinking that their shoes were wet and dirty and now Elfride was unlikely to allow either of them inside unless they entered in stocking feet. He could not abide the thought of having a stocking-footed craniologist walking over his polished floors and sitting in his chairs.

It began raining harder.

"Eva, I've heard," said Heidegger, "has intelligence."

Heidegger intended this statement as a test of the craniologist's own intelligence. He was not going to waste his time out here in the rain talking to an idiot. Eva *Who? Which* Eva? Those were his two questions, and the stuffy craniologist would either know the answer or not know the answer.

But the craniologist was not aswim in the dark.

"Eva has brains," the man said. "I stand corrected."

Heidegger scrutinized the craniologist's features more closely. *I stand corrected* were not words he could ever imagine himself uttering, any more than he could imagine the Fuhrer uttering them; it proved that the craniologist, however much he wore the mask of public esteem, perceived in his heart that he was very much an underling.

"Eva Braun and the Fuhrer are properly suited to each other," the craniologist said.

Heidegger had the impression the man was suggesting he had dinner with the Fuhrer and his darling every evening.

"Move a little," Heidegger said, elbowing the man.

But the craniologist did not move.

Every now and then the wind was blowing the rain's spray into their faces.

The Heidegger house was set well away from the street. Under the thick hedgerow by the street a deformed cat, refused by the neighborhood, was trying to find a dry spot. The soaked cat, to Heidegger's eyes, had a slimy look. The cat had been tormenting him for months by hopping up on the outside sill of his study and moaning at him.

"The effect this rain is having on our soldiers at the front is God's own misery," Heidegger said.

It had been raining in Freiburg and over all of Europe for a full three weeks. There were times when Heidegger felt he would never again see spring. He longed for his cabin in the Black Forest, at Todtnauberg. It was isolated there.

At Todtnauberg he could don Swabian peasant dress, brew tea on the stove, and think.

The craniologist had no comment to make on the war effort.

The craniologist had with him a leather satchel in which he obviously transported the tools of his trade.

He seemed concerned that the satchel was getting wet. A moment ago the satchel was between his legs; now he tried stuffing it beneath his coat, though the satchel was much too large.

"How do you measure your brains?" Heidegger asked.

The craniologist looked surprised. He looked as though he thought this was information which should be under everyone's province.

"Various means," he said.

Heidegger snorted; he hated the vague.

"By eye, by feel, by—"

The cat abandoned the hedge in a run; midway across the grass, it stopped; then it scurried off in a new direction.

Good, Heidegger thought. The cat had developed a limp.

A week before, the cat had given birth to a single kitten.

"A cloth tape," the craniologist said, hardly opening his lips.

"Cloth or wood or German steel," said Heidegger, "you do not have measuring apparatus of sufficient girth to measure *Heidegger's* brain."

The craniologist smirked.

Heidegger told him: "The time that lapses between one Heidegger thought and another can not be measured any more than the content of the thoughts themselves can."

It seemed to Heidegger that the craniologist sneered. Someone, he thought, should report this man.

"I show you two spoons," the philosopher said. "One filled with lead, the other with gold. In the dark you would say both weighed the same."

"I beg your pardon," the craniologist said. "That is not true."

Heidegger's mouth dropped open. Not since old Husserl, whom he reviled with all his heart, had anyone spoken so to him.

Edmund Husserl, right here in Freiburg, had invented phenomenology; Heidegger, celebrated, had but scratched the bare bones of time and being.

The rain was splattering up as high as their knees now. His shoes were sodden.

The critique of words by yet more words, Heidegger thought. Before Heidegger that is all philosophy was.

"When I sleep my brain swells enormously," he said. "Elfride has noticed this. She has the visual proof not only of her own eyes but also in the wear and tear of my pillow."

The craniologist nodded. The statement did not seem to amaze him.

"When I am teaching, or talking to certain people — Lowith, for instance, in the old days — I can feel my brain swelling large as a melon. If I sat on a wall you would think me Humpty-Dumpty."

Elfride would have smiled at this joke; the craniologist didn't.

"The Heidegger brain is the potentate of the metaphysical," Heidegger said. "How can you hope to measure the metaphysical, when Heidegger has himself grappled with it each instant of his life? Even if your cloth tapes could span the metaphysical the hand meant to hold those tapes could not hold the volume of tapes required. Your cloth tape could not even span so much as the Greeks who relentlessly toil inside Heidegger's brain. How could you measure the one brain in the world which alone in the world charts the scope of time and being?"

"I can," the craniologist said.

Heidegger laughed. He was unaccustomed to doing so. His laugh sounded like a snarl.

The cat was meowing in the rain. Heidegger could not determine where it was meowing from. The cat was skin and bones. What kept it alive was a mystery.

"You could set around me a ring of buckets and I could pour my strange syntax into those buckets but you could never bring enough buckets to hold even my syntactical leavings."

A tick had developed at one corner of the craniologist's thin mouth.

"Am I losing you?" Heidegger asked.

A phrase hopped into Heidegger's brain: *from me and yet from beyond me.* Later he would endeavor to sort out what this meant.

The craniologist closed his eyes, as though in pain.

In his research on Heidegger he had learned that the philosopher had spent the summer of 1918, twenty-nine years old, as a soldier in the Verdun district. He had hoisted and studied balloons. With data gleaned from these balloons weather forecasts had been made, necessary for the success of poison gas attacks.

The philosopher had not shown himself gifted. After two months influential friends had finagled his release.

"Look here at this shoe," Heidegger said, removing the same from his left foot.

"I don't want to look at your stupid shoe," the craniologist said.

Stupid? Heidegger's eyebrows lifted. The man was insufferable. Even so, Heidegger persevered.

"Notice how the heel of this shoe has worn inwards. Now look at this other shoe."

He removed his other shoe. His feet sank a few inches into the wet soil.

"The heels of both of these shoes, and the soles as well, are worn to the inside. How I walk is a thing you can measure but what this means, the relationship between the walking habit and the workings of the brain, is a thing your cloth tapes can not reveal."

Heidegger paused, tapping a stiff finger hard against his brow. He could feel his brain expanding, and wondered whether the craniologist would have the wit to notice.

The craniologist looked at him. Heidegger looked away. He had never with ease looked into another person's eyes. Something he saw in those eyes was disturbing to him. Elfride sometimes gripped his collar and shook him. "Look at me!" she would say. "Look at me!"

In his family they had never looked at each other; in that regard he was a victim of his humble origins.

"Also," Heidegger went on. "Also, look how worn both these soles are up in the toe area. You likely have never seen this before, not even in Eva Braun or the Fuhrer. When Heidegger has a thought, a brain wave — about nothingness, to mention but one example — his toes dig holes through the toughest leather. Before he knows it his toes are leaving bloody imprints on the streets. Every other month he requires new shoes. It is driving Elfride insane. But that, my friend, is called concentration. It is called *thinking*."

The craniologist looked to the ground where Heidegger was standing. He looked at the wet black socks on Heidegger's feet, at his narrow white ankles.

At their feet lay a bed of empty shells, black walnuts left by squirrels.

The door opened and they heard Elfride say, "Put your shoes back on, Martin. There's a war on. I am not going to spend the whole of my life tending to a sick man."

The cat appeared from nowhere, streaking between Elfride's legs into the house.

Elfride screamed.

The door slammed.

The craniologist flattened his satchel, then tried buttoning his raincoat over it.

"In the cat world which has the biggest brain?" asked Heidegger.

The craniologist did not answer. He was listening to raucous sounds emanating from the house.

A week ago, the pregnant cat had assumed its position on the sill outside Heidegger's study. It had stalked back and forth and scratched at the screen, meowing ferociously. Heidegger had just scribbled in his notebook, *No shelter within the truth of being.* Then the cat had again showed up, a slick, black, ugly kitten, newly born, dangling from its jaws. The kitten's entire head was in the cat's mouth. With its claws the cat ripped a hole in the screen. It stepped through and settled itself down in that space between the screen and the window. Heidegger had just written, *Elfride's stomach was last night made queasy by wine.*

The ridiculous cat, fortunately, had produced but one very small kitten. Horrified, Heidegger had watched it eat a second one, or the afterbirth.

"How do the Jews fare?" Heidegger asked the craniologist.

The craniologist remained silent.

"Who sent you?" Heidegger asked.

"I am not permitted to disclose that information," the craniologist said.

"What is your name?"

"That too is confidential," the craniologist said.

"Goebbels?" asked Heidegger. "Or someone higher?"

The craniologist's face remained indifferent to these questions.

"The Fuhrer sent you?"

The craniologist pressed himself flatter against the building.

"I have every right to know," said Heidegger. "The higher the office you represent the less reason I have to question your credentials. You will agree there are a lot of crackpots running about."

It seemed to Heidegger that the craniologist did agree to this.

For a moment they watched the rain. Heidegger put his shoes back on. The trees were heavy with rain. Rain was coursing down the street beyond the hedge and flowing in thick grey curtains down the facades of the facing buildings.

From his cabin windows at Todtnauberg Heidegger had a sweet view of the Swiss Alps.

The Swiss were a durable people but theirs was not a fated nation.

At Todtnauberg he could wear knickerbockers and his peasant caps. He could tread the slopes on snow shoes.

At Todtnauberg, until recently, he had enjoyed the company of Hannah Arendt.

Christmas time two years ago he and Hannah had unsuccessfully attempted cooking a goose dinner.

The craniologist was studying him; Heidegger caught himself licking his moustache. He had got into this habit lately, one infuriating to Elfride, whose own alienating habits were confined to those inflicted upon her by her father, the high-command Prussian officer. A dozen times each day he would hear her saying, "How did these crumbs get on the table!" She saw imaginary ants everywhere. She saluted the stove, the cupboards, the light fixtures. She could stand for hours on end mesmerized by the sound and sight of water running in the kitchen faucet.

Her taut body was accustomed to upholding her father's rigid standards on posture; when they made love her spine emitted cracking noises.

"I measured Einstein's brain," the craniologist suddenly said. "When he was in Berlin." The words seemed to spurt from his cramped lips. His eyes were blinking fast.

"I measured his brain twice. Once before his property was confiscated and again before he was born."

"In the womb?" said Heidegger. "You took his measure in the. . . ?"

The philosopher's tone suggested that not since his honeymoon had he been so amazed.

Then he remembered that he and Elfride had succumbed to two wedding ceremonies, Lutheran one week and Catholic the following. That had amazed him. He would have to think a while now, to recall why it had been so important.

He and she had prayed together in those days.

"Trotsky," the craniologist said. "Lenin. I've done them all."

Nietzsche, Heidegger thought. I'll bet the son of a bitch will next be telling me he's done Nietzsche.

"Nietzsche, also. Now there was someone a man could talk to."

"You conversed with Nietzsche?" Heidegger could not believe this. For years he had himself been conversing daily with Nietzsche.

"We were. . . intimate," the craniologist said.

Something in the sound of the rain must have led Heidegger's mind to wonder. He became aware suddenly that the craniologist had mentioned a dozen more names of those immortalized.

"Wagner?"

"Wagner, of course."

They were both silent a moment.

"Napoleon, too," the craniologist said.

Silence fell again.

Heidegger stepped away from the wall. He didn't care how wet he got. He was excited.

"Who didn't you do?"

"I don't do Jews. Einstein was the last."

"I hear Julius Streicher is insane. Is the insane mind larger?"

The craniologist rolled his eyes.

"Have you done him?"

"I have done the highest echelon of Reich officials."

"Whose is biggest?"

"I am not permitted to divulge that data."

"Holderlin? Our greatest poet? I would be curious to know whether you have done him."

"Too much decay."

"Holderlin? Decayed? Our greatest poet!"

"Unlike Napoleon. Perfectly preserved."

"Jesus? What about him?"

The craniologist stared at Heidegger.

"Pardon me," the craniologist said. "But I would not walk in all that shit."

After a moment, Heidegger nodded. So here was another who had shed his faith.

"But I did Pontius Pilate. *Very* impressive."

Clearly this craniologist, built like a scarecrow, as emotionless as history, was another time- and-being man.

The door opened.

Elfride stood on the landing, hands on her hips. They waited for her to say something about the cat. But she did not speak of the cat. She had perhaps dealt with the cat as she had with its kitten.

She had dressed. She had done up her hair and put on lipstick. She had put on an alluring frock, with a silk scarf folding from a pocket, and had the niceties adorning her throat.

"Come inside," she said. "Both of you. Come inside *now*."

The two deposited their shoes by the door.

"Take off those wet socks," she said.

They entered.

"Your office called," she told the craniologist. "I had no idea this project was all so scientific. I had a nice chat with Goebbels himself. He was most gracious. *Quite* an enchanting man."

Heidegger stared at her red lipstick.

She was wearing stockings. Stockings were precious. Something of significance must have transpired over the phone, for her to put on stockings.

"Did he say anything about me?" Heidegger asked. "Did he offer any hints?"

Elfride was studying the craniologist's head. The heels of her hands rested against her slim hips. A cigarette burned there between two fingers, the nails still damp with red paint.

She seemed mesmerized by what she saw behind the craniologist's thick brow.

But a moment later she emerged from this state.

"The poor man needs a towel," she said. "Martin, get our visitor a towel. A nice one, from the guest room."

In one thin hand the craniologist was holding up his dripping socks. Elfride, her face flushing, the flush spreading to her ears, suddenly lunged, snatching them from him.

"I'll give them a quick wash," she said.

Heidegger was still by the doorway, holding his. It stupefied him that Elfride would wash another man's socks.

"What about mine?" he said. "What about me?"

But Elfride was already scurrying away. They heard water running in the sink in the kitchen.

The craniologist entered the living room. He looked about for a second, then settled himself into the room's most comfortable chair.

From the hallway Heidegger watched him cross his legs; he watched the craniologist dangle his naked white foot. The skin was hairless. Raw scabs, spots of blood, showed on the nubs of his toes.

Beneath the chair crouched the deformed cat. Its lunatic eyes were staring fixedly at Heidegger.

Heidegger felt a shiver steal over him. A thought had just come to him, bewildering and frightening.

Hitler would lose the war. The Volk would not claim its rightful greatness.

[The Speaker falls silent. He drains the last of the cognac in his glass. He rearranges the judicial robes, buffs the toe of one black shoe. A door is heard opening. A new shadow is seen. A soft voice is heard. "Gentlemen. It is time to reconvene."]

OLD MOTHER

Mother said call the dog Mother, since it clearly had known the hard life. It was not a dog seen in these parts before. So the dog was called Mother, which made two of them.

Years passed. Mother, not the dog, took to referring to herself as Old Mother. "Your old mother," she would say. Old Mother one day said let's call the dog Old Mother too.

Now when they called, "Come, Old Mother," six legs came running. Ten were these years that had passed. They had been looking up the road all those years for the rightful owner to show up and claim the dog. They had been calling the dog Mother, and Old Mother, but the owner would arrive and call him something else and the dog would go running.

Benji bet pony. He will arrive pony-back, Benji bet, and every week was made to wash the family britches, for losing. "Listen to this," Benji would say. He would put two fingers in his mouth, sound his whistle, and more often than not six legs would come running. In the beginning, the dog was faster, beating their mother by a full twenty to thirty lengths. A clear victory. A raccoon bit off the dog's left hind leg. That changed that.

The family gathered on the porch each Sunday, in mild weather, and looked up the road for the pony. The owner would be coming from a mighty distance, and be cold and hungry. Benji wanted to make sure an extra plate would be set at the table, so the man could eat scrambled eggs. Benji was himself partial to such eggs and would not talk to his family if the eggs arrived over-cooked or had a herb anywhere near them. He let the dog always lick his plate. The family objected to how he pampered Old Mother, and praised him endlessly, until the night of the fire. That night was the coldest night the family, and the dog too, so far as is known, had ever seen. The family would have frozen to death, certainly, without they had a house to shelter them. They would have had to stand up close to the burning house, with one side cooking and the other side frozen. When the house was ashes, they would freeze, or venture out becrazed into the wilderness.

But this terrible event did not come to pass. Old Mother barked, and licked Benji's face. He did this even with his fur smoking. Old Mother, not the dog, shouted, "Shut up that dog!"

Benji figured it was the dog saved the family's bacon; other family members stressed it was their natural mother had raised the general alarm and roused the whole bunch, with her yelling, "Fire, fire!" and flapping her bedsheet. Benji was nice about this, granting her the extra credit.

They got to the fire quickly enough, and three of their four rooms were saved. The kitchen stove, Benji said, was where the fire started. No one argued this even a minute, some claiming they could remember hearing the explosion. Benji said he opened his eyes and all he saw in the smoke was Old Mother's tail ablaze. Even so, Benji said, Old Mother was licking his face. Some few in the family did not credit this, and looked askance at Benji, which made him argue Old Mother's heroics all the louder.

The kitchen was gone. It was a black cinder-post room, Benji said, made totally of the heaven's windows. The family tramped through the room's burnt space over the ensuing cold and snowy days, along with the dog. No roof, no walls, wind and snow whipping.

"You can see here," Benji said, "where Old Mother's tail is singed."

Old Mother, not the dog, said to the assembled family, "We are all alive. We have known wicked misfortune, though I think it can fairly be said that this family is blessed."

The whole family, not known for its religious convictions, said Amen.

She then told them of her time around a campfire in her younger days when the earth was a peat bog of revolting gasses and men were like unto beasts rising from the quagmire.

She told them the story of her life, and how hard it had been, and how she had picked the family name out of slips of paper in a stranger's hat. "I am old now, and have eaten humble pie," she said, "but these are family secrets you need to know about, in order that your descendants realize whereof they spring and the why-fors of their existence on this earth."

She then told them a good deal else about the family, and the perils of her younger life, much of which no one among those assembled had ever dreamed.

The boys clasped her about the shoulders and the girls kissed her face.

Benji, looking up the road, and at the shiver of ice on the trees, was first to make out the pony. The whole family came running to his whistle, in time to see the man riding pony-back crest the nearest hill.

The rider was old, and the pony was old, and he had come so far and for so long that none seeing him could imagine he would ever reach the end of his journey. They came on, he and the pony, in fading light through the high snow and the ice-field of trees.

The pony-man called the dog's name, some common name no one in the family liked or would ever repeat, and the dog, old as he was, took off on his three legs like a shot, and both of them — owner and dog — went out of their lives forever.

THE WOMAN FROM RED DEER
WHO WENT TO JOHANNESBURG,
SET HERSELF AFIRE,
AND LEAPT FOUR FLOORS
TO HER APPARENT DEATH

*I*thought they were children. I saw their heads over the fence and then the gate rattling. They couldn't open it, which was stupid of them, then their heads appeared again. They were looking over the house, passing comments back and forth. A narrow service alley runs behind the back yard, and that is where they were. A boy and a girl. The boy pointed to the apple tree growing beside the closed garage, and both laughed. A few seconds later they were up on the garage roof, crouched within the tree limbs, staring intently at the house. Children, I thought. The roof is rotten, they will fall through and hurt themselves.

But they looked old enough to know what they were doing, and so I went on with what I was doing. In the kitchen, bathing my feet in a pan of all but scalding water, into which I had mixed Epsom salts. This treatment seemed to my mind to control the swelling; it soothed the skin and eased the relentless ache of a thousand shattered bones. As the water cooled I poured in more hot water from the kettle and continued my watch of the two intruders. But they tired me. They were on my roof, they were spying on my house, but this had nothing to do with me. I couldn't see how it did.

I closed my eyes and let my mind follow its own slow, crooked path. My thoughts had no destination. I forgot their presence. It wasn't until I had both feet down on the white towel on the floor, the breeze like quick hot matches to the skin, that I looked back at the roof. It was vacant. They've gone, I thought. They've come up with something new to do.

Would, I thought, that I could do the same.

The time was close upon six o'clock. Darkness would be falling soon, and in fact inside the house it was already darkish. The windows all placed against the light. A mad person had built this house. My father.

I smiled not unhappily at the thought. I jacked up my feet into the high stirrups, since the doctor has advised this. I do find it relieves the pain somewhat.

The pulsing blood. It disrupts the flow of pain, sends it shrieking into less familiar joints, muscles, organs, appendages.

I wheeled myself through the door into the sitting room, and paused there. What next? I didn't know. In an hour or two I could take my pills and knock myself out for the night. But I willed myself to wait. Otherwise, I would be awake before dawn, and another of these empty days would poke into view.

I wheeled over and turned on the radio. It was a Beethoven symphony on the one station I could get. Good enough, I thought.

I put on the earphones, set the volume. Closed my eyes.

How long they were inside the house before I was aware of it, or how they made their entrance, I didn't know. I wouldn't have known at all had the girl not switched on the light.

She was standing not a foot away, her back to me.

Blue running shoes, shredded jeans, a formless sweater. Brown hair cropped close to her head. I must have made a sound, because she spun quickly, her fists raised. She fell back the second she saw me, her mouth open. I slipped off the headphones, and said, stupidly, all that it came to me in that second to say:

"Hello."

She screeched out a sound, and darted away. I heard the boy running, and then the two of them whispering with some urgency, and a second later the back door slammed.

Gone.

I rolled myself into the kitchen and stared at the open back door. They were both at the back gate, struggling to get it open, cursing, shoving each other aside.

It is a simple latch. I couldn't understand why they were having such difficulty.

The girl looked back and saw me. She had a look of panic in her face. But the next second her left arm

shot up, and I saw she was giving me the finger, in that instant before the gate finally swung outwards and the boy shoved her through.

"Up yours, Jack," the boy yelled.

They were out in the alley now, running, their anxious laughter floating back to me through the dark.

I was asleep when the phone rang. It had been ringing a long time, so it seemed to me, before I roused myself.

No one spoke.

For the longest time no one did, including myself after the initial response.

I was still reclining back on the pillow, sedated by my medicines, the room dark. I didn't want to wake up. If I waked, then what? More of the pills, and another long wait, staring into the dark, until they took effect.

Then a woman's voice, or a girl's, said, "You don't know who this is, do you?" A high-pitched voice, unnatural.

I tried placing who it was. But I kept my eyes shut, willing indifference, content to wait for more.

"Did you call the police?" she said.

And I knew then who it was.

I didn't say anything. I wanted not to wake up.

"Did you?"

"No."

"Why not?"

"I don't know."

"You sound groggy to me," she said. "You sound like a dope."

She laughed nastily and hung up.

An instant later she rang back.

"D," she said. "We saw your name on your mail box. D. For dope, right?"

I sat up, rubbing my head.

Two o'clock.

"Miss Cripple Pants," she said. "You live in the ugliest house I ever saw."

"What do you want?"

"Nothing. What's it to you?"

I reached for the glass of water and the pills. My feet were throbbing, and my head too. I felt hungry, but I didn't want anything to eat.

"I couldn't sleep," she said. "I kept thinking you'd have the pigs kicking in the door."

"I am not a great admirer of the forces of law and order," I said.

"Well, oodle-dee-doo. Pin a medal on you."

"I'm sorry," I said. "I'm not feeling well. I've got to go back to sleep."

"Dope," she said. "Do it, then. Asshole."

She hung up.

*L*ater on, wheeled up to the bedroom window, staring out into the night sky, I tried considering why she'd called. Tried remembering what she looked like, tried fixing her age. Tried imagining her life.

Tried imagining my own life whenever I was whatever age she was.

*M*y sister arrived at ten the next morning, angry to find me asleep in the chair, unwashed, puffy-eyed, sore through to my bones. The house cold.

"Turn up the heat," she said. "My God! You don't want to take care of yourself, do you? No, you want to make it as hard on me as you can."

She made me breakfast, and fumed as she wiped the counters, watching me poke at the eggs.

"You need a full-time maid," she said. "You need a lunatic perpetually at your beck and call. What's the matter with you? Why won't you eat?" She crouched beside me and spooned a forkful into my mouth.

I sealed my lips to the second bite, and she trounced about, remarking on this and that.

"You think I'm bossy, don't you?" she said. "You've never liked me. I'm vapid, I'm silly, my life is meaningless — that's what you think. Well, I don't care. So what?"

She disappeared, came back carrying an armload of dirty sheets, complaining that I'd left the radio on all night.

"Practically ripped out my eardrums," she said.

"Small wonder you can't hear a normal word anyone says to you. Eat! For Godsake, why don't you eat? I've got to hurry. I can't spend all my day babying you. They're going to fry my ass if I'm not back at work in twenty minutes."

She flung herself down the basement steps with the sheets. I heard the washer lid bang, heard running water.

Then she was back in the doorway, staring.

"You've got a cracked window down there," she said. "Glass all over the floor. I could have cut myself. What gives?"

I feigned surprise.

"Jesus," she said. "Now I'm a goddamn glass-cutter? You expect me to fix that thing? I'll put cardboard over it, that's all. How do you manage to break everything you look at? You throw something at it? Never mind. Never mind, it's just something else for me to do, though why I should bother is beyond me. Do you appreciate my help? No, you appreciate nothing. Do you know why? Yes, because no one is as good as you. Morally, ethically, we are all strangers to that breeze. Right? No one comes near you on the goodness front. The strike-a-blow-for-humankind front. Right?"

Another sally, minutes on: "That dress looks hideous on you," she said. "Drab. Drab. When last did you make up your face?" She came near. Sniffed. "You could use a wash, too. Too bad, honey-bunch. Little Sister doesn't have the time."

She opened the windows, mindless of the chill.

"Airing-out time," she said. "Spring is coming early this year. Have you noticed the buds? Look at that sun: a beautiful day!"

It was cloudy outside, a drifting overcast, with only small flits of sunlight.

"You're looking better," she said. "Your skin, I mean. It's healing nicely. Do you still use that salve? No? Then use it. Pacify me. You were never a beauty, but you could hold your own in a crowd. Not in *my* crowd, mind you. But in that riff-raff bunch you ran with you were quite the little orchid."

She dumped the uneaten breakfast into the garbage, complaining viciously, "Why do I bother? Why put myself out? *Why? Why?*"

"Mother can't come today," she said. "You depress her, she says. You depress her until she wants to scream."

"Do I?" I said. "I hadn't noticed."

"What's there to notice? She's as asinine, as crazy, as you are. Sickies at both ends. She calls you *Mother's comet,* when in a good mood. Rare, I tell you. *Rare,* those moods. I fly from one to the other of you. That's all the life I have. Fred says I'm the little hummingbird he never sees. I'm the one sane person in the whole family. Wouldn't you agree? Thank God for small favors. Thank you, thank you. All of you, the entire family, drives me around the bend. Look at you! Look what you have done to yourself. Why? Has anything improved? Did you solve all our problems? No, damn you. Jesus, it tears me up just to think of it."

"I'm sorry."

"Oh, you are, are you? Well, don't sweat it. Am I sweating it? I promise you, I am not sweating it. Here, put this pillow behind your head. Let me see if I can do something with that hideous hair."

A little later she got into her car, gave her two quick beeps of the horn as the rusted Austin pulled away from the grassy slope, and motored off, waving happily. Pleased with herself. I was pleased with her, too. Hearing her talk, seeing her rush hither and yon, always gave me a jolt. She had been that way as a kid, ever in dialogue with herself or with anyone within her vicinity. And racing, racing.

Her whirlwind visit left me panting for breath, as her visits always did.

*I*have a routine in the afternoons, if the day is sunny, which this one, to my surprise, turned out intermittently to be. I roll myself down the ramp and sit out in the back garden with my two-cup teapot of tea. The pot is earthen-colored, flecked with ashy-white, fired by my mother when she was in her potting youth, done with a salt glaze in the old way, and shaped with an elephant spout, since she was in her decorative phase at that time. The sun steals over my face. The breeze enchants. I comfortably elevate my feet on an old stump there. Birds feed and fly, dart and whip. I contemplate the speedy advancement of vines, the encroachment of tall weeds, the stealth of small blooms, violets, within this wildness; mysterious squeaks, rustlings, pulings in the leafy overgrowth.

I watch the swaying tops of trees, the sparse patch of color. The sky. The slow rearrangement of sky. I nap. My mind and body, they steal away. It is the one time of day that I truly enjoy, these sunlit afternoons, when sleep and the waking state coalesce, connive, in delicious harmony. To produce a third reality of being whereby a kind of web, or net, intricate and weightless as those a spider weaves, settles over the world.

I welcome this, as one would a luminescent voyage above a seamless untroubled earth, or the rapture one might find if cast within a timeless spell.

I was aware of whispers, of nearby movement, for some time before I opened my eyes and saw them. The girl was seated on a rock, leaning back on her arms the way models often are seen posed on billboards.

The boy was drinking from a milk carton and looking at my ruined feet.

"What do you want?" I asked.

"Nothing," the boy said. "You don't have anything in that ratty house I'd want."

"That's my milk," I said. "You took it from my refrigerator."

He finished the milk and pitched the carton into the high grass.

The girl picked at something between her teeth.

She smiled.

"Last night you broke a pane in my door."

"So. Prove it was me," he said.

The girl walked over. I flinched, thinking she meant striking me in the face; she took my face in one hand, pinching my cheeks.

"Show a little life, lady," she said. "Be polite."

The boy strode into the house, slamming the door. I could hear him opening and shutting cupboards. Going through the house.

"Tell him not to break anything."

"Tell him yourself."

I said nothing.

"He's looking for money," she said. "You have any cash hidden in that rat-pile?"

I shook my head. "A few coins in a bowl," I said. "Mostly pennies, unfortunately."

"Yeah. We found those."

The boy came outside with the radio. It was an old one, with a broken aerial.

"It only gets the one station," I said.

"Yeah, I noticed," he said. "Brahms and sleepy shit like that."

"You won't get much for it."

He laughed, looking at the girl. "Fuck it, then," he said, and looped the radio underarm into the apple tree. "You coming?" he said to the girl. "This places sucks. It depresses me. *She* depresses me." He sauntered over to the gate, glancing back our way a few times.

The girl waved him on.

"Suit yourself," he said.

But he couldn't get the gate open.

"Use the latch," I said.

He kicked at it, and pulled. The gate held.

"The latch," I said again. "And lift a bit."

He did so, and stood there a moment marveling at the ease of it all, before he went on through.

The girl moved over and closed the gate.

"He's hard to take," she said. "Two hours in his company and I'm ready to hang myself. What's in the garage?"

"It isn't locked. Why don't you look in and see?"

She went inside. She was gone maybe five minutes and during that brief spell I must have fallen asleep. I was feeling very tired. One moment there seemed to be a haze before my eyes, and the next moment the haze was seeping within.

She was shaking me.

"Please," I said. "Don't do that."

"Is that your car? In the garage?"

"Yes."

"It's covered with dust."

"Yes."

"It won't start."

"No. The battery, I expect."

"You don't drive, you don't do anything. All you do is stare at your stupid feet. Were you born mangled like that?"

"No."

"How did you get those burns on your face?"

I didn't reply.

She stepped closer and snatched open my blouse. Her face wrinkled in surprise.

"What happened?" she said. "Somebody set you afire?"

I sipped at the cold tea.

She hopped behind the chair and commenced to push me slowly about the bumpy yard.

"Why don't you give me your old car?" she said. "Small good it's ever going to do you, in your piss-poor state. I bet it was some man set you afire. Yeah, probably some man. You're not so old as I had figured."

I could see how her mind was running but was unconcerned with what she thought.

We came to the dirt street. To the south it sloped downhill. She could swing me that way, and push, and everything would be over.

"What's your plan?" I asked.

"Relax," she said. "I'm all generosity today."

"Do you live around here?"

Scarcely more than a dozen or so houses were in the district, most of these lined up along the alley. A few others strung out over the distant hills.

"None of your business," she said.

I rode with my feet in the stirrups, hoisted high in the air. It felt silly, but the truth is I was enjoying myself.

"Not far," she said. "Carl and I live in a broken-down hunter's shed in the woods. No heat, no lights. No nothing."

"How did you make your phone call to me?"

She stopped and pointed off.

"That house over there. With the red roof? The people who live there are on vacation, I think. Last night I went in through a crawl space. I slept there. Imagine my surprise when the phone worked."

"Where is home?"

She spread both arms and shrugged.

"You got it, Sister. What you see is what I call home."

She pushed back her sleeves, stepping to the side of my chair.

"See these marks?" she said. "They're from when I was a baby. We had this big wood stove, which heated the house, and in winter my mother would wash me on the stove, in this speckled pot she used for cooking roasts."

She abruptly turned and started pushing me back up the alley.

"One day she forgot me and the water boiled. I was practically cooked alive. Underneath these clothes, my skin looks raw, just like yours. Carl nearly gags."

"Do you hate her for it?"

"Hate her? Why should I hate her? Anyway, she's dead."

"How did she die?"

"You won't believe it. Something fell on her from the sky. She was out working in a beet field, and this thing came down on top of her."

"What thing?"

"No one knew what it was. It wasn't anything anyone had ever seen. It wasn't *earth*-made. Everyone agreed on that."

"That's terrible," I said.

"*Aliens*," she said, under her breath. Then laughed. Her fingers brushed my face. "I've bruised your cheeks," she said. "Little rouged spots to make you pretty. You might say I've fallen on you from the sky. Is that how you feel?"

"I don't know how I feel."

She opened the gate and we re-entered the yard.

She gave my chair a shove, and I bumped three or four yards over the weedy ground. When I caught my breath she was over by the garage, with both doors flung wide.

"I can drive," she said. "I've got a license."

"You're not old enough to have a license," I said.

"Maybe not. But I've got one."

She went out of sight and when I had wheeled myself over, all I could see of her was a skinny elbow poking from the window. A thick layer of dust covered the windshield.

"*Zoom-zoom,*" I heard her say.

I went into the house and lay down on the bed. My feet and legs were hurting. I placed two pills under my tongue and waited for the pain-killer to take effect.

Later in the day I heard the car motor fire up.

I propped myself up and through the window saw the car roll slowly out. The tires were all but flat.

She sat erect behind the wheel, a ludicrous joy brightening her face.

When next I looked she'd found a hose, had soap in a bucket from my kitchen, and was washing the car.

Later yet, I looked out, and the car was gone.

"*Zoom-zoom,*" I said.

At six my sister showed up. She flitted about, helping me into the chair, wheeling me into the kitchen, spreading dishes of take-out food onto the table.

"Shanghai chicken," she said. "You used to eat this stuff by the peck. Mother never cooked a day in her life. You remember? Even then, I had to do all the cooking, all the cleaning. The goddamned ironing, too. I set out rose bushes that never, *never,* survived the freeze. Let me see you eat now. You'll want tea. Where's that frightful old elephant tea jug our mother-the-potter made?"

She was sounding terribly gay.

"Out in the yard," I said. "Will you bring it inside? My radio is out there, too, lodged somewhere in the apple tree."

She raised an inquisitive brow.

"Actual sentences," she said. "How do I rate such loquaciousness from you?"

But she didn't go outside. She rushed into the sitting room, singing this back over her shoulder: "I've got a surprise for you. A big surprise. Close your eyes."

Some seconds later she settled a heavy bundle into my lap. She'd done it up, or had it done, in wrapping paper and a bow. Her hands clapped together. "Your *boots!*" she cried. "Finally your boots! Do you know they cost a fortune? But Fred and I went in together on them, so you're not out one red cent. What do you say?"

She was dancing around the table, radiant with glee, waiting for me to unwrap the boots.

"Speak. Say, 'Thank you, little sister.'"

There had been much discussion between the surgeon and the shoemaker about these boots. If made properly, with high sides and steel reenforced, tightly laced, thickly cushioned in the soles, elevated, the instep molded to my own, and instilled throughout with something akin to the magic on duty during my fall, they would somehow act as extra bones. They would provide what my feet couldn't. They would absorb the pain my feet refused. Theoretically, I should be able to walk. Not far and not fast, and not often for a while, but I, theoretically, would be able to perambulate about in them.

They were huge, and hideous. They were a monstrous weight. But I stroked the cowhide, tears suddenly streaming down my face.

"Guaranteed, the shoe-maker said. Guaranteed A-Number One Mountain Goat boots!" My sister danced about, hugging my neck, dropping to her knees in front of me, saying, "Put them on! Hurry up, let's see if these dillies work."

I was shaking. I couldn't stop crying. I was clutching her hands, her shoulders, unable to speak. I was seeing myself all the way back to Johannesburg.

"Don't think about *then,*" she said. "Think *now!* Wait! I forgot. Wait one minute. I've got you these special socks. My camera, too." And she rushed away again.

A year. It had been a full year since my feet had been inside footwear of any kind.

They were clunkers. They were weighted stones. They were like magnets nailing me to the floor. But I hobbled, bent over and perspiring, using the chair-backs as crutch, around the table while my sister crouched and spun, snapping off her pictures.

"See the dead arise!" she cried. "This woman talks, she walks! See the woman *breathe!* Smile! Smile!"

She wanted a thousand smiles.

I sank back breathless into my chair. My hips and legs, my feet, seemed all but numb. I had put a crimp in my neck. My face felt flushed, my shoulders cracked with fatigue. I couldn't halt the shudders raking my bones. These boots *worked.* They actually *worked.*

I gave her her smiles.

"Now eat," she said. "Eat!"

The chicken was cold, but I ate it. I ate the cold chicken, and gnawed and slurped at the bones.

She raced around me, clicking her pictures. Ducking and weaving.

"One more for mother. Fuck apartheid! *Comet seen again! Comet takes off!*"

Late night. I am in my chair, buffing up the shoes in the dark. The phone rings. It is a collect call.

"I stole your car," the girl says.

"Good," I say.

"Not so good. I'm out of gas."

"Where are you?"

"In another country."

"Do you have any money?"

"Just those coins from your bowl."

"Gas up. Come back."

"Why?"

"I don't know why. Why do people do things?"

"Did a lover set you afire?"

"No. I did the setting."

"Like those monks?"

"What monks?"

"Those monks in Saigon, before I was born. I read about them in school."

"Yes. Good Lord. I'd totally forgotten those monks. Like them."

"Why?"

"To make a point. To stop people from doing what they were doing."

"Did it stop them?"

"No. Maybe it made them go about their work that much more urgently. Come back."

"We don't even know each other."

"Yes we do. Better than you think."

"Who made you so wise?"

"No one. Come back. You can quit your shed and move into this ugly house."

"And care for you? Fuck that."

I laugh. She laughs, too.

"I've got new boots," I say. "I can walk."

"Yeah," she says. "But you can't drive."

"You can drive," I say.

"Do you know what they were doing while I was boiling on the stove?"

"No. Do you? Do you know what brought you back? From the boil, I mean."

"I know what you mean. No, I don't. Do you?"

"No."

I can hear her breathing in, breathing out. From wherever she is, I can hear her.

"Okay," she finally says. "Look for me when you see me."

I put down the phone, holding my breath.

Through the window, the witless array of stars.

I am thinking of unknown objects, forms, substances — of things organic and inorganic — in chaotic tumble from the sky.

I am thinking of my sister, who has saved my life. For one entire year she has painstakingly sought to revive me, nourish me, instruct me. Return me from the dead. Now I am passing the favor on. I am throwing out the lifelines.

THE LITHUANIAN WIFE

Cordelia, a philosophy student studying at one of Europe's oldest universities, Jagellonian, at the start of a rare visit home to America, struck up a conversation with another traveler, a man, in Krakow's Central Station. He was good-looking, wealthy — as she judged that issue — but old enough to be her father. While both were waiting for their train to be called, the man told her that long ago one of his brothers, named Tadeusz, had brought home a new wife from Lithuania.

The new wife had taken one look at the house where she was to live, and had told everyone, including her new husband, that she would not live in such a place. She sat out on the road on her suitcase, which was no more than a rotted sack, while the day waned. The new husband tried to reason with her.

The rest of the family watched this, initially in silence, because they could not understand her speech any more than they understood why one of theirs had to go all the way to Lithuania to choose a bride, and one not that pretty either, should the truth be known.

Once in a while the family dog, which was named Tadeusz also, as were half the men in the village and a good number of dogs, would trot up the road to where the new wife sat on her sack; the dog would sniff and nose her up and down, and sometimes drop down and sit beside her, as if she were another dog or merely a human being under his protection.

Then the dog stopped making the trip and simply stayed where the girl was, both of them quietly encamped on the road.

The man telling Cordelia this episode from his family history had got this far in the story when he suddenly picked up the chair in which he was sitting, and without moving his buttocks from that chair, arranged it and himself nearer to Cordelia's own. Cordelia's hands lay unclasped in her lap. The man took hold of her hands, and kissed each in its turn. When Cordelia did not remove her hands from his, or scold him, he went on with the other story.

"If that dog can understand my new wife," the new husband told his family, "and make room for her in his heart, then surely it would not be asking too much for you to put yourselves out a bit."

His youngest sister said, "Now he is comparing us to dogs."

The husband's mother asked him how old this Lithuanian wife was.

"Eighteen," was the reply.

"Eighteen," his mother said. "Yet she knows no better than to sit out there in the sun without a hat. Do you love her?"

"Yes."

"If I loved a Lithuanian woman sitting out in the road bareheaded in the sun, I would at least have the courtesy to take her a glass of water."

Here Cordelia interrupted her friend.

"How old are you?" she asked.

"Seventy-three."

Cordelia was astonished. She had thought fifty.

The man calmly watched a cleaning woman working a cloth back and forth over brass rails in Krakow's Central Station. The woman was barefoot, had high, rolling hips, and looked quite elderly. Her hair was tied with a rag identical to the one in her hand. A wide patch of the floor where earlier she had been working with mop and pail was wet with sudsy water. People were having to walk around it.

"Seventy-three," Cordelia said.

"Last November."

Cordelia could not believe she had been flirting with a seventy-three-year-old man.

The cleaning woman finished with the rails. She was again at work with her mop and pail. A cake of the cleaning woman's brown soap slipped from her hand and they watched the soap slide a long distance over the floor. People executed little dance steps, or jumped, as the soap skidded beneath their feet.

Cordelia and her seventy-three-year-old gentleman laughed. Then he glanced at Cordelia, lightly stroked the back of her head, and resumed his story.

The husband took his wife a glass of water. He had a long trek to reach her, because over the recent hours the girl had been occasionally springing up from her sack and retreating down the road another hundred yards or so, as if she meant through this method to effect her return to Lithuania. She was now about a half mile from the family house and no more than a speck. Each time she had moved the dog had moved with her, so actually there were two specks on the road for the family and everyone else in the village to see.

Then for a time there were the three specks, after Tadeusz had finally reached her with his glass of water.

At this point in the narrative the man telling Cordelia this story had to break it off. Their train had been announced and they had to hurry between the gates and find their proper car, with their baggage bumping the man's knees, since he was such a gentleman that he had insisted on conveying his own many bags and Cordelia's rucksack also. He was old enough to be her father, even her grandfather, Cordelia thought, stealing glances at him, but appeared to be in good physical condition. He was certainly good-looking.

Once on the train the man stowed this baggage in an overhead rack and he and Cordelia took seats together. Again the man held Cordelia's hand, since she did not discourage this; in a little while — actually, before the train was even out of the station — she was resting her head on his shoulder and aimlessly stroking a button on his suit jacket, as he continued his family saga.

When Tadeusz returned from his trip down the road with the glass of water, the family asked the new husband what had been his wife's reaction to this little kindness.

"She dribbled a few drops of water over her head," the husband said. "The rest she poured into the palm of her hand, so Tadeusz, the dog, could drink."

"My God!" everyone said, for this had not been the expected response.

"Then she pitched the glass into the nettles by the side of the road, picked up her bag, and she and the dog went a little further down the road."

"Life must be good in Lithuania," said the new husband's mother, "if they can afford to throw away decent glasses."

"I never knew Lithuanians liked dogs," another brother said. "It is not a thing I have ever heard about them, although I am by no means versed in the subject."

"A Lithuanian woman can be very dramatic," someone else said.

"Maybe," a sister said, "it is less that Lithuanians like dogs and more that dogs like them."

At this remark, Tadeusz, disliking their tone, put up his dukes and squared off to hit anyone in the mouth who had a single word to say either against his wife or her people.

Cordelia, on the train, nestled close-by the man telling her this tale, laughed rather merrily and kissed him on the neck. He was wearing a nice fragrance.

The man then told Cordelia that by this time both the girl and the dog were altogether out of sight. Even when the family members walked as a group out onto the road, and pivoted up on their heels, nothing could be seen of the pair. This was in part because the girl and the dog had long since retreated over a far hill, and also because night was coming on.

"If it was me," the father said, "I would put down my fists and go up the road with something good to eat and several warm coats. From the look of things, we are in for a cold night."

"Yes," the mother said, "but it won't be as cold here as it is in Lithuania."

A sister asked the new husband what it was the girl had in her sack.

Tadeusz blushed, and everyone knew from this that one item she carried in her sack was a flimsy nightgown, or some such women's paraphernalia.

They all then turned and looked back at the house, asking themselves why the girl had refused to live there.

"It's the graveyard," the mother said. "It should have been tended but we have let vines and thistles grow up all over the graves. She thinks this family does not show sufficient appreciation for its dead."

Others pointed out the reason could be any one of a number of things, including, for instance, the new bride's homesickness for Lithuania.

They stopped talking then because the dog could be heard barking in the distance. They watched to see the dog come bounding over the hill, but the dog didn't appear and soon they realized it was no longer barking either.

A large white bird, surely an eagle, could be seen in stately perch upon the limb of a distant tree. Perhaps the dog had been barking at the eagle.

The new husband, having lost himself for some little while in the house, now showed up again and joined his family in the road. He had ragout in a jar and something else in a greasy bag — bread, most likely — his form all but hidden away by a dozen bulky coats.

"Those Lithuanians," someone said — but quietly — "have always been a lot of trouble."

"You best take good matches, too," the father said, and rooted in his pockets until he found a box of matches made in Sweden and not those Soviet sticks which would spit and fizzle and rarely light.

"You will have a devil of a time finding dry wood," someone said, because just then it started raining.

The new husband was now about ten feet up the road, where he turned.

"Your lot would scare me, too," he said. "I've never seen such a scruffy bunch of useless Poles."

A third brother in the family, who had not spoken until this point, now decided that he would. "Jews through that door!" he cried. "Poles through the other!"

No one said anything to this. The brother who had spoken had been a tram conductor in the city when the Nazis invaded the country, and again during its Sovietization, with time out at Majdanek, and now he could no longer remember when he was driving the tram and when he wasn't.

Here the man paused again in this story, embracing Cordelia, who had shivered at that remark about the Jews.

"What was that all about?" she asked.

"It is a long story," her friend said. "I am not up to its rendering."

"Try."

After kissing Cordelia's warm throat, he said:

"Let us go back two thousand years."

Cordelia tightened her grip on his upper arm, preparing her mind for this journey.

"It is now two thousand years ago," he said, "and I am being born on one side of that same road, while you are being born on the other side."

"Must we be so old?" asked Cordelia.

"No. This is just my way of telling you this is a story that has been going on for a long time."

She scrunched herself tight against him and told him to continue.

"Now we have both been born and are feeding at our mother's breasts quite contentedly. Your mother, however, is a Jew. You, and your whole family across the road, are Jews. Mine are Poles."

He fell silent, as if he had completed the story. After a moment, Cordelia raised her face to his, looking at him expectantly. He smiled, but still did not speak.

"I don't understand," Cordelia said.

Her companion shrugged, as if to relay to her the information that at issue here was not anything having to do with something so cumbersome as logic.

She pinched his leg, letting him know by this act that amplification was required.

Sighing, he took up again his story of their birth two thousand years earlier.

"Two thousand years pass, and, let us say, enough of our two families' stock, with luck, survive all the wars and invasions and insurrections, all the rezoning and partitioning, all the treaties inflicted upon us by other nations, and our two families continue to produce babies."

Cordelia's head swam with the flux and flow of these two thousand Polish years, but she remained attentive.

"Through all these two thousand years, with Poland sometimes to be found on a map and sometimes not, these elementary facts remain steadfast. My family, on one side of the road, are Poles. Yours, on the other, are Jews."

Cordelia reared up in her seat, quite excited. "Which is why," she said, "one of those babies on my side got fed up with it all and decided to found Israel!"

The man patted Cordelia's knees, which were clad in black tights. Still in place on her head was her black Greek seaman's hat. On her feet, a pair of black, thick-heeled boots, heavily-laced, which came up over her ankles.

After a moment, Cordelia's excitement subsided and she settled back down beside him. She did not know, now that the moment had passed, what had brought on her sudden exhilaration. She felt languid now, at ease with herself, and in a mood to be cuddled. This man she was with was old enough to be her father, even her grandfather, but he had dimples when he smiled, and warm eyes, and was every inch a gentleman. If he proposed they go to a hotel when their destination was reached, she would say yes.

She looked out the window. The train was ascending into the mountains, where ice had piled up in the crevasses and fresh snow glistened in the sunlight on the forested slopes. She could see, far off, at the top of the mountain, people skiing.

"Is this train cold," she asked, "or am I only imagining it?"

The man stood up and rescued his coat from the overhead bin, plopping back into his seat in such manner that the coat spread itself completely over both their laps. He placed his hand between her thighs; Cordelia, closing her eyes, considered whether she should ask him to remove it.

He took up again the family saga.

"The wedded brother," he said, "was now at the crest of the hill, looking far larger than a speck, with all the coats he was carrying, though the family was still able to make out his arm flapping over his head in a gesture that signified his departure."

A few seconds later they saw the dog trot up and sniff at his heels.

Then he and the dog disappeared over the hill.

For a time they heard barking, and reasoned this must be because of the eagle which had abandoned its perch in the distance and was now an invisible presence in the swollen sky.

The brother who once had driven the tram in the city and survived the ovens at Majdanek, shouted, "Hold the potatoes!"

It was all but dark now, and the rain a steady drizzle.

"We never even got her name," the mother said.

"Sometime this week," the father said, "if any is to be found, I am going to paint this house, and you lazy boys are going to get busy cleaning up the graves."

The entire family trooped back into the yard. In a little while the dog Tadeusz came running home with his tail between his legs, nosing everyone's legs and crotch for sympathy. The dog had always been nervous at nighttime and never liked to stray far from home.

THE BOY FROM MOOGRADI
AND THE WOMAN WITH THE MAP
TO PARADISE

"*A*re they crazy?"

"Yes."

"I think my officers would like to shoot these crazy people."

"Of course. But their deaths would reflect badly upon me."

A white woman and two white male companions lay unmoving on the ground, on their bellies, their hands tied behind their heads. They lay in swirling pools of mud and water, rivulets coursing about them and gushing down the mountain side. A handful of soldiers, dressed in rags, dark skinned and solemn, armed with knives and rifles, stood guard over them, displaying only marginal interest.

"If my officers shoot you as well, then your honor would be salvaged."

The speaker had given his name as Raoul; he was questioning a boy of about twelve, who had not yet been asked how he was called.

A heavy, warm rain was falling, with great monotony, as had been the case for the past several weeks.

"Tell the crazy people if they move my officers will shoot them."

"They will not move."

The man poked the woman with his rifle, lifting her hair so that he could see her burnished neck. He stood between her spread legs, his shoulders slumped under the drenching rain. Around them there existed a gnarl of twisty vines and trees, and leafy, swollen vegetation, and mountains rising another ten thousand feet, though they could not see beyond their own weary group because of the rain's steady downpour.

"What is the journey of these crazy people?"

"Their mission is to find Kolooltopec."

"But Kolooltopec does not exist."

"I agree."

"It does not matter whether you agree. I could agree also, but this would not change the matter."

"Yes," the boy said. "Because Kolooltopec still would not exist and you and I would both be as crazy as these gringos."

"Yes."

"Good. Then we are in agreement."

The man stepped from between the woman's legs and stretched his naked arm around the boy's shoulder. They remained that way for some minutes, the three on the ground silent and unmoving, their faces all but buried within the coursing water, and the swarthy officers with their rifles muttering to themselves as they watched the rain and each other and their bedraggled prisoners on the ground.

"How long have you been on this journey with the crazy people?"

"Five days."

"Along the river?"

"Two days along the river. Then we began our ascent of the mountains."

"In the rain?"

"Yes."

"Then you must be from Ooldooroo. Or Moogradi."

"Moogradi. It is the village of my people."

"Does Ooldooroo still exist? We have heard rumors."

"I do not know."

The man fell silent for a moment, as a few of the men nearby spoke nervously of the apparent destruction of Ooldooroo.

"One of my officers came from Moogradi. He spoke well of the river basin and its people."

The boy nodded.

"He is dead three years now, this man from Moogradi."

The boy made a quick, violent sign of the cross, and each of the several officers within hearing did likewise, with murmurs of pain and astonishment that lifted above the rain. One of the prisoners coughed and made to stretch his legs, but quit this when he was nudged by one of the officer's rifles.

"It is a poor place, Moogradi."

"Yes."

"An affliction. Do you agree?"

"Yes."

"Nothing stinks so much as Moogradi."

"Yes."

"The men of Moogradi do nothing all day long, while the women work. Is this true?"

"Yes."

The man laughed.

"But the women are all ugly in Moogradi, especially the young girls. That is what I have heard."

"It is very true," the boy said. "But bless them anyhow."

The man laughed harder and pounded his hand merrily on the boy's shoulder. All the officers were laughing now and passing lewd comments back and forth.

"Whereas, Ooldooroo."

All fell silent.

The three on the ground lay as though stricken and the warm rain continued to fall and the rivulets to course noisily down the mountainside.

"What is your name, boy from Moogradi?"

"Toodoo."

"Is Toodoo a good name?"

"It is my parents' good name."

"But you have ugly sisters."

"Yes."

All laughed again, including the boy, although his face was strained and he looked on the point of exhaustion. He did not believe this man standing beside him, with a hand on his shoulder, was the famous desperado Raoul.

"My dead officer from Moogradi was a Frooloo. Do you know the Frooloo family of Moogradi?"

The boy looked out into the rain. The entire Frooloo family, a long time ago, had disappeared; if the officer

asking him so many questions was the famous desperado Raoul, he would know this.

The man took his hand from the boy's shoulder and
once again stood between the woman's split legs. He
regarded the woman's backside solemnly for a while,
before kneeling and doing something with the ropes
binding her hands. Rainwater coursed down his face,
which was without expression.

"No? Then perhaps my dead officer lied. Perhaps
he had never seen Moogradi. Or perhaps the Frooloos of
Moogradi also are in journey towards Kolooltopec."

The man smiled. The boy tried to smile back, but he
was too tired.

The woman lifted her shoulders somewhat and covered her face with her hands. Then she slumped down
again and lay motionless.

A number of the officers slung their rifles and
threaded their way carefully through the underbrush
and sat down out of the rain, under a rocky precipice.
The boy watched them remove some spit of stalk from
their pockets and thoughtfully chew upon these.

The man leaned upon his rifle and with his free
hand turned the woman's head about so that she was
suddenly looking up into his face and the rain. She gave
a silent moan; her face was slick with mud and ravaged
by a terrible swelling. He lowered his face and said
something to her. She keened softly and closed her eyes.

The boy crouched down, hands circling his knees.
He was looking with fascination at the three prisoners.
The isolated pools of water had now become one large
pool of muddy, gushing water, eroding the soil and
chewing away at the lip of this small plateau, with the
result that the three bodies were ever so slowly sliding
down the incline, their boots now all but touching the
edge of the cliff. They would soon tumble to their deaths
in the great valley below.

The man knelt by the boy, also absorbed in this phenomenon.

"Kolooltopec?" the man said to the boy.

"Yes."

"Kolooltopec, which does not exist?"

"Yes?"

"How is it that a Toodoo boy from Moogradi has come to be in the company of these crazy people in journey towards Kolooltopec?"

"I am their guide."

"Then you are not the best of guides or you would have known not to come by way of this jurisdiction."

"Yes."

"My officers are much disturbed."

"Yes."

"It has occurred to them that you and these gringos may be spies."

The boy regarded the officers in silence. They were at first few in number, now they were numerous, all assembled under the small protection of the rocky overhang, chewing on whatever dried meat or vine they had to chew upon, and jabbering softly among themselves.

"Are you spies?"

The boy reached into the puddle at his feet, and pitched a small stone out over the valley.

The woman had risen to her hands and knees. They watched her hold to that position; she seemed unempowered to do more. One of her companions let out a helpless moan as water coursed about him and slid him another few inches out over the cliff.

"A Toodoo does not spy," the boy said.

"No. He only journeys towards what does not exist."

The officers under the small overhang had broken off twigs from a nearby bush, and were now comparing them for length. The longest was perhaps two inches. The shortest could barely be seen.

The man turned on his heels and made a gesture towards them. "How long before our unfortunate prisoners hurtle to their deaths?"

The officers displayed their various sticks. They were jabbering and laughing among themselves. The rain had momentarily slackened; it now drove down again in a renewed burst.

The prisoner nearest the edge gave a strangled cry.

The boy touched the officer's arm.

"They have a map," he said.

"Oh?"

"A map which purports to show where Kolooltopec may be found."

The man considered this statement. He rubbed his eyes and wiped both hands across his face. The boy noticed that the skin on the man's hands was deeply scarred and that none of his fingers were longer than his thumbs. They had been cut away, the boy thought, probably with an axe.

"'Purports,' the man said. "I do not know this word. What does it mean, this 'purports,' and how does it come to pass that a boy from Moogradi makes use of the unknown word?"

"School," the boy said. "I was a student."

"Ah. So the famous Moogradi village now has a school?"

"My village once had a school. But the teacher vanished and the school was torched."

The man nodded.

"And did your great village have a fine clinic where the sick could come?"

"Yes."

"Which was also torched? So that now your clinic and school and the school teacher, along with the Frooloo family you have never heard of, is lost to the world? Does not exist? Like our fabled Kolooltopec?"

"Yes."

"But your adventurers have a map, you say?"

"Yes."

A couple of the soldiers ventured out from their overhang and dragged the two male prisoners a few feet forward from the cliff-edge.

"You have seen this map?"

"Many times. They have studied it unceasingly."

"'Unceasingly'?"

"Yes."

"Is this map a good map?"

The boy shook his head. "It is a worthless map. It is a map to Kolooltopec."

"I wish to see this map."

"Of course."

They sat in their crouch, side by side, for some while before saying anything further.

"Which of these fine prisoners possesses the valueless document?"

The boy pointed at the woman. She sat folded over, her head at droop on her knees.

She had cropped her hair close to her skull the second day out from the village; the boy had some of this woman's shorn hair still in his pocket.

"Does this prisoner, who possesses the famous map, also possess a name?"

"They call her Emma."

"Emma. I have never known anyone purporting to possess this name."

The boy shrugged.

"Has Emma been good to the guide from Moogradi?" asked the man. He circled one hand lazily over his groin.

The boy grinned.

"Unceasingly."

The officers under the protection of the overhang laughed merrily. Some few of them now had their shirts off. They would step out into the warm rain for a few minutes, wash themselves, and then step back into their dryer environment. Then they would step out into the rain again and for a few brief seconds furiously scrub and flap their ragged shirts. The boy studied these half-naked officers. He could count their ribs. One had a filthy cloth wrapping his chest; the blood flowed red for a second, then went pinkish in the rain, before the red stain showed again. Another of these officers was a boy not much older than himself. He tried catching this one's eyes, although it was clear the young officer had no interest in one of his experience. Several of them were women. The soldiers now numbered a dozen or more, a fresh face frequently arriving, although the boy could not see how this was possible unless they had burrowed a tunnel somewhere through the mountain and its mouth was nearby.

"Where are these crazy people from?" the man asked. "America."

The man weighed this, watching the woman. He seemed amused.

"I had a young cousin who went to live in the country of America. Perhaps I and these prisoners are related."

The boy smiled half-heartedly. "I hope your cousin in America is well," he said.

"I thank you for your good wishes. But I expect this young cousin is now dead. He returned home, you see."

"It grieves me to hear it."

"I thank you. Yes, he is dead. My village was not so fortunate as your Moogradi with its teacher and clinic and the vanished school."

The boy shut his eyes.

"But I have my officers and it is not wise to dwell upon those sorrowful deaths."

The boy was crying. But he reasoned that no one would notice this in the falling rain.

The woman had moved again. She had crawled in the mud to a spot somewhat removed from her two companions. She lay with her head between two large rocks, her muddy hands covering her head.

The rain had turned cold. The sky was darkening.

It seemed to the boy that there now were as many as twenty officers milling about the tiny encampment.

"These crazy people," asked the man. "Do they have food?"

"Yes."

"Is it good?"

"Yes. Although it is of a kind I have never tasted before. They call it hiking food."

"Hiking food? You are right. I have never heard of hiking food."

The officers were busy under their little overhang. They were on their hands and knees working with knives and sticks and an assortment of other tools. They were enlarging their little pocket in the mountainside.

"Tell me this," the officer said to the boy. "In your five days' journey towards Kolooltopec did you come across soldiers wearing the uniform of our republic?"

"Yes. In their camp at the headwaters. But they let us continue when your prisoners showed them their documents, and after prolonged inquiry."

"Because you were on your way to Kolooltopec, which does not exist."

The boy shrugged.

"Which meant that our prisoners were not to be taken seriously?"

"Yes."

"Or perhaps your three friends are peacekeepers from the famous United Nations, and the soldiers of the republic did not wish to offend their benefactors."

"I do not know."

"And because the soldiers of the republic were given money."

"Yes."

"And what was the view of the soldiers of the republic as to the merits of the boy from Moogradi?"

"I do not know."

"My officers have heard there are informers in Moogradi. Some, so it is reported, express sympathy for the cause of the soldiers of the republic, while others align themselves with our movement. The Frooloo family, for instance. Have you heard these reports?"

"I have heard whispers."

"Did these soldiers of the republic harm you?"

"Not excessively."

"What does this mean, this 'not excessively?'"

"They twisted my arms. They beat me about the head."

"But not excessively."

"No."

"Since I see no visible wounds."

"Yes. No." The boy was confused.

"No cigarettes to your skin. No finger in the electrical socket. No axe to your hand or your head in the vice. No threats to put the torch to the whole of your wonderful Moogradi as you and your family are asleep on your mats."

"No."

"Because you were the guide for these people from the country of America who are now my prisoners and not because you are a spy in the employment of these soldiers of the republic?"

"Yes."

One of the officers strode over and slapped the boy hard in the face. The boy tumbled into the mud, and lay still until the man who said he was Raoul helped him to his feet.

"You will excuse him," he said. "My officers are distrustful of boy-guides from Moogradi. He thinks you have been making a count of our members."

The boy looked at the coursing ground. His shoulders were shaking.

"How many would you estimate are among us?"

"I do not know." The boy took a deep sigh and squared his shoulders. He looked into his inquisitor's eyes. "It was out of curiosity only. But your officers seem to come and go."

The man smiled sadly. He lay his hand over the backside of the boy, and said, "Yes. Yes. I agree. They come and they go."

"I am sorry," the boy said.

"Yes, we are all sorry." He held the boy's cheek in the hand with the shorn fingers, and lifted the boy's head into the rain. "Look up there," he said.

The boy squinted his eyes and looked up into the cold rain. The mountains here stretched another ten thousand feet, but the sky was all but black now and the boy could see nothing of that vast height in the blinding rain.

"We are as numerous as the rain drops," the man said. "That is how many." The man allowed him to lower his face, and affectionately tousled the boy's hair. The officers wove in and out. The boy was now convinced they had burrowed some crawl space through the mountain. But it would have taken them many years to accomplish this; perhaps the task was begun even before he was born. The war had been going on a long time.

The man and the boy watched as the two male prisoners rose and staggered over to the rocks and dropped down into a heap near where the woman was lying.

"Why are they so spiritless?" the man asked the boy. "We have not harmed them."

The boy peered at his thin ankles puddled in the muddy, streaming water. "No, you did not harm them. But they did not believe it would be so difficult as this, reaching Kolooltopec."

"Then they are crazy."

"Yes. They are crazy."

The woman seemed to be trying to scramble away from the two men, but her feet kept sliding from beneath her as rainwater sluiced its trails down the mountain. There was no place she could go, in any event.

Some of the officers were still digging into the mountainside. Others were laboriously attempting to get a fire going beneath a teepee of small, smoking sticks erected within a ring of stones.

The boy found he had fallen asleep, because when he opened his eyes the man was shaking him.

"My prisoners whom you are guiding to Kolooltopec, do they have money? How is it they are funding this elusive expedition?"

"I do not know. They are very strange on the subject."

"In what manner?"

"They bargained long hours with my family before my fee could be settled. They feared they might be cheated."

"What was the settlement, may I ask?"

"My family received one thousand moolees. A second thousand is to be paid upon my safe return."

The man's face brightened. "Two thousand? Two thousand moolees is very little. Such a sum, I believe, would amount to no more than ten or so of your friend Emma's American dollars."

"Yes. But since the Koo does not exist then the expedition to it is foolish and thus has no value. So my family did not wish to charge extravagantly for my services."

"Agreed. But there is still the issue of your time and expertise. Do you know the word, 'expertise'?"

"Yes."

"Or there might also be the extra remuneration to your family for the small informational services you are meant to provide the soldiers of the republic."

"No."

The man smiled and playfully ruffled the boy's hair. The boy shivered.

"On the other hand, you are serving your explorers as guide through a terrain totally unknown to yourself. Do you agree?"

"Yes."

"So the sum of two thousand moolees is perhaps fair."

"Yes. Such was my family's determination after long deliberation of the matter, and after much imbibing of the pulqoo."

"Ah, the pulqoo! Did your adventurers admire the pulqoo?"

"They became very merry. They could not stand up. The woman said she would return once she found Kolooltopec, and marry any handsome man in my village who could provide her with an eternal flow of the pulqoo."

"She said this!"

"Many times."

They looked admiringly over at the woman. She was holding a flat wedge of slate over her head, this slate providing shelter of a sort, under which her downcast face was hidden by multiple curtains of rain and a fine mist now steaming up from the earth.

"Yes, many times," the boy said. "But the next day she repented."

He pulled the woman's wet hair out from his pocket and showed it to this man who might or might not be the legendary figure Raoul.

The hair was examined at length although the man would not touch it.

"Did the soldiers of the republic do this to our Emma?"

"No. She clipped the hair herself because of the heat."

"It was not the best hair, to begin with."

"No. It is not the best hair."

Finally he was told to return the woman's hair to his pocket, and the boy quickly complied.

"And our other prisoners, what did they do under influence of the pulqoo?"

"They argued and shouted. They danced and sang."

"As did your own people?"

"Yes."

"And how is it your poor family in the insolvent village of Moogradi chanced to have such a wealth of the wonderful pulqoo?"

"The jugs had been hidden, along with my sisters, when the soldiers of the republic occupied our village. It did not take much pulqoo to arouse the enthusiasm of our distinguished visitors."

"My officers would give much to have this pulqoo in front of them this minute."

The officers who heard this left off their digging and fire-building to shout out "Pulqoo, Pulqoo," while thrusting their arms time and time again into the air.

"But alas," the man said. "Alas, the pulqoo is all hidden away in Moogradi, side by side with its young daughters."

"Alas."

The officers had succeeded in getting a fire going. It was a high blaze now, with thick smoke pummeling above the flames and vanishing moments later within the ceaseless rain.

"Excuse me," the officer said.

The woman's head was down between her bent knees, her shoulders scrunched. She looked up, startled, when his hands touched her. He said something to her and the boy, incomprehensibly, heard her laugh. The man helped her to her feet and led her over to the fire. One of the many officers milling about there dislodged a large stone and rolled it up by the fire. The man seated her upon the stone and after a moment her face lifted and she held her hands up to the fire. Several officers thrust their little spits of food upon her, but this she refused.

The other two prisoners arose and staggered towards the assembly.

The man returned and stood by the boy, who had given up trying to follow the movements of the officers and could no longer even guess at their numbers.

"We will first warm them," the man said. "Perhaps then we will shoot them."

"The Toodoo family thanks you in their behalf."

"On the other hand, if my officers shoot them the Toodoo family of Moogradi will be denied their next one thousand moolees and our adventurers will never reach Kolooltopec."

"They will not reach it in any case."

The boy's eyes snapped open. For a moment he had imagined he saw doors opening in the mountainside and a stream of officers, endless in number, entering and leaving.

The man knelt beside him.

"These soldiers of the republic, in their garrison at the headwaters, were they many?"

"No more than fifty."

"Well-armed?"

"Yes. With heavy weapons, including artillery. Many trucks, and armored vehicles without number."

"Yes. More vehicles than they have soldiers to fill them. But such vehicles can not scale these mountains. Are they well-fed?"

"They have much food, and more cargo arriving by the hour."

"Which cargo they will not distribute among the people for whom it is intended. Is this correct?"

The boy spat into the mud at his feet.

"These goods are stamped in what manner?"

"The usual."

The man was quiet for a long time.

The boy heard some little noise from afar and thought he saw a trip of goats at graze beyond the clearing.

He closed his eyes, hugging himself against the rain.

It was a very cold rain now, and he could not stop his limbs from shaking; his buttocks were all but numb in the icy, flowing water, and a wind was whipping the rain against his face. He had his shoulders turned towards the fire and he imagined he could feel some little heat against the skin.

"And what did these heroes of the republic say to you of my officers?"

"They were contemptuous. Raoul's forces were puny, and cowardly, and beneath consideration, they said. His officers were of diminished capacity, without weaponry, the daughters of rodents, and were at final rot in the jungle. The insurrection would soon be terminated, they said, and your heads afloat in the river."

"Yes. Yet they are frightened and dare not venture outside their garrisons, except to pillage and burn innocent villages, and rape and maim our sisters. What is the news of the latest atrocity?"

"We saw fresh burning along the river. The villagers at the headwaters spoke of many corpses. Some say it is the work of your officers. Most believe otherwise."

The officer unslung his rifle, yanked back the bolt, and showed the boy his rifle's empty chamber. He stroked the wet stock before returning the weapon to his shoulder.

"Lamentable, yes?" he said. "But do not surmise from this deficiency that we are unempowered."

The boy did not speak of that other matter of which he had heard whispered speculation, even within the household of the Toodoo family of Moogradi: of the many villages, up and down river, largely deserted now. Of the great secret exodus of his people to a sanctuary high in these mountains.

"My teacher spoke of Raoul's cause with much reverence."

"He who has vanished."

"Yes."

"And is likely rotting in the jungle."

"Yes. Or his head afloat in the river."

"Perhaps your scholar has found bliss in Kolooltopec."

"That is doubtful."

"I agree. That is all but impossible. But your friends, you say, have with them a map."

"Yes. It is wrapped in skin inside the woman's pocket."

"In Emma's pocket. And what is in the pockets of her companions? Money? Tobacco? Beads? The pulqoo?"

"I do not know. They have a card."

"A card?"

"Yes. A gold card."

"A card made of gold? I do not believe it. For what purpose?"

"I am uncertain. They took their gold card to the bank in Foolderoo and came out with a fistful of our moolees, one thousand of which they presented to my family. I saw this with my own eyes."

"I must see this card of gold."

"Of course."

"And the map."

"Naturally."

"My officers are expert readers of maps."

"Yes."

"And we know the country."

"Precisely."

"You do not think our presence would diminish your own guide's assignment?"

"Quite the contrary."

"A thousand such maps distributed wisely along the river might prove profitable for those hidden away beside your pulqoo."

"Yes. If Kolooltopec exists."

"But it does not exist."

"No. Even so, the woman asleep by the fire has the map."

"Yes. Perhaps we should join her."

"If you are satisfied a boy from Moogradi deserves this honor."

"I can not attest to the boy's honor. But I will extend to you our welcome."

"I am grateful."

They could see steam rising from the flesh of the three outsiders, and their wet clothes smoking. Some few other fires were alight now and the officers, some thirty or more, huddled around these, on this craggy lip of mountain.

For a moment the rain thinned and the boy thought he saw a thousand faces strung out over the hillside, and fires from a string of other such encampments carved into the mountainside; in these could be seen the stark faces of mothers nursing their babies, and old women tending the fire pots; he could see bony children of his own age and younger at kneel upon the stone shelves, and goats, and pigs, and burros, and an ancient, bedraggled figure with hollow eyes seated upon a bird cage.

But he blinked and shook his head and when his eyes cleared they had all vanished. There was only loud, coursing water, and great sheets of rain splattering like gunshots all about them.

The boy slumbered by the fire, his body at rest among the three adventurers for whom he was guide. He was thinking of the one thousand moolees paid and of the one thousand more his family in Moogradi would likely never receive, since Kolooltopec was only a figment of the crazy imagination.

He slept. Then it was morning, and blinding sunlight, and the earth already baking, and considerable activity in their encampment.

"Onwards," the officers were shouting. "Onwards to Kolooltopec!"

Up and down the mountainside came the same cry. "Onwards. Onwards to Kolooltopec!"

RALEIGH
IN THE NEW WORLD

We hastened over the dunes and up to the hill where the watcher stood hollering.

A white bird of magnificent span had skirred in and was beating its wings above a large dog. The dog was the bird's exact white hue, the dog leaping at the bird and yapping furiously.

Raleigh said nothing.

Out on the shoals our ship was listing; the wood was bursting as if under cannonball, the air skimble-skamble with volleys of flying splinters.

The rigged sails were whipping.

The bird dropped lower, hovering inches above the dog, which now was whining and spinning in diminishing compass.

Raleigh said nothing.

A black lay panting at the water's edge, still shackled to his oar.

The bird stabbed its talons into the dog's ribside and the dog twisted and yelped and scrambled with a moan into deep sand.

Then bird and dog lifted away.

The black clawed to anchor himself into the churning sand.

Raleigh said nothing.

The seaman guarding our sideboat screamed as high waves lifted and scurried the craft forward.

The great bird was struggling to get itself and its catch airborne.

Raleigh said nothing.

When we looked again where the slave had been the space was empty, though some dozen yards back we could see, like the fin of a fish, the tip of oar.

Raleigh said nothing.

The bird climbed seawards.

The wind was swirly.

Wind ruffled the bird's feathers, the dog's legs tucked up forlornly under its belly.

Then the sun struck our eyes and, lo, we were blinded.

Raleigh said nothing.

Then bird and its catch plummeted.

We trudged the deep sand to a forward incline.

The sideboat guardsman was gone, and the sideboat gone also. The black was gone, though his oar was floating.

Some eight or ten others were bobbing in foam, and going.

Raleigh said nothing.

The dog's head rolled; it batted its eyes at us most entreatingly. The boat cracked. Only its withers held above water.

Shrieks one upon the other sounded out over the expanse.

"Can ye eat a bird of this disposition?" the man holding the bird requested.

Raleigh said nothing.

"Can ye eat the dog?" entreated another.

Some thirty or fifteen of our crew were washed up and floating.

Never had we seen such a mush of sea ivy.

The dog whimpered and ceased its struggles. The bird scrabbled about on its beak and broken wing in vain attempt to soar into the heavens. The seaman holding the bird cried out and fell back into the sand, kicking himself away with a flurry of heels.

Some ten to twenty of our crew laughed our cajolery.

When another large wave receded, our sideboat receding with it; the guardsman clung to its mounts, shouting most peculiarly, while further down the black we had seen earlier was beheld beached and alive, the oar gripped by both hands and groping himself forward inch by inch, with his oar as crutch or anchor.

Raleigh said nothing.

The tide reclaimed some twenty or fifty and still he said nothing.

The dog wheeled its bereft eyes upon us, moaning.

The cripply bird sighted us angrily.

"Fetch a stick and kill it," one in our party said, though we remained as planted.

Raleigh said nothing.

A monstrous creaking was heard out upon the water. Next, the masts popped clean and the sails corkscrewed off into the hereafter.

Up hewn to the foredeck was our Queen's apparition. She was looking our way with longing. Then the vessel heaved itself flat-over and quickly went about its sinking.

Some quartermile downshore a cadre of survivors were firing musket into the bushes.

Right and left without pause the tide condemned our members.

Raleigh said nothing.

THE JUDGE:
HIGH PLAINS ART

*T*hey told me the judge was coming. They said he'd be pulling in about midday. I walked up around the mesquite bushes where the dead men slumped down to their knees, one pair, the other pair down on their sides, the legs tucked in. I looked out over the plains but couldn't see the judge or anyone else coming.

I can't wait all day, I said. I got other business to be looking after.

Ye best wait, they said. Ye don't won't to git on the judge's wrong side.

I'll give him an hour or two, I said. Then I'm riding out.

Hours later, the judge still hadn't come. There wasn't anything to see out on the plains except a half dozen meatbirds hanging and gliding.

I'm going, I said.

Ye best not, they told me. Ye best think twice and three times on that question.

Hell, I said. The judge don't scare me. He's a human being the same as me.

No, he ain't, they said. He's the judge.

Near sundown, he still hadn't showed. I'd sent out a rider to spot for him but the rider hadn't come back either.

The meatbirds, brazen as you please, scooped down and got a beak or two into the dead before we could flutter them off.

The judge won't like that, they said. The judge don't like the evidence tampered none. He don't mind it so much though when he knows a person is telling the truth.

How can he tell, I asked, if a man chooses to lie?

He can, they said. He's right gifted in that department.

I went out and studied a minute on the men I'd killed. I had four of them, bad men all, trussed up back to back in two pairs. I'd stood them up and put the bullet in the brow of the one facing me so that bullet could go on through the head of the one tied up to him, so that with one bullet I could kill the two. Then the other pair done the same way. They were all four older than me.

My bullets were on the dwindling side. That's why I done it that way. If the judge was any kind of judge he wouldn't find no fault in this.

Maybe he had some ammunition I could buy off him.

That was one reason to wait for him. I couldn't care one widget about his right or wrong side.

Not that I hadn't heard of him and wasn't curious. I'd heard of him for most of a thousand miles, through much of the nine months I'd been crossing these high plains. How nobody had elected or appointed him, how he carried no law book under his arm or otherwise, but how he rode up to a place where trouble was or had been, said he was the judge, and settled the matter in whichever manner occurred to him. If you crossed him or spoke your disagreement to his face, then he settled that too. The word was he had killed upwards of a hundred, some with his bare hands, before folks started accepting as a matter of course that he was the judge and nothing to do but accept whatever decision come down.

So in that regard he was the same as every other judge.

I wasn't worried none. I'd been within my rights killing these four and if the judge didn't like it he was in for a battle. With him dead I might go on and take up his judgeship myself. God knows there was money in it and hot baths and that wouldn't hurt me not one little bit.

I got to thinking along these lines and wishing the judge would come and he'd come down on the side of the four dead men, so then I'd have to kill me a judge, there being no more right nor wrong to it than that.

I had me enough rounds left to finish him off.

The thing was to shoot where he'd be ducking and not where he was.

When he hadn't arrived by full nightfall I sent me out another rider to scout for him and wean him my way, and the three of us left set by the campfire drinking and telling tall tales. I kept my eyes on my compatriots throughout, for I didn't trust them and far as I knew they were only waiting for me to turn my head, since the one was weasel-eyed and the other with a horse had gone lame and I'd seen that one whose horse it was eyeing mine and studying the empty notches in my belt.

We're ye witnesses, the one said, by that time drunk, and me and him will tell that judge you done exactly what ye had to do in killing them four.

We saw the gun battle from start to finish, the one or other said, which was a lie, for the battle was all over and the men dead by the minute this pair rode up.

I felt like the judge must feel, knowing they were lying, and I thought about killing them on the spot because of the falsehood, but I slowed down on that consideration when recalling me my skimpy ammo. I thought about killing them with my bare hands the way the judge did his, but we just instead passed the jug back and forth and now and then running over with a stob of lit firewood to scare off the meatbirds feeding in the dark, the two I'd first killed still sitting up back to back on their heels like they were having a powwow, while the other two was rolled over, the one with his hat squashed and his boots wrapped in buffalo cord.

We might should bury them dead, my two compatriots said, but the judge, it's said, likes to take note of the aging process, so he'd have more trouble than wanted, fixing the exact time you put your bullets into them.

He'd git right riled, the one said.

He's that careful is he? I said. This judge of yours, he don't let nothing slide?

Well, they said, if that's his mood. Ye can't never tell what will be the judge's mood, and I wouldn't bet hard silver on it, one way or another.

My horse pawed the ground and we all jumped, though it won't nothing more than a rattle snake.

We said no more, but crawled off and had the light dose, with one eye open or mine was.

In the morning it was one riderless horse reined up by the dead fire and about a hundred meatbirds out where the four dead men had been, their flesh already picked to the bone.

Oh God, my two compatriots said, the judge is going to be fit to be tied, he sees this turnaround. He will likely convict us everyone on the spot and kill us off one by one with his bare hands, as a lesson to one and all that his will is not to be denied.

They were jumpy, sure enough. For some minutes they palavered in hot whispers, and the next minute they were riding hell for leather across the high plains, the one with the lame horse left behind and now astride the good horse, though not mine, God knows.

I picked them off clean with the Winchester, having no choice in the matter, then rode out to claim what now was mine, which was property owed to me, as I reasoned the issue, since their skedaddling had exhausted me near the last of my ammo.

The one's foot still hung to the stirrup and the horse skittish, but I calmed the horse with soft words and strokes along the neck before I could empty the dead man's pockets and search among the saddlebags. But here was lean pickings, as expected, though in the other man's belongings I found gold medallion from Mexico, it bent and a hole poked through it, and the bag jam full of trinkets wrapped in a white garment such as women took to wearing way back yonder. An underneath thing, flimsy to the touch and a glory to behold, though right moldy and the trinkets rusting, and why my compatriot should have these in his possession a startlement to the mind.

All morning of this second day I waited around, me on a high shelf behind rock, the horses staked, and still the judge didn't come.

I wondered if the whole shebang hadn't been concocted in the whirling dust, the judge a figment in the minds of these few souls you ever come across out here on these desolate high plains.

I wondered did I dare give over the last of my ammo to the demise of the lame horse, or should I let the horse pace after me when I vamanosed, since it would do that, pace after me long as able, till it give out and the meatbirds swooped down and feasted.

I wondered could I afford the lame horse pacing behind me, what with the meatbirds in pursuit, and what then if my own horse went lame? This was a humbling position to be in and frankly who I blamed was the judge, for in waiting for him my grub had give out, and my water and strong drink, and my patience, and I didn't hardly perceive how I could journey through to civilization given the few cartridges remaining in my gun belt and my foot tender through snakebite and every man and his brother, including Injuns, out to smite you.

All day I watched the sagebrush roll and the mesquite blur in my vision, the heat slamming down in waves so thick a better man could have walked them straight up into paradise.

Such was my thoughts as I struck off, sore at heart, and cussing the lame horse, which came on after me despite my kicking its face. It seemed to me after a spell of long thinking that the judge had planned this every step of the way, his decision drawn from afar, from the unknown beyond, convicting me of the killing of the four dead men, not to mention my compatriots during my bivouac, and all without a shred of evidence or me without a single opportunity to speak up for my actions or defend my good name.

That varmint, I thought. Now wasn't that one sorry trick for him to pull on me who never once has set eyes on his face, but isn't that just what you would expect from one calling himself a judge?

All I hoped was I'd cross him somewhere up ahead, before I gave out or he gave out, and I would shoot the bastard upon sight or he'd drill me, one or the other, whichever way it come out.

Then I rounded a turn up by the Black Coyote mesa, and there he was, obstructing my path, him afoot, all strung with bandoleer, his rifle jacked, his every finger ringed, wearing porkpie hat, a tight eastern suit, his face bright, him smiling like he'd known me since my very first step. Saying, "Son, did ye think you could escape me? Did ye not adhere to the view that justice was blind? Have ye not sneered when ye heard my name? Will ye now plead the case of the beggar's mercy or will ye take your medicine in the same potion that ye so readily have give it out?"

NATIVE ART

One Foot and I and our beset tribe found ourselves on the lam through the Dakotas, and many yesteryears removed from those encounters here I am alone floating upriver on the Nile. The Nile? They said it was the Nile and took my passage money with nothing back. At night this was, off a black pier. You walked a shaky plank and hoped it was a boat at the end. Stay in line, they said. No bickering. Yes, Princess, I will assist you with that trunk. You don't mind I drag the bitch?

The river banks were a dark entanglement, as I remembered, but in fact you do not see much when you are slung over the deck and sick to your very footsoles still from the crossing. Down below this was, where you could see nothing of what might be out there, including entanglements.

Some wondered what we would do, what would happen to us when we landed, and where we might land — the captain being vague, in fact silent on this issue, though I did not inquire myself, being more the willy-nilly type who goes where gunshots, fate, or romance decrees she must. My main concern was my wardrobe, and for that matter it still is, so long as I have my head, because my wardrobe with my tattered princess dress is all I have brought with me from my marriage to One Foot in the Water.

One Foot. Oh, One Foot! One Foot is in retreat from civilization's memory now, but once he was the famous leader of his people and husband married to the beautiful princess in her boned and beaded dress. I say this proudly. A certain dispersement of beings brought him all the way to Yale University on a professorship, which by one measure was that point in our lives where ascent and descent, happiness and unhappiness, had their bridge. A Chair this was called, the Jefferson Chair! But the hellhag bride was discovered aswim in her princess dress on the savage's arm and every weathercock and slubbergut mobbed the streets and we were shouldered back to the train. Scat! Never let us see your faces again! Or else!

Which was how we found ourselves again in aim for the Dakotas, our entire tribe in the meanwhile out there in a state of collapse and desuetude without their leader One Foot to harangue them or muzzle the extreme faction bent on the suicidal cause.

But all this trading of the aged news is discouraging to me now, as it might have been then, for we were both without our sap and listing in the wind after our long flight from the Chair zealots.

Our child arrived during the return journey from Yale and the commotion surrounding this natural event put great strain on every person in the six cars constituting that train, especially following an episode with a man who called himself Luther. This man flung burning fuel at my husband — this in the form of a torch that some attested appeared flaming from his very mouth — and did his best to slit our throats during the conflagration and hubbub, with everyone shouting and sliding fast as they could through the windows of the train which was hurtling at top-most raucous speed across the continent.

It was the swaying of these cars, I believe, and the constant clickety-clack, the heavy air, the stink of boots, which brought on our child's early birthing. I was already sore from the sticks hurled at us at Yale and hearing so often the Whiffinpoof song in rendition by groups of boys assembled on each street corner, and confused from the beginning by the endless talk of the Chair, the Chair.

Oh, I can make light of it now. Now that I am ten thousand miles removed from those shores and am beginning to breathe the sweet moisture of home. Usumbura we passed yesterday. Ruana Urundi tomorrow. They can't fool me. It is something in the blood.

My husband, pursued by these chair forces through the Dakotas over the span of three summers and winters, repeatedly had sent word to Yale's tireless posse that he had no interest in their Chair, or in the wealth that accompanied this appointment, as Jeffersonian democracy was neither his specialty nor a concept in total arrangement with his liking.

I would not recommend acceptance of this Chair, should the offer come your way.

I would be wary of any invitation to show yourself upon New Haven's public green.

Avoid the whole of this uneasy state, if you are able.

My husband told the Chair's emissaries that he under no circumstances could accept the Chair, even a Roving Chair, or ambassadorship, and in reaction to this sentiment we were ordered out of the Dakotas, advised that we must not step foot into any adjacent state or territory, nor think that we might take leave by water, for that ocean was under sovereign jurisdiction as well.

So all right, I lie. I veer from strict truth.

But we were on the lam through the Dakotas for some many seasons, the Chair's supporters in hot pursuit and our tribe decimated and factions arising at every turn, since none of us knew that much about why it was that such hoards of influential and moneyed people were willing to sacrifice so many lives or effect such widespread deprivation all in order to bring about One Foot's ensconcement in the deplorable Chair.

A council of elders was called and in one voice, after but a few minute's deliberation, they summoned us before them and said, "One Foot in the Water, take the Chair."

Take it before all our people are dead and only our bones are left to rattle through these Dakotas.

Off we went to Yale for receipt of this honor.

Until our arrival that rain-soggy day, we had not known even of the existence of violent and powerful forces simultaneously at work to prevent just this occurrence.

Yet also at Yale, in the president's house where we were in the initial days lodged, some kind and consummately patient person sewed scores and scores of roses onto the lining of my princess dress. These were of the old York variety, with each thorn carefully removed and fine invisible mending done on the hem, where my heels back in the Dakotas had time and time again caught the beaded and boned fringe.

Every bead polished, every bone wiped, our bed-covers folded back, the pillows bestrewn with further displays of these blossoms.

Two bleached antelope shin-bones also crossed over my pillows, which sign made me tremble, for they spoke of home. Decades in the flow since and me but a nip-pling when uprooted.

I wore these petals next to my skin and wept, for it had been a long time since we had enjoyed privilege or mercy of any kind.

One Foot cried, to see me bathe, these lovely petals at float on the scented water.

Our bed and the floor about that bed ablaze with York blossom, and the air afire with the airy petals as we loved. Us little expecting these times to be our last hours of bliss in each other's embrace.

At five the butler's bell rang and we passed down the stairs to a gay reception and dinner.

"Perhaps you will get accustomed to sitting in this Chair," I said to my husband.

"Good bed," he said. "I like beds." And went on to explain his view that the entire westward expansion owed everything to the presence of these eastern beds. So I saw he was putting good face on this Chair issue, and thinking better of Jeffersonian principles in the aftermath of our couplings.

A stone occasionally strikes the deck of this boat, and skids off into water. We are told black infidels are ashore in the bush, tracking our passage, and to be watchful for poisoned arrows, though I have yet to see any proof of this menace. Only these small bouncing stones or harmless splats of mud which a child might mindlessly fling.

A crew-member sent by the captain stands solemn-ly beside me and after a long interval presses a warm glass in my hands. I drink its contents without inquiry, and return the glass to him. He does not quit my side.

"What was in the glass?" I ask.

He cocks his head indifferently, standing close by on spread legs.

"A soporific," he says.

"It had the taste of rum."

"A soporific, Princess. With rum, to settle the stomach."

He smells of monkey. I have seen any number of these animated creatures at swing in the wheelhouse or scampering along the deck. But I will not satisfy him by stirring even one inch, and my little knife as always is at the ready. I have stuck it through tougher beings than this one man.

"The captain wishes I should report to you that your trunk is secured."

Although he smiles, I am not deceived. He would pitch me overboard and be done with me, without the smallest qualm.

"It is in the wheelhouse?"

"Yes, Princess. Padlocked under heaviest chain." He bows witlessly and tosses the glass my lips have touched into the Nile.

"Then how am I to have ready bargain with my clothes?"

He does not reply.

I thank him and at last, reluctantly, he goes.

I hang over the deck again, retching into black water, as night-birds thrash and squawk in the trees.

Curiously, our train-car had palest-blue balloons in danglement from every inch of ceiling, these aloft at a level equal to the heads of those men and women standing in tight press along the aisles. Each few seconds a smoker's cigar would burst one or another of these, and each man in the vicinity reached for his blade or hand-gun. One Foot could not remove his gaze from this display of dancing blue balloons, the presence of which puzzled him greatly and elicited endless whispered commentary into my ear. He sought to find messages in this armada of balloons as he did in the night's sing of stars, and was vexed by his inability to conjure same, although he laughed mightily each time a balloon popped from the ceiling and on its own accord shot at dazzling speed its wild orbit above our heads.

The child was coming; I was in considerable torment and retained my composure, I hope, although One Foot was sorely incensed that no one in the packed car would surrender his seat or even squirm so much as an inch to right or left. But he was already hobbled in one leg from the fray on the public green at Yale, plus suffering dog bite which now was festering, plus carrying in addition deep wounds in his side from his youthful wars.

He could do little to right the matter beyond arranging some little rope's length of comfort for me in that space on the cold floor beneath the gentlemen's feet. I lay on this slab of grit and boots and food spat from the traveller's mouth, shuddering with the clickety-clack of iron against iron and in the grip of deepest anxiety and pain, for this child was my first and coming early and my attendants all scattered in result of the fray at Yale.

Pity me, to have been so senseless as to wear my princess dress.

It worried me that my dress should not survive the ordeal, or that my child might not, and between bursts of pain and the dizziness of balloons, I had mind to consider my great wardrobe of seven steamer trunks long since reduced to the one, and One Foot's worry that he could no longer provide for me. It is a pitiful thing to see this recognition sap a prideful man, and I wept bitter tears for his misery and for my own and my laboring child.

These gentlemen pressed their boots about my head and chest and limbs through the entire birthing process, their cigars in ceremonious toil and their ash in steady cascade about my face. Their boots kicked and prodded my flesh at every turn, some perhaps unconsciously, to render them that justice. My floor space smelt of pigshit and piss and the eastern civilizations enough to make me gag. Soldiers in attendance to see to our safety were at cards, or bent with drink and frivolity, or such obscenity as betokens handshake with the uniform. They lifted not the one hand, but instead inflamed the matter, which did not in the least surprise us, given the discord in surround of the Jefferson Chair.

Oddly, a gentleman sharing our cramped compartment sat in study of an Eastern paper though near the whole of my birthing throes, often kicking his boots against my head and body in his excitement as he discoursed upon the rights and wrongs of the Jefferson Chair, and its rich endowment, which investment seemed to his mind to exist in contrary fashion to the democratic ideals the Chair's very creation was meant to promulgate.

Mr. Jefferson had never been a piece of God's creation that he could champion, he said, and had Mr. Hamilton shot the rascal, as so often had been his desire, the country would have been saved much grief.

There was something cunning under way with this business, he said, and it was his guess that European monarchists were behind the whole of it; they had put up the coin, no doubt about that, he said, and duped the intelligentsia at Yale, which institution had sorely declined since its removal from old Saybrook. But what could you expect, given the tenor of these times. A great debauchment of the people's trust was in the wind now that the laws of entail and primogeniture were at lapse. Much claptrap, he said, was being put about with regard to the requirements of education for the poor and uncivil, with slave and redman and pick-pocket rising to assail one at every turn. Women strutted in secret, arrogant rule up and down every corridor of power from the Potomac to Yale, and the country would suffer calamitously if the citizenry did not soon come to its senses and cast off the foreign yoke. Hang the scoundrels at home, who knew not where their bread and butter did come. Cast off this puerile exercise in freethinking, which rewarded only freeloading rodent, chimney-sweep, and slubberdegullion. The county must forsake its restless clamoring for art and the snooty ideal and the luxurious life for every upstart or fieldhand with tongue to flap or arsehole to fart it out of.

A great boomswell of "ayes" sounded in aftermath of this speech, and heavy trampling of boot where I lay in dire sweat, huffing and puffing, with thrusting pelvis, my water sloshing beneath me and the flesh of poor One Foot's palm between my teeth chewed into rag.

"Aye!" they said. "All the evils of this nation's business can be seen in this episode of the Chair!"

"Aye, the Chair, heaven help us!"

But now my husband forced some little extraction of space between my legs and slung my limbs high upon his shoulders, for he took news from my shrieks and thrusts that the child was in its daylight chamber and he must be my woman and my midwife now.

The gentlemen through some precious moment or two fell silent, and stayed their feet.

I shrieked anew to see my heels at lock about my lover's neck and to glimpse his bloodied hands at work between my naked legs. Sweat roiled upon our skins and the jolting pain now was without surcease. I closed my eyes and locked my teeth on whatever came between them, as for instance the toe of the talkative gentleman's boot. But he grappled this away from me, with a show of bad humor which found release in a stream of lurid comment upon the vileness of travel in this ignorant age.

With each new siege my feet thrashed against my husband's face and chest, my great belly heaving and my buttocks at slushy romp, until at last he was made to force them into the grip or brace of whatever man of quality would consent.

The men, at crowd upon us, by and large, seemed bored with our activity, or assumed attitudes in antipathy with our goals, and soon went on again with their scholarly perquisites.

"Women should not ride the train," one of these said, "and there's the proof."

Another chorus of "Ayes" sounded, and much toasting to this chap.

The man with the newspaper announced that he held exalted status with the Halls of Transport and Railroads, and that he normally would be found riding in the owner's caboose, with mugs of hard cider in each hand and comely Chinee wenches in slit red dresses showing ample ankle or even garter belt to see to his every need. There followed a great tipping of hats and a flood of inquiries about the availability within that office of other exalted jobs.

On this occasion, the man said, the caboose had been turned over to that Chair savage from the Dakotas who had incited the riot at Yale and trampled innocent children underfoot. Yes, thanks to government intervention and outright laxitude, lawless, irreligious hoards could usurp a fine man's seat anywhere in the land, and it was high time a Cotton Whig took hold of the realm and hung this low-life from a tree, wherever they be found.

Yes, yes, the savage was riding this very train, he said, and likely coupling this very minute on the owner's divan with his black princess who, as was well-known, had cavorted shamelessly with a thousand men away there in the Egyptland she came from..

"Aye, aye!" the others said. "'Tis well known."

There's some as should hold the line, he said, as to which raw whore they'll take aboard a good slave ship.

"Aye!"

Profit or not, there's principles at stake here!

"Aye! We ought to go ourselves and plug the bitch!"

But at this moment the vulgarian's attention was drawn to One Foot, as if he had but just noticed my husband's presence for the first time. He offered his fatted hand for shaking, and for some protracted seconds that hand hung at mean jiggle above my eyes, One Foot's own hands being at busy engagement between my legs.

"And what is your opinion on these matters, sir?" this magpie asked One Foot. "Do you have views, I mean, as a redman and savage, on this treasonable business with the Chair?"

At this very moment my child's head slipped loose of all encumbrances, sorely irritating this unsavory clown. I strained and huffed, certain I was being torn apart limb by limb. One Foot planted his legs anew, forcing my legs wider yet; a snarl was fixed upon his lips and glitter showed in his eyes and for an instant his sight locked with mine. "Push, bitch," I heard someone growl; One Foot's fingers probed inside me deep as a barge pole; he spat and yanked as I howled; I was aware of a great sucking, slurpish sound which seemed to arise from the entire car, and my guts ripping, then a swoosh, and then a great vacuum or hole suddenly opened inside my womb; this emptiness swept onwards and in the instant took hold upon my brain. My very bones seemed to have been scoured. Heaven help me, yes. My eyes opened and I saw the newborn gliding smoothly upwards, flowing like a skein of syrup between my bloodied legs into One Foot's nimble, fraught, embrace.

"Aye, duckie!" someone said. And henhouse cackles all around.

My husband held the child high in the one hand, smacking rump.

"Sir?"

One Foot's hand at last shot out and shook Big Mouth's lingering paw.

"Indeed, sir," One Foot said to him. "Indeed I have views."

I arose —"You will move the buttocks, sir"— and took back my seat.

But that our child was a beauty to behold and born in perfect health despite the setting I have described, I leave to more proper and learned annals in our history to chronicalize in detail.

We named her Oryxes II, in my tongue, and Foot of the Dogs, in our shared language, with more than a few exchanges between ourselves of the mirthful code.

Some little aftermath of tranquillity must have followed this birthing, for I do recall I was asleep when this Luther person disconnected himself from that throng of travellers occupying each dot and parcel of seat and aisle. My eyes blinked, I mean to say, and in the next moment I felt the crush of One Foot's body slung across mine and our child's, though not before I saw the flaming torch in arched flight upon our very selves. And every man and woman screaming and trampling away from the fire's orbit, without regard for neighbor or friend.

From this attack I suffered a few unremarkable burns, together with nose bleed from one or another wild elbow, plus tintinabulation, plus gore everywhere, and nothing to do with that dress except fling it at the first bush. But later I gave this decision second thinking and coerced myself into reclaiming the garment with a good wash, plus tincture of lye, plus needle and thread. Oryxes was unharmed, and One Foot's diminishment only the little greater, though the nature of his disfigurations in body and spirit did have weight upon me wearisome unto my depths. His mind was in deep cogitation of these Jeffersonian principles thrust upon him, and this study tired him mightily. What had seemed obvious now seemed arguable, he told me, and the vice-versa. Each simple issue or statement of plain truth now arrived in his mind with interminable codicil, or long-winded preface, with gazette and appendices, or contrary council and allegation, and footnotes that went on into eternity. He feared his new scholar's mind was now in session with the full academic committee, and it tired him, it tired him, *it lays me low, my darling.*

Through the oily, coal-dusted windows could be seen vultures at glide with our traffic. They gobbled flesh as they sailed. When morsels fell from their beaks, crows swooped in from nowhere, with raucous chatter, to claim what was theirs.

At Yale, a woman wearing a scarlet bonnet had asked my husband which of these many eastern inventions he was witness to had most impressed him.

"The hammock," he said.

The president of that institution had taken us aside and said how sad he was that Meriwether could not be with us to celebrate my husband's ascension to the Chair. "Villains struck him down, you know. Years ago. On the Natchez Trace."

"Yes. My princess and I were much enriched by our association with him during the Expedition, as with our correspondence through the years."

"I understand you were most helpful to him during those difficult Louisiana years."

"Princess was."

The president bowed and kissed my hand. "We have much to learn," he said. "I understand your lineage can be traced as far back as the Middle Empire's Amenehet." I bowed to him, fluttering an impervious hand.

"Mr. Clark, alas, is also in the grave," he said to my husband. My husband fidgeted. He regretted Mr. Clark's demise, but had never forgiven him his decisions in the nasty Black Hawk affair.

"What do you hear of Sacajawea?" he asked us.

Ah, I thought: dear old Sacajawea. Even Whig bankers loved Sacajawea.

"She is toothless now," I said. "Though still the charmer. Her grandchildren are strung throughout the Dakotas and Wyoming. They are all great warriors."

He sniffed. "I smell roses," he said.

At that minute a rock crashed through the window; agitators were assembling on the lawn.

*T*he Captain's man again appears by my side. A monkey clambers about on his shoulder. The monkey regards me with merry, attentive eyes, looking over my attire to determine if I possess anything that can be put to its own use.

"The Captain regrets the food aboard-ship is all contaminated," the man says. "It is all at rot."

"Your Captain has never heard of salt?" I ask. "Of smoke?"

"Unfortunately, the pineapple does not smoke. Regrettably, the orange does not salt."

He scratches the monkey's belly. The monkey gyrates on his shoulder, then produces an orange.

I snatch at this fruit and have my teeth sunk into it almost before it has left the monkey's hand.

"To your health, Princess," the man says. He spins on his heels, the monkey chatters, and both are gone.

This man is not so bad after all.

Juice drips from my mouth. I have not eaten in a month.

Minutes later, the monkey returns. He hops about in noisy agitation at my feet, making horrendous noise. But he loses not a drop of what he has brought. A rum bottle bobs atop his head. He settles the rum glass in my hand, pours from the bottle, dances about once more, then rolls away like a wheel.

I hear gee-gaws of muffled laughter from the wheelhouse, and smile my own appreciation into the dark.

*I*mean not to dwell on my vicissitudes, being not the whiner type and finding such a parade of memories repellent to my nature, as earlier said. But there it is: history must be composed, if lessons are to be extracted and life ever improved, and the winds again to sing.

All history, I mean to say, is not written in blood. To cite an example, I will mention the Night of the Trees. Soon after our train had crossed the border into Canada, it braked to a sudden, lurching stop, and steam and dust engulfed us all. Urgent whistles rent the air and the very earth shook. The next moment passengers of every description were surging forth, the cars all but instantly emptying. Up and down the track people by the hundreds poured into the darkness, as though possessed by some claim of enthusiasm or madness beyond our normal call. Before one could make account for this, large beds of fire ba-roomed into being, these flaming campfires or outposts of light spreading far almost as the eye could encompass; in the shadows of these great flames an incalculable array of bodies swarmed this way and that, each man, woman, or child among them, it seemed, hastening to his or her objective as by some predetermined course and cause. Their heads and shoulders, sometimes the whole of their bodies, were soon obscured by their loads: massive trees, shrub plants, and flowering bush of every variety. These bodies in phantomish assembly, silhouettes at flow in graceful symmetry beneath the blackened sky. Others roved about in mysterious dialogue with pick and shovel, while numerous wagons pulled by horses barely larger than dogs arranged themselves in strange procession over the barren, ghostly plain, each of these instruments of transport piled high with mounds of black earth. In this

rich cargo blinked pinpricks of mirrors all at steady
flash, mica-chips, my husband observed, and over these
wagon loads rode a lattice-work of cages big and small.
An extraordinary convergence of wild, plumed birds
were at flutter within these cages; birds swayed upon
the creaking carts with their heads under wing, or held
forth as statuesque sentinels transcribing shrieks and
clucks and throaty, rapturous song into the dark,
implausible night. Still other conveyances arrived, some
as though dropped from the starry sky. In these prowled
a montage of beasts large and small, many of a species
heretofore unseen in the new world, you would think;
these beasts arranged either in quiet curiosity as to what
mercies it was that awaited them, or in wild roar of outrage at what travesty already had ensnared them. Men
and women of oriental cast were everywhere to be seen,
come from nowhere to sound out their strange tongue to
one another while applying tong and hammer to some
spot immediately beneath where they stood.
Transforming that spot in the instant and moving on
decisively and with fierce muttering of excitement to the
next chosen place; and the whole of this teeming terrain
lit, as I say, by moonlight and torch — this flood of souls
released to some higher plain of endeavor.

Oryxes nursed, cutting her eyes to right and left.

The night wore on. The mysterious work on the
great plain beyond our windows continued without
letup.

Six white butterflies hovered at my window. They
disappeared the instant my eyes claimed them. Scant
seconds later they were at soft circling wing in the air
above my child's head. As one, they descended, settling
on the baby's brow. I sped them away with a wave of
hands, but the second my hands stilled they again
dropped as one upon the child's brow.

"She will live sixty years," my husband said.

Or die, I thought, in six days.

One Foot grasped my wrists to hold them quiet.

"Six days or sixty years," he said. "Do not wage war
against the stars."

I watched the butterflies traverse my newborn's face.

At this point in our journey we were days from even the smallest hamlet or outpost and indeed knew not where we were, or were bound; in the darkened coach, with all this before us, my husband's spirit had revived; he sucked at my one breast as Oryxes suckled the other.

"You will bring great scope to the assignment," I told him. "You will bring honor to us, and to Yale, and to the Jefferson Chair. In the spring I will take Oryxes home and walk with her among our pyramids."

So much was the sense of goodness upon us that we swore anew our vows, pledging a strengthened loyalty to all in nature that was tranquil and harmonious.

Through the night the army worked beyond our windows, and at daybreak when the great fires were nothing more than ashen piles a great virgin forest stood in seemingly endless stretch towards the horizon; the arid plain was no more. Birds were in bivouac in the trees, or in summit each to each, and beasts and fowl at roam among the foliage and dazzlement of blossoms.

Something unyielding in the heart had finally yielded, I thought, and created this amazing oasis.

In the distance one could hear mighty waterfalls, and witness their wet haze in the clouds.

Morning, now.

Those who had disembarked came on again as the sun rose. They wore their previous composure now, and showed no evidence of toil; they were eastern loud-mouths in suit-coats and boots, in quaint round-topped hats and string ties. They were demure ladies in unsoiled travellers' dress, in high-top shoes that still carried shine; they were strutting schoolboys and young gentlemen in apprenticeship to a latitude of professions and trades. Boisterous soldiers, as drunk or obscene as they had been earlier, trooped in noisy combat or comradeship up and down the aisles, to fling themselves into whatever empty seat or lap their province of thought led them. Old men and women hobbled aboard, as bent by ache and disfigurement as when they had disembarked. Hardly the crew, you would think, to have wrought what they had wrought through this wondrous night.

The fat impresario of the railroad swung elbows, fitting himself again beside me into his old seat. His bloated, immaculate hand thrust itself One Foot's way.

"Now," he said. "You were saying. As a redman and savage, and one who has known the unblessed life, what might be your thoughts about that infernal Yale Chair? Every scalawag and dog to have his day? Is that your tune?"

"Them coolies," I heard one woman whisper to another, passing along the aisle. "I couldn't make out the single word! Must we have ignorant foreigners in pigtails building our railroads?"

Our boat chugs on through the night, aimless as a plank tossed into water. Our stomachs have soothed and we repose on the deck like bundles of hay dropped haphazardly over the rail. Wind rakes at old cuts in the flesh, and my bones acknowledge their age. The sky has blackened, we can see nothing. Our boat scrapes bottom, brushes invisible foliage, and one can feel the lean of a thousand trees; we lift uncertain hands to dislodge drooping vines. One hears an occasional splash in the water, nearby or in the distance, and the heart quivers: is it fish or one of our own, sliding away into the black mystery?

The captain's man again returns, on shoes as silent as the evening's character.

"A pillow, Princess? The captain desires you should be comfortable."

Something else scrabbles across the deck, approaches me; already I have raised my knife. What does it want?

"It is only the monkey," the man tells me. "Come with a blanket."

Indeed, it is the monkey. I can smell now the raw smell. I can hear the monkey scratching its fur.

"Cover the princess," the man says. The monkey chatters a polite reply. I see the waves of yet a blacker darkness, and cool air, and the blanket settling lightly over my legs. The hair on the monkey's hands brushes my face.

"No rum?" I ask.

The rum glass finds my fingers. I hear the slosh of liquid in the glass. I drink.

"Tell the monkey thank you," I say to the captain's man.

"No need to," he says. "You already have. You could talk that Egyptian tongue, he'd likely understand that too."

They start to go.

"Should be quite the show," the man says. "Quite the celebration. Whole country at feverpitch. You're coming home, Princess."

It seems to me I can feel some timid increase in the boat's speed. Some added play in the waves. Some extra force in the breeze.

It occurs to me that I must have the captain's monkey. I must walk through the capitals of Europe, Asia, and the Far East. Through this continent and back again in the New World. I in my princess dress and the monkey at my side, our hands intertwined.

Oryxes the First, I seem to recall, had monkeys and birds sealed with her in her golden tomb.

The railhead at Winnipeg, where we took on the cattle and into whose terminus we had been re-routed, was not an improvement, although it was here a man named Riel, said to be a rabble-rouser and menace to the earth's inner-tuning, furtively boarded and sat with us and recited his name. He spoke into his chest, although his eyes darted everywhere. He was an outlaw, on the run. Branded a traitor. His friends dead. So many of his people homeless, on their knees, or dead. Gutted end to end. The Great White Father was The Snake With One Belly and Two Heads. One head lived on the Potomac, the other up here. The snake's belly was fat with the dead. It liked the lard. The two heads saw little of each other. They did not need to. Such brains as the snake possessed were located in the belly. Or was up its arse-hole, *forgive me, Princess.*

Riel wore a bell on a rawhide cord looped around his neck. He drew back his coat to show us this. A handgun hung by the same cord. He had never fired this weapon, he said, without first ringing the bell. The ringing bell made him feel easier about the matter. It soothed his conscience and brought peace to the swans at swim in his head.

"What was decided with the Chair?" he asked.

Yes, he had been approached in the early days. The offer had chagrined him; he had believed himself unworthy. He was too angry. Although in those days he had trod about with six bells round his neck, and no handgun, or even a knife or stone in his pockets.

"Try One Foot, I told them. He's the bigger fool."

We shook with laughter at this.

"What news of Sacajawea?" he asked. "She always excited my blood, though her own ever ran clear. She was ever trimming my nails, inserting sticks into my hair or slapping tree bark onto my face. Correcting my French. I see her now, walking Paris streets under a gay umbrella, white poodles dogging her heels. Quite the savage, eh? Sacajawea could read one page of Latin in Clark's book, and thereafter speak the tongue with a sauciness and grandeur the match of Cicero's."

Ah, we all thought. The old days.

"Where do you go now?" we asked.

He laughed, and waggled his head.

The baby wriggled on my lap, wanting to join in.

"A child shall lead them," Riel said. "Onwards into light." He tickled the infant's chin. "Never fall asleep on a tree's mossy side."

A man stalking the aisle paused at our chairs and leaned his face into Riel's. Riel tinkled his bell. The man straightened and hastened on.

"And what news," he asked me, "of the empire? Of the darker continent? How fares the princess, her heels raw from the Dakotas' lam. So far from home, and for so long?"

"Upriver, slave ship oars thump out the iambic beat. More and more vessels thicken the water. High tide is ever higher."

He withdrew a white handkerchief, and with it daubed his sugar under my eyes.

"Downriver, there's talk of a canal."

"Ah," he said. "The innocent life."

For a time within his environment our spirits lifted, and we smoked and spat and dwelled on the eternities and toasted the baby.

He slipped away, and our train rattled on, again in ungainly lurch towards the Dakotas.

A night and a day passed. The vultures once more plied commerce with our route, gliding calmly by like gulls at a seaport.

Three days, four days, five.

Then there was this same Luther underfoot again and the train at crash against a boulder set up across the rails. By Plum River this was, and it engorged, and somehow in the stew of this my newborn's throat being had at, plus Luther's gang at pile between my legs.

You can see here my sketchiness, for I have little stomach for the chronicle. A body tires, it wants relief, and the mind, too, desires the pruning.

Then this mucous scampering away into grass.

But One Foot was wounded and his head a hollow bell and his eyes sightless in the aftermath.

"More rum, Princess?"

"I thank you, yes."

"More?"

"Yes."

"To the top?"

"Yes."

We survived in these conditions and made on again, on foot now and following a path of stars, accompanied by the maddened cadenza of wolves at rove on the plain. Some two hundred of Luther's sordid fireboilers drove in hot pursuit, as we nightly reconnoitered the matter from our moonward levels. This, thanks to a scurrilous document nailed to tree stump and post by our enemies, affirming that the Chair brigade had under

face of darkness routed that institution called Yale, mur-
dering every woman and child while they slept and
leaving in their wake naught but the stench of rotting
flesh in which maggots of a special Egyptian-Injun variety were at swim, with the whole of civilization now at
peril. And these blackguards now loose in unprejudiced
liberty through the continent, with more of their infamy
to follow. And all this at the will of a moneyed claimant
to the French throne, in conspiracy with the English
Influence along the Potomac — and many a decent ket-
tle-tender, pig-swiller, blackie or redman the dupes of
these knaves who dared make use of the Jeffersonian
name. These despoilers of his hand-writ Constitution
and defilers of the *of, by, and for,* who would usurp our
land's very foundations.

"More rum, Princess?"
"Dispatch the monkey for another bottle."
"He's asleep, Princess. I believe yer know that."
We reside now in the wheelhouse, our features at
dance under the globe of yellow lanterns. I sit on the
captain's stuffed horsehair sofa, cold inside my bones,
mindlessly rubbing the monkey's scalp. The monkey
groans in his sleep; he has the sound of one grown
weary and old from the drone of my voice.
The captain is attentive to the wheel and only intermittently shows notice of me. He cares for his boat and
would have nothing harm her on this journey. "Yer has
the mission, yer takes it," he has told me. "Yer hopes to
effect no damage to yer vessel what brings yer to or from
it."
"Yer does?"
"Yer. Yer does."
I have been here the past hour, the pair of us saluting ourselves with each drink we pour down our gullets.
"Skaal!"
"Skaal!"
"Prosit!"
"Prosit!"

"To yer nanny."

"To yer nanny!"

"Pura quanzu!"

"Pura quanzu!"

"A votre santé!"

"A votre santé!"

"Down the hatch!"

"Down the ruddy hatch!"

The captain is a piece of cloth new to my experience. I cannot make him out.

"I told yer," he says. "Yer takes on a mission, yer . . . "

Another lantern illuminates the boat's bow and some few feet of grey water. It illuminates the captain's weathered confederates. Ropes are entwined about their torsos as they dig in their heels, as they sway and pull. We are in shallow water; this tub is scraping bottom.

"We'll get yer through," the Captain says. "No problem."

The monkey yawns, stretching his limbs. I notice the right foot jiggles as he sleeps.

"I meant to ask," says the Captain. "How's that Sacajawea? There were a woman could come at yer like oyster on the half-shell."

"You knew Sacajawea?"

"Why, my Lord yes. Like this us were."

He snaps his fingers behind his back, his torso at lean through a window. "Onward, boys," he shouts. "Another league onwards!"

It sounds silly. I help the monkey scratch at fleas, thinking that this monkey and I are walking down a Paris Street. We are creating the sensation, and why should we not? I shall not let the low-life deter me. Go away, I will say. You with your small minds. Who else will flap warm blankets over me when I am cold? I will sit on a bench and debate with the monkey Jeffersonian ideals and the Napoleonic Code.

"That Riel fella were hanged, yer know. Captured at Batoche and strung up — " The Captain pauses to gnash the gears, to kick at some hum of engine irregular to his ears — "Oh, not so long ago. Quite a fella. My old side-kick, in my rough-and-ready days."

He turns and looks at me. It is the first time I have seen his face near a lantern, in good light. His face shows the cascades of a thousand years.

"Didn't know yer husband. Knew his father, though. Old Two Foot, yer know. Two Foot in the Water. Now there were a man could chew yer up and spit yer out. Yer give him cause. Not the man for that Chair, though. Not a Jefferson man. The way yer husband was."

Beneath the wheel, where the captain rests his leg, is my chained steamer trunk. I started with seven, and now am returning with one. I have gone up and gone down.

I root a finger into the monkey's ear; I ream the knobby flesh.

"Yer can go on with yer tale, yer know," the captain says. "Anytime yer like."

Yer. My infant daughter ripped from my chest and flung into the Plum, even as these same tormenters tore away my dress and dropped down astride me. Shouting insane currency in my ears. Another of Luther's gang standing by at the ready. *"We'll show you democracy!"* My child at squall in rapids and no shriek too many to proclaim the atrocity.

Jackals at gnaw upon our bones.

Later on, my child at float, head down and much bloated. I pushed the swollen child along in the tide. Go, I said. Why do you tarry?

I observed her spirit rove ashore some further distance along; it arose sprightly, and joy flooded my heart. But then her legs kimbered and the arms spun as in a cripple's dance and the head sailed loose of her frame and one arm spiralled eastward and the other westward and in the sky I saw lips nose eyes ears all disassembled and whirling in wind and the next moment the form that remained in the water toppled backwards and sank into that fathomless bottom.

"Ujiji," the captain says. "Kigoma. Yer. By daylight. Then only three thousand more miles. Yer see slave ships in yer mind, Princess?"

Yer. And the cry of the birds when their wings are axed and the sky is no longer theirs and the slave ships slip away with the bird wings stacked one upon the other and the night of all nights has come down.

"Yer. I thought yer was."

We are entering a lake mouth. A soft rain is falling. The leaves are dripping.

"More rum, Princess?"

I think not.

A hush of people, come from nowhere, are lining the bank.

"Yer dress, Princess? Yer think?"

Already he has unlocked and opened my trunk.

"Yer are their princess too, yer know. Yer are the Chair."

Yer. My bones, my beads, my princess dress. Sticks in the hair. My face painted.

Yer.

RAPHAEL'S CANTALUPO MELON

*T*wo men in farmer's workclothes, their faces scrubbed clean, stood by the road leading down into the long valley of the Ebo, or Eboli. Behind them at a distance flowed the placid waters of the Ebo River, wide fields rife with yellowing cantaloupes stretching all around. The high Ebo mountains in the far distance shimmered in the white heat.

Now and then either of the two men, or sometimes both simultaneously, would snatch bright scarves from their throats and wipe their faces. The cloth each had was identical, clearly cut from the same throwaway material.

A woman wearing a red dress reaching past her knees, and flat-heeled shoes, sorely worn, was trampling up and down the road — a dozen or so paces one way, then to turn and stride the other, looking sternly at the men's faces each time she passed by.

A small flat parcel wrapped in paper, tied with a string, leaned against a tree by the roadside.

"I am tired of this," one of the men said. It was the first time any one of them had spoken in some while.

The pacing woman paused, wanting to see what the other man would say, but he did not say anything.

A wagon rattled up Ebo Road to where they stood. The driver made a clucking sound and the animal pulling the wagon stopped.

"Going to Ebo?" the driver said.

The two men did not reply to this overture and after a moment the wagon man said, "I thought to God not."

He touched the reins and the animal, which was an old mule with shortened rear legs, moved along.

The wagon was piled high with cantaloupes bound for the Ebo market.

The two men on the road studied with some interest the cantaloupes as the wagon passed, then looked with heightened curiosity at the driver's backside a few seconds later when he halted the wagon beside the woman.

"Every woman in this county seems to have a new red dress," they heard the driver say. "Now I wonder why that is."

"Ask your wife," the woman replied.

"Ask her?"

"Why not?" the woman said. "She can talk, can she not?"

"Oh, yes, she can that."

"Then ask her."

"I might do that," the driver said.

The driver reached behind him and probed among his load. He lifted out a cantaloupe and twisted in his seat to present this to the woman.

"Three parched people like yourselves might want something refreshing on a hot day like this," he said.

"Then wouldn't we want three?" she replied.

"Now that by God is a point," the driver said.

He reached back for another two cantaloupes and handed down these to the woman.

The woman accepted the yellowing fruit and the driver touched the reins and the wagon creaked on along the road.

The woman briefly walked alongside.

"If you see a man in a motorcar," she said to the driver, "you tell him to hurry along."

"In a motorcar?" the driver said.

"Yes."

"I hope to God I don't. This mule here cannot abide motor cars."

The woman fell away and she and the two men watched the driver's backside and the load of melons until they were out of sight and the creaking no longer heard.

The woman placed two of the melons by the side of the road and strode back to where the men stood leaning on sticks they had picked up from the road. The third fruit she held to her chest by one slender hand, on her wrist a narrow bracelet decorated with purple stones.

The men looked at the bracelet and at the fruit against the red dress, then looked at the two melons she had placed by the side of the road.

"Have you settled it?" the woman said to them. "I hope to God you have settled it."

The men looked at their feet.

"I hope to God you settle it," she said, "before our Emissary comes along." Her voice rose tendentiously on the word *Emissary,* as though the word was strange to her ears but had received some practice with her tongue.

Then the one man said to the woman in the red dress, "I can't see why you took that fellow's melons when by God there's a thousand right here rotting in the fields."

He spread his arms and all three looked off at melon fields which embraced both sides of the river as far as one could see, the vines climbing some distance up the Ebo range and growing right onto the road where they stood.

"More like a million if you ask me," said the other man. "But that by God is how she is."

The woman narrowed her eyes and a second later walked away from them.

The two men darted faintly satisfied glances at each other. Then they both sat down together on a boulder on the high side of the drainage ditch running along Ebo Road.

The woman stood off from them now, looking from one to the other, kicking the ground and making a face.

"You're going to ruin those shoes," said the one man.

"She's ruined plenty," said the other.

"By God!" said the woman, stomping the ground.

Someone down in the valley, unseen and far away, shouted a name, but although they listened for it the sound did not come again.

The woman began her pacing again, now and then pausing to shade her eyes and stare up the road.

"The Emissary is not coming," she said.

"No, by God," one of the men said, "and why by God should he?"

The other man retrieved tobacco from his pocket, together with rolling paper, and proceeded in measured pace to roll a smoke.

"She don't care," he said. "Not about them shoes on her feet. No, her heart is set on a red pair to match that new dress."

The woman stopped kicking the road long enough to hear how the other might reply to this.

But the one man only watched the other tamp the tobacco, roll and lick the paper, and twist the smoke's end.

The man rested the finished smoke on a knee, then began the rolling of another.

The two men sat out on the boulder, smoking.

The woman walked over to the tree where the parcel rested. She untied the string and carefully unwrapped the paper and for some little while seemed engrossed in what she saw within the paper's wrinkled folds.

The men nudged each other.

"I don't see why," one of them said, "you can't just hang that picture on a wall."

"Seeing," the other man said, "that you cannot stop looking at it."

"*Which* wall?" the woman said.

The men shrugged and once again regarded the sweeping melon fields.

The woman propped her picture uncovered against the tree. It was an old painting she had found wrapped in skins among a mound of stones up high along the Ebo slopes. The painting showed a single melon on a thick green vine in a surround of leaves lit by the sun. Something had pecked or gnawed numerous holes into the melon, birds perhaps or rodents of some kind, and in the fruit's depths could be seen a moist yellow center containing whitened seeds. In the background, shrouded by a cloudy mist, rose what the Emissary on an earlier visit had identified as Cantalupo castle. The painting was signed with the name Raphael.

The woman carefully rewrapped the painting and tied the string and leaned the picture back against the tree.

The men looked at the woman. They would not look at the picture.

An Irish Setter came trotting along Ebo Road, the dog's long red fur glistening in the sun. The dog passed between the three of them without a glance.

"Oops," one of the men said. "Someone has left the door open."

"Yes," the other said. "There goes that dog after that wagon."

The woman paced up and down the road. Sometimes she would say to them, "You two are birds of a feather," and sometimes the words would be, "Well, are you making any progress?" and sometimes she would not speak or look at them.

Sweat stains had formed under the arms of the red dress and her worn shoes were the color of the road.

Sometimes the men's eyes would openly follow her passage; at other times they would stare at the baked ground beneath their feet. Once in a while they would look up and down Ebo Road to see what might be coming; they would stare off at the endless melon fields, or scrutinize a nearby tree that had been old before they were born but in the recent past had been split by lightning. The lightning had split the tree's trunk in half.

They would gaze through white heat at the presiding mountains.

Later on the woman planted herself by the side of the road in front of where they sat, and said, "By God I hope to Mercy I am not letting you two kill my appetite."

The woman split the cantaloupe on a rock and with her fingers eased away the seeds.

The men with rapt attention watched her hold the one half up to her lips and eat the melon down to the rind. Then they watched her pitch the gnawed rind away and burrow her mouth into the other half.

Then they watched her swing about and prance around on Ebo Road's grassy shoulder for something she could use to cleanse her hands and chin.

Each of them unloosened his neck rag and silently dangled it out at her, but she ignored this.

They saw her lift the hem of her dress and next the slip hem, each time thinking better of this and in the end wiping the backside of a hand across her dripping chin. Then she stooped and cleaned her hands on a patch of grass.

"Was it good?" the one man asked.

"As good as ours?" asked the other.

"Better anyway than that awful thing in the picture," said the first.

She looked at them with narrowed eyes and with the toe of one shoe calmly rolled the remaining two cantaloupes into the ditch.

The Irish Setter was seen returning from up the road, running low to the ground, its tail between its legs.

When the dog came near to them it left the road, taking a wide arch across the melon field until it was well past them, when again it took to the road.

"Wonder why that man wouldn't let that dog go with him?" the one asked.

"Now that's the million dollar question," replied the other.

The woman brushed dust from her dress and examined the spreading stain under each arm.

The two men looked at her naked arms golden in the sun, stealing quick, apprehensive glances at each other.

"If this dress is ruined," she said, "by God I'm going to light with a stick into both of you."

The two men grinned.

She took off her shoes and shook gravel from them.

"Well," she said, "you two may have this time to waste, but I have work to do. When you reach a decision I hope to God you will let me know."

They watched her put on her shoes again, standing on first one leg and then the other while flapping her arms.

She picked up her wrapped painting by the tree and started down the road.

"What if that Emissary fellow comes?" called the one man.

"What about those red shoes?" called the other.

The woman stopped.

"I wish to God," she said, "I had never heard of that Emissary fellow or of either of you."

But she walked back and replaced the painting in its original spot against the tree.

"It is out of my hands," she said. "I am by God going home."

Then she hastened along the road again.

The two men watched her follow the road until she reached the tree that had been split by lightning, at which point she climbed the vined embankment and struck out across the first of the many melon fields.

After a time all they could see of her was a spot of red moving through the distant growth.

"Wonder *which* home?" the one said.

The other leaned on his stick, nodding.

After a while each rooted inside his hip pocket and flattened out crumpled one-thousand lira bills onto the ground.

"Wonder how much?" the one said.

The other placed down on his stack a few more bills and the first man then did the same to his pile.

"That ought to do for those shoes," the one said.

"Right," said the other. "She can go into Ebo next week and buy herself the brightest pair to be found."

Then they put the two stacks together and debated which one should carry the money.

"You carry it and I will present it to her," the one said.

"No. You carry, I give."

They walked over to where the two cantaloupes lay in the ditch. They picked up the melons, appraising each for weight and color and aroma, the texture of the ribbed skin, before placing them down again, not ungently.

From the long dip in Ebo Road ahead of them they saw plumes of smoke rising as if from a moving chimney. Moments later they heard the putt-putt of an engine, and then the vehicle's high carriage crested the hill.

The Emissary, his face obscured behind goggles, wearing the same bright yellow scarf and yellow motoring jacket worn during his previous visit, brought the vehicle to a stop near where they stood.

"I am a man of my word," the Emissary said, alighting from the car.

The three stood palavering a moment within the field of smoke emitting from the jouncing motorcar.

Then the man picked up the painting from where it leaned by the tree. With some anxiety he ripped away the paper, but then seemed satisfied and quickly walked over and carefully secured the painting inside the vehicle.

From the car's confines he lifted out a shoebox.

He approached the two men, lifted the lid, and all three looked inside at the pair of red shoes.

"I can't promise her," the Emissary said, "that they will be an exact fit."

All three shook hands.

The Emissary returned to his vehicle and motored away.

"Now that by God was a brisk piece of business," said the one man.

"So by God it was."

The man carrying the stack of bills they had intending presenting to the woman pulled the bills from his pocket and each took back again his own money.

They walked up Ebo Road as far as the split tree, which had thrown up new branches along each of its two trunks. Then they loped on off across the field, the one sometimes carrying the shoebox, and sometimes the other, and sometimes pausing in heated argument until the issue was temporarily settled. Then both going on again, taking care to avoid the great spread of melons ranged upon the earth, as they took that same route the woman had taken earlier, each in his mind wondering which house it was that the woman would today be calling home.

WY WN TY CALLD
YOUR NAM YOU DID NOT ANSWR

Marucha was six when she decided she would no longer employ the eighth letter of the alphabet either in writing or in speech.

"Wy?" asked her father, Huidobro, in his woodshed hard at work with hammer and chisel on his newest pig. "I don't compreend."

"Very good, Uidobro," said the girl. "You can see ow muc fun it will be."

"Wat if you fall in te river and must call for elp?"

"I will call '*Elp! Elp! Elp!*' and you will bring me to safety."

"Fine," said Huidobro. "But I am apreensive."

The child's mother Astrada, when it was her turn to be informed, was not instantly amused.

"Go aead, toug," she said, "if you must be a lunatic, because wat am I in tis ouse but a mop and pail?"

At her prayers that night Marucha said to God, "God, tis is Maruca Figueroa Jotamaria of eigty eigt Calle Noces de la Mil Lunas in te village of El Flores, Micoacan, Mexico, putting te bug in your ear once again. Save my sister Gongora Azurdia from furter umiliation on te sow-grounds and see tat Uidobro's soes are polised and please do someting about my moter's air."

That day Gongora Azurdia had fallen from the thoroughbred Egoro on the fifth jump and was now in the bed beside Marucha, covered in nasty bruises, one arm on a white board elevated from her hip by a metal rod.

"And pray God in te morning you will assure good fortune to us all."

"Stop tat talking to eaven," her father shouted from his own bed.

"I am sorry you do not like my air," shouted the girl's mother, who that very day had been a guinea pig at the Estrella de Oro Beautician's School. "Doesn't anyone like my air?"

"*Elp! Elp! Elp!*" shouted Marucha, and in an instant Huidobro was by her bedside conveying a glass of water.

In the night the girl dreamed that the "h" was a comet whirling the heavens, mad as could be for having been forsaken, and it was decided in her sleep that "E" was a letter of similar inconsequence.

Thus at breakfast the following morning, when Huidobro asked what Marucha would like to eat, the words that poured from her mouth made no immediate sense.

"I will at a ors," she said. "I will at a lim or a jalapna pppr or drink juic until I pop."

Mother and father stopped what they were doing.

Each patted a foot, waiting for Marucha to continue.

"I don't know wat I will at," she finally said. "Unlss you av somting trrific for m to at it may vry wll b tat I will at noting. Wat ar you ating?"

Mother and father suddenly beamed, clapping their hands together.

Her sister Gongora Azurdia sat stiff at the table with her arm elevated from her hip on the white board.

She was not happy to be in this family.

"I wish someone would tell me what is going on," she said.

The previous day she had pitched right over the stallion Egoro's head into a muddy pool of water.

"I wis somon would tll m wat is going on?" quoted Marucha Figueroa Jotamaria.

The parents had slept well; they felt uncommonly rejuvenated this morning. Huidobro had arisen early and in his woodshed with hammer and chisel had finished work on his newest pig. The pig now sat grandly on a fifth chair drawn up to the table like a regular member of the family.

The Huidobro pigs were famous throughout the region. Every village in the mountains where they lived had to have its Huidobro pig.

"I fl uncommonly good tis morning," said Huidobro.

"Tis as gon far noug," Marucha's mother said. "If no on is willing to improv rlationsips in tis ous tn as usual I must myslf pick up th gauntlt."

Huidobro kissed his wife on the lips.

"You ar t most fascinating woman I av vr known," he said. "I lov you madly."

"W all lov ac otr madly," Marucha said.

Her sister was in the act of writing something on the white board elevating her arm.

"Wat ar you doing?" the others asked.

She had been writing, 'Of all the animals in the animal kingdom I like horses best.' But she had written this in letters invisible to everyone but herself.

She would hereafter speak invisibly as well, since no one in this house ever paid the smallest attention to her.

"I am going out now," she said, rising from the table.

The other three looked at her with blank faces.

"Did somon spak?" asked Huidobro.

"I tink it was t wind," said Astrada.

"I saw r lips mov," said Marucha.

At the doorway Gongora Azurdia turned, looking back at her parents and her impossible little sister.

They were chattering away at her empty chair.

"Wat did s say?" she heard Marucha ask?

"I don't know," said her mother. "Wr did s go? S is always disapparing witout a word to anyon. You would tink s wantd to liv wit tos stupid orss."

"On of ts days," she heard Huidobro say, tilting back in his chair, "I man to gt to t bottom of tis affair. I guarant to you all tat I will discovr ow s pulls ts disapparing acts."

"I op s dosn't try riding wit tat arm," said Astrada.

Marucha was no longer listening. She was eating as fast as she could. There was much to get done this day, in her view, and already it was getting old.

Huidobro had not yet eaten even a crumb, and wouldn't now, because Astrada was busy stashing away every little morsel of food.

Gongora Azurdia, fully invisible, was racing as fast as she could to the stables.

Later, everyone in the village was struck dumb with amazement to see that devil horse, Egoro, galloping one

way and another, jumping everything in sight, sometimes even their own crouched and trembling figures.

As for Marucha, she had decided to abandon all letters of the alphabet. She filled the house with silence,
which proved a great comfort to everyone.

THE WEEPERS OF VICENZA

*T*he Weepers were having a problem with their most noted member, Benito. There had been problems with Benito since the movement's early days, but these problems had worsened during his long relationship with Fruhöffer, the mad Austrian. They had worsened more yet when the impossible woman presented him with a baby. And just yesterday Benito's behavior reached new depths when he attacked a nun at the opening of his show at Svengali Gallery.

Now there was scandal.

True, the nun had come at one of his paintings with a chopper.

The nun's attempt had been partially thwarted. The gallery owner, Svengali himself, had interceded, deflecting the nun's aim. The nun had wanted to mutilate that portion of the painting she found most offensive, which was Benito's wicked and high-handed depiction — grossly anatomical — of the Holy Virgin.

The nun's deflected chopper had flown instead through the brow of Jesus, impaling itself into the gallery wall, where it still remained by police order.

At which point Benito had splashed champagne into the face of the luckless nun, and called for the abolition of the papacy and of Catholic zealots worldwide.

This impaling together with Benito's scurrilous remark precipitated the riot which — it must be said — had all day been brewing.

Today the Vicenza paper, and those throughout Italy, were filled with reports of the shameful incident, together with accompanying photographs of the nun's chopper embedded in the Savior's skull.

This morning the Weepers — an appellation borrowed from that name applied to those small, usually insignificant, always countless mourners found on ancient Italian tombs — arrived in force at Benito's home in the hills above Vicenza.

They included:

Old Pietro, the silk and satin miniaturist;

Old Pettifoggi, a sculptor specializing in winged serpents common to the Jurassic period;

Old Bellicosto, known for sporting pictures in the British style;

Old Marinetti, said to be a relation of the infamous Futurist of the same name, who now painted only buttercups.

They had come bearing a document drawn up during the night, called The Weepers' Declaration of Solidarity. The solidarity the document spoke of, however, was not with Benito. It disassociated the Weepers individually and collectively from any remarks that ever had passed the painter's lips; it offered profuse apology to the Vatican powers and to Catholics worldwide; it urged Benito's removal to a distant isle where he would be without artistic supplies or human fellowship for a period of not less than fifty years.

This contingent of elders had expected to find Benito in a mood of contrition and disrepair. Instead, they found him in a state of elation. He had been painting all night, he said, with unbounded fever, for the event with the nun had unleashed in him powers alike unto those of Moses parting the Red Sea. Bring him a loaf, he declared, and he would feed thousands. He was perfecting new techniques, he told them, " — more revolutionary for our times than those in theirs of Raphael, Michelangelo, and Leonardo combined."

His fellow Weepers suspected this involved more of his Pittura Metafisica rubbish or perhaps even a jump into the deep end such as had taken place when the Novecento bunch had sought glory through a return to the great Italian past. Benito, the villain, each thought — he has more systems than the universe.

In the kitchen, sitting on a chair upholstered in the manner of Matisse, sat the mad Austrian, eating a melon. Through the expanse of windows the Weepers saw a naked child of five or six executing endless cartwheels in the grass by the lemon orchard.

The old gentlemen hastened in to pay their respects to the dreaded Austrian.

They kissed her ringed fingers.

They kissed her frozen cheeks.

Each in the Weepers contingent had at one time or another fallen under the spell of Mistress Fruhöffer.

But that had been decades ago — half a century — and now Mistress Fruhöffer's sky-high sculptures were to be seen in every world capital. Just recently, her "Woman with Bread Basket in a Laundered Dress" had been installed alongside a Cucchi work on the grassy slopes fronting Monte Carlo. Her "Woman with Flat Feet," some ninety feet high, composed entirely of a pair of legs, competed with Brancusi's column at Romania's Tirgu Jiu. The Bolognese master, Pomodoro, was said to kiss the page whenever he read her name.

The Weepers commiserated with Mistress Fruhöffer over Benito's assault yesterday of the nun and the resulting clamor in the press — the nation's grief, the thirst for revenge.

"Nonsense," said the Austrian. "The nun was not a nun. The 'nun' was that crackpot art critic, Tassi, wearing nun's attire."

"But . . . "

"Nonsense."

"All the same, Benito's sacra-religious statements, his . . . "

"Nonsense," she said. "Whenever did not the public labor to fry the true artist in hot oil?"

"But . . . "

"Nonsense. I will hear no more. You Weepers, out of my house! I have work to do."

Outside, the daughter of this madwoman continued her endless cartwheels in the grass.

The old gentlemen found themselves being herded towards the door.

Pettifoggi, to deflect the mad Austrian from this goal, embarked upon the telling of an elaborate story involving each of the many painters of his acquaintance and in history's ledger who had fallen drunk into one or another of the canals in Venice.

"I do not see," said the Austrian, "how this story pertains to my situation."

Weeper Pettifoggi reminded her that both she and Benito, as riotous youths, had fallen drunk into a canal in Venice.

"That," she replied, "was to prove a point."

They waited, but she did not feel compelled to elaborate upon this point.

Old Pietro then thought to speak of a new theory he had been advancing over the years. "Blue eyes are not lucky in an artist," he said. "They are apt to induce an insistent romanticism in the artist's work; they steer the artist into adoption of the rhythms of the Flemish School."

Fruhöffer's eyes were a startling blue.

"Out!" cried the woman. "Go and paint your old bones into heaven!"

*B*y the gate a young girl of incomparable beauty was daintily kneeling, arranging diminutive plants in the black earth with a Matisse-colored trowel.

She batted her eyes at them from beneath a wide-brimmed yellow hat.

"Voila!" she said, standing. Her hands spun in the air. Instantly the plot of earth where she had been working was filled with a profusion of flowers.

Then sunlight flashed over the grounds, instilling such radiance upon the scene that both the girl and her little garden of flowers became invisible.

"Pay no mind, messieurs," the Weepers heard her say. "I am a spirit, you see. The poor Muse."

"A muse?"

"Oui! In the employ of my betters."

Gradually, she was reappearing. In her wide yellow hat and yellow smock and yellow stockings, her yellow shoes and with her white porcelain face and silken hair, she looked — in the eyes of the Old Weepers — completely charming.

Old Pietro, with a glint in his eyes, asked if she might join them for a coffee, or drinks, in Vicenza's old quarter.

To their surprise she said oui.

"Oui! It will be like having four fathers."

The aches and pains of the old men slid away. They were enchanted. Young again. Chatting with a muse heretofore had been a privilege denied them.

"Your name is . . . ?"

"Suissé," she said.

"You are . . . ?"

"Parisian, ah, mais oui..." said the girl. And for the next several minutes, quivering with apparent excitement, her tongue rattled on in the language of the French people — words that the Weepers as a group could not begin to comprehend.

That she was French altered the matter somewhat. Even more did they warm towards her. The French, after all, during their brief history as a nation, had produced one or two gifted artists.

"How old are you, dear one?"

"Ageless, monsieur! I am but sixteen!"

A youth!

"Suissé? That is your name? Such a lovely name and not unknown to the art world, certainly. In France you have the *ateliers libre,* do you not? Walk in, pay the price, paint the nude. Suissé, founder of the first *atelier,* such a model she was! Or so I am told. All the Impressionists — Monet, Cezanne, Pissaro — where would they have been without their Suissé?"

A breathless "Oui, monsieur" fell from her lips.

"Oui. Oh, oui. You are speaking of my beautiful mother."

They strolled as one happy family down Vicenza's winding hill.

Old Pietro in his younger days, before finding his niche, had dallied about with Cubism in the French capital. He told her this.

"Ah, Cubism!" exclaimed the girl. "It was my sister's great enthusiasm! That Picasso, he would take her to bed every night!"

*T*he girl was in a gay mood. On the way down the long hill she sprinkled the air with her laughter. The morning mist had lifted. The day was beautiful. The Weepers, hobbling on crutches and canes, felt young again.

"I like to get out from time to time," she said.

"I like to see the sights. I like to sit in the cafés with my legs crossed, wearing my yellow hat and yellow stockings. Everyone wants to look at me. They want to talk and flirt. I am not above such frivolity, although at heart I am a serious person. I want to marry one of these days, though not to any of you. You are all too old and probably have not a franc between you. Though that would concern me not in the least. I hope very much to fall in love with a pauper. My own family is exceedingly rich, you see, and I have always believed the rich have it as their duty to marry the poor, and vice versa. That is the one thing I have picked up from my study of philosophy, although to my knowledge no philosopher has ever suggested this course of action. Am I charming? Do you like me?"

It seemed to the Weepers that the very dwarfs adorning the white walls at the Villa of the Dwarfs burst into song as the girl passed. Their old eyes swam with visions. Beneath them in the distance lay the whole of beautiful Vicenza. Often had they sat up here painting *vedutisti — veduta ideata, veduta capriccio.* It seemed to them they could see the many dwarfs on the high walls dancing about like pole-vaulters.

Lilac scented the air. Their very lungs sang.

"If one of you makes a proposal to me this minute," she said, "I might find myself accepting. That is because I am walking on air. I am in promenade upon the air because I like artists so much. I find them so unpredictable. One artist is never like another artist except when they are talking about their technique. From the way one artist talks about his or her own technique you would think every painting painted would be only so much technique, as when a French boy makes love, but that is not how I see it. Oh, but you Weepers are so solemn! You Weepers have such heavy eyes. Your very heart is like a stone. If I just once met an artist with a sense of humor that pertained to the true purpose of art I would hold his hand and kiss him deep in the mouth. Over and over I would do this. That is the kind of artiste *I* am. I like to show my feelings. I would give this artist all my love and he would never again feel poorly about his art. His very paint would walk on air. His brushes would have as many legs as the caterpillar. As when Degas said of Monet, looking at a Monet, Degas said he felt chills about his neck and had to raise his collar, so much did Monet's visceral eye define the "Haystack," the "Poplars," the "Waterlilies" and compose them in the heart. You Weepers cannot say *I love,* you can only say *I look, I judge, I abjure.* Oui, I am a person of opinions too, no? You can realize from this what a dangerous spirit I am.

"I have it in me to ruin lives, though I would say I am saving them from themselves. I feel a desperate affliction riding my shoulders. I must marry someone soon, perhaps even tonight, though I have every intention of remaining a virgin until the day I die."

"Then what?" asked Old Marinetti.

"Then what, what?"

"What is to happen on the day you die?"

"I shall then give myself wholeheartedly to my husband. He shall breathe fire through his nostrils like a dragon and rattle the walls and cry unto the gods that it was worth the wait. His passion will restore me to life and my cheeks shall remain rosy for a thousand years."

She gnawed at her fingers, saying this, spitting out her nail ends upon the cobbled stones of Vicenza's medieval heart. Here Palladio had worked. He had sailed his Palladian theory over the oceans to bestow the colonial style upon the Dixie Americans; he had ruled the Brits for a century.

"All this from little Vicenza," she said, *"mon dieu!"*

*A*t Café Garibaldi the group sat outside on blue chairs and ordered drinks. The gay yellow hat floated from the girl's head to her heart, to her knees, and back again to her heart, as rapturously she contemplated the Vicenza sights.

"Bon, bon bon!" she exclaimed, "this is so good! I am having such a good time with you gentlemen. *Bon, bon, bon!"*

She sounded like a church bell, and the Weepers hung on to her every sound, in a state of rapture.

"We will sketch you, mademoiselle, if you please."

"Bon, bon, bon, certement!"

The Weepers sketched. They had not felt so alive in years. The sun was shining. A soft wind blew.

From time to time, when the sun struck the café tables in a certain way, it seemed to the old Weepers that the enchanting girl would again fade into a state of invisibility. But then they would hear her gay, rippling laughter, and she would reappear to them with her yellow hat and yellow stockings brighter than ever. In stalls along the way fruit and vegetable vendors were time and time again rearranging their produce in the manner of Matisse.

Birds clucked along the rooftops.

Signore Plevano, the retired banker, stood in the doorway of a gadget shop, greeting strollers. At Plevano's gadget shop one could buy amazing objects: a yellow plastic bird, for instance, that could be set upon the rim of a water glass. When that glass was filled with water, the bird would drink. Then it would throw back its head and sing like Mirella Freni. Then it would drink again, throw back its head, and once more sing like Mirella Freni. Like Fiamma Izzo D'Amico. The bird could do this all day, requiring only a good battery, a full glass of water. Similarly, a blue bird dressed in a tuxedo, could sing like Domingo. For a fancy price Plevano could provide you with birds capable of rendering entire operas, orchestra included.

Bicyclist swept speedily over the stones.

On the doorknob of a yellow palazzo nearby someone had tied a beautiful silk scarf. The scarf had been found in the street. For four days, unmolested, the beautiful scarf had been tied to the doorknob.

"I don't know which one of you I shall let walk me home," the girl said. "I shall have to do the eenie meenie."

The Weepers smiled. To look into the girl's joyful face filled them with misgivings. She excited their thoughts to flit hither and yon. They wondered whether their movement's blood had not for too long been sapped by insidious melancholia. They had begun their careers with such vigor.

At an adjacent table sat three people in nuns' regalia, teachers at the nearby high school.

The waiter was summoned to their table for a second round of drinks. He was a boy no more then eight, wearing a filthy apron.

"I want a drink that approaches the color of blood," the girl said. "That is my mood today."

She settled for Pernod and when it came the boy brought a plate of cherries in a dish with legs colored in the mode of Matisse.

A woman of advanced years crossed the tiny piazza under a gay umbrella, as though walking through invisible rain.

"There goes my wife," said Old Pietro. "I wonder where she is off to at this hour."

The Weepers watched Old Pietro's wife wave down a taxi at the traffic turnaround; they saw her demurely shake and close her umbrella as she stepped into the taxi.

As her taxi departed another stopped in the vacated spot. An elegantly dressed woman, alighting, was heard to say in a beseeching voice to the man occupying the back seat, "What will I do without you, Giuriato?" Then that taxi hurtled away.

A priest and a man in a leather jacket stood in front of Liberia due Ruote waving newspapers containing photographs of the chopper embedded in the head of the Savior. They were shouting at each other.

They watched Giuriato's elegant woman stand heartbroken on the pavement, weeping into a lace-trimmed handkerchief. Pigeons fluttered around her red shoes.

"What will I do without, Giuriato?" the woman wailed.

"I love women," Old Pettifoggi said. "I can love them without pretending to understand one syllable that ever issues from their lips."

"With women it is always the soul that is speaking," said the Weepers' young Suissé. "And how much is it that is in you to understand about the soul? So there is the mystery of your ignorance explained."

"The soul has never been sufficiently arrested on canvas," said Bellicosto. "Two thousand years of valiant attempts, ten thousand cathedrals, and so little to show for this endless soul-searching."

"Do not despair," said the girl sympathetically.

She shoved back her yellow hat, lifting her face into the sun.

She said she was reminded of that little episode Alberto Moravia narrated in his story, "Bitter Honeymoon." A woman went to the doctor and the doctor right away saw that nothing was wrong with the woman. 'Go and lean out the open window,' the doctor told his patient. 'Lean your elbows on the sill. When you go home do this every day at your own open window, and in three month's time you will be cured.'

One of the nuns at the adjacent table leaned her elbows into their group.

"You have forgotten the most important action in Moravia's little episode," the nun said to them. "While the hypochondriacal woman was leaning at the window, the doctor kicked her in the buttocks."

"*Merci*," replied the girl. "But I had not forgotten. I preferred to leave these gentlemen Weepers with our image of the sad woman at the window."

The nun nodded serenely. "Ah, a romantic," she said. Then she withdrew to her own table.

"Everywhere in Europe," Suissé said, "you see women at windows. It is how she replenishes her spirit."

The Weepers turned as one to scan the piazza façades, and those narrow streets emptying into the piazza, but not one woman was to be found at any of the hundred windows.

"Such silly talk," Suissé said. "It has made me sad. Someone hold my hand."

The Weepers' hands stacked high upon the table, holding the girl's hand.

They watched tears dribble slowly down her cheeks.

"Thank you," she said. "I am improved now. "Look!"

Across the way, Vicenza's ancient poet Branko Gorjupo had appeared at his window, his wizened shoulders wrapped in a woman's black shawl, a cigarette drooping from his lips.

He held aloft a cage filled with pigeons.

Those occupying the tables at Café Garibaldi, indeed everyone in the vicinity, turned to study Vicenza's famous Croatian poet at the window. They watched him settle the caged birds onto the sill, smoke his cigarette, extract a bird, smoke his cigarette, look up at the sky, smoke his cigarette, extract another bird.

When all the birds were strutting the sill minute scraps of paper appeared from beneath the old poet's shawl. These scraps, one by one, he attached to the birds' legs.

Then the poet waved his bony arms and the birds lifted away into Vicenza's sunny heavens.

In this way, every day at the same hour, did the revered master release his poems upon Vicenza. Upon the whole of Italy.

"Bon, bon, bon," sang the girl, as distant church bells erased another hour.

One of the birds skidded to earth at the Weepers' feet. They unrolled the poem:

     ON MARRIAGE
     Ask for the hand
     of one
     and then the other.
     Just shout your proposals
     through every window.

"My wife's mother is ill," said Old Pietro. "That is where she was going in her taxi."

The Weepers lowered their faces, hastily inducing the sign of the cross upon their bosoms. Old Pietro's wife's mother was Vicenza's oldest living person. She had been old when they were born and now they were themselves visions of antiquity.

"We all live lives of mystery," Suissé said. "Even the simplest among us."

The Weepers nodded agreement to this falsified claim. The sun was hot. Their blood ran hot and cold.

"Another drink, messieurs? I have worked up such a lovely thirst."

The boy waiter was not to be seen.

Finally they sighted him out in the piazza by the fountain. He had taken off his waiter's jacket. He was bare-chested, playing with a small blue boat in the water.

Suissé at once flung herself off. At the fountain she grabbed the boy's face in her hands and kissed his cheeks. Then together they contemplated the boy's boat, the cascading water, the naked splendor of the seven nude women over which it flowed.

The old Weepers' shoulders sagged. Their heads drooped. They watched the girl and the bare-chested boy play with the boy's boat in the water. Seconds later they were asleep.

The fountain sculpture was called "The Seven Naked Wonders of the Underworld."

When the gods had created the underworld, the boy told his new French friend, they had created it without women. But the fires the gods had created burned so intensely that the moment a sinner died and his body transcended into the pits of hell his flesh was instantly consumed. And the fat of these many sinners only made the fires burn more intensely. The gods felt thwarted because their underworld had been meant to be a place of eternal suffering. And so if the flesh was consumed so instantly, what then was this hell's effectiveness?

So the gods assembled on the Vicenza hillside and devised a plan. Already there existed a group of sisters known as the Seven Naked Daughters of the Sunlight. Each of the Seven Naked Daughters of the Sunlight had been born with a body more beautiful than the other. But the sisters bickered endlessly among themselves as to which possessed the perfect body. The sisters bickered among themselves so endlessly that the gods could neither sleep by night nor converse by day.

In addition, the boy told the girl, even on the Vicenza hillside the gods could feel the heat rising from the lower depths. The heat singed their garments and smoked their tresses and the ashes from the burning sinners in the underworld drifted up into the heavens and into the gods' golden dishes as they ate their food.

So the gods decided the Seven Naked Daughters of the Sunlight must be called by another name. They renamed the sisters The Seven Naked Wonders of the Underworld. They ordered that the sisters take their bickering into the pits of hell.

So this was how women were first admitted into the underworld.

The tears of the bickering sisters would ever control the raging flames. As with Sisyphus doomed to convey his eternal rock up the eternal mountain, so too would the sisters spend eternity combatting the underworld's eternal flames.

But it is because they are beautiful, the boy told the girl, and because they are women, that some little good has come out of this, for us here in Vicenza.

It is their tears falling upon hell's fires, the boy told the girl, that we see proof of each evening when the sun sets. The evening radiance that we see in the sky has nothing to do with the rotation of the sun and the earth. The glow is made by the fierce brooms, the incessant tears, of the seven sisters ever working in diminishment of the flames — that our bodies should not burn instantly when we are sent there, but have instead the eternal punishment promised us.

*T*he boy returned to his play with the boat in the water. The girl returned to the Weepers' table. The Weepers instantly awoke. They felt amazingly refreshed.

"Why did you kiss the lazy boy?" they asked.

"In reward of virtue," the girl said. "Which artist executed this most memorable work?"

Alas, the Weepers said, the creator of the Seven Wonders was Anonymous.

"Some attest it was the great Donatella, while in partnership with his friend, Michelozzo. Whatever the case, by common consent the 'Sisters' artist has produced the most erect nipples in all of Italy. A man has only to look at these incomparable nipples to fly into fits of ecstasy."

The critic Tassi strolled by, his nose in the air.

Out by the fountain a starving artist had been sketching caricatures. The critic sat down in the sketcher's empty chair. The artist began sketching him. It was said of Tassi the critic that the only art he appreciated was just these caricatures — -portraits — of himself. *"Art is dead,"* he had written. *Those disavowing this argument need only peruse the funereal melange of Weepers' Work on show at Galleria Svengali, where each day this death takes place before your very eyes."*

At night, it was said, the critic Tassi haunted the graveyards. They were the one place he could sleep.

"If that Florentine Torrigiano could break the nose of *il divino* Michelangelo and escape hanging," Weeper Belacosto said, "then surely we can break the nose of that cur."

But they remained seated, their old bones too brittle now for the pugilistic endeavor.

"Artists are the most generous creatures on earth," the girl Suissé said, peering out at the Weepers from the lowered brim of her yellow hat. "While I am so stingy I would not part even with the dirt beneath my nails.

"Look!" she said. With a forlorn cry, she showed the Weepers her fingers' hoarded dirt.

The day waned. The Weepers and the lovely girl stayed on at their table.

"Oh, my friends!" she said to them. "Were you not yourselves such powerful personalities I should very likely fall asleep. Only sixteen, but always so tired, *pauvre, pauvre!* The air, you see, is always rearranging itself over my head. With every breath I feel I might disappear. You will recall that Rembrandt's pupil, Gerard Dou, likewise suffered in this respect. The countless hours Dou would sit on his hands in his studio at Leyden, still as a rat, waiting for the dust to settle. His every move a whisper, every window tightly shut, hardly daring to breathe, less the enervated dust consume his very body."

Up Via Veneziano where the silk scarf had been tied for four days to the doorknob, strolled a pair of young lovers. The man stopped. He untied the scarf and looped it over the woman's neck. The woman laughed. Then the woman looped the scarf over her lover's neck, and they both laughed. Then the man retied the beautiful scarf to the knob and the two continued their lovers' stroll up Via Veneziano.

About this time Café Garibaldi was invaded by the family Formicidae of the order Hymenoptera.

Oh, my god, *ants!*" cried someone at another table. Within seconds every person seated among the café tables was slapping at his and her arms and legs and dancing about. *"Ants! Ants!"*

The word *Ants!* rang through the piazza like a chorus: *"Antzantzantz!"*

In a matter of seconds Café Garibaldi was deserted.

The woman who had alighted from the taxi and shouted in a distressed voice, "What will I do without you, Giuriato?" was the sole person in the piazza taking no notice of the scurrying ants. She sat on at her table, sobbing. "What will I do without you, Giuriato?" she cried. "Oh, Giuriato, my love!"

The Garibaldi work force, with brooms and cloths and pails filled with hot soapy water, waded in, laboring to rid the establishment of its pests.

The proprietor himself approached the Giuriato woman to take her order.

The woman looked gravely up at him, her eyes filled with tears.

"I will have an ant," she said.

The crowd cheered.

As quickly as the café had cleared it was full again. To the proprietor's chagrin, everyone ordered ants. Even the Weepers did.

So Vicenza's Giuriato Ant was invented that day, adding new luster to the city's fame.

W oman's talk. Suissé sat down at the bereaved woman's table; in a matter of minutes it became clear that the Giuriato woman was unburdening herself of the full story.

The Weepers, observing the sacred conversation of that pair, found cause to speculate upon the tribulations of true love. Old Pietro said it put him in mind of the Venus Bicycle Company. Each year, since his youth, in celebration of the Italians' fascination with romance, spectacle and heartbreak, the Venus Bicycle Company had manufactured one thousand two-seater bicycles known as the Lovers' Special. The front wheel would only roll forwards while the rear wheel could only turn backwards.

Two women, their arms linked, strolled by, singing:

I had a man, his name was Mary
He was so so ordinary!

From time to time Suissé, her arms encircling the Giuriato woman, could be heard casting aloft such phrases as these: "The brute!" "The rat!" "What a pig!"

The Giuriato woman was gradually regaining her composure. Entire minutes passed during which she did not once moan or burst into tears, or cry out in ragged pain, *"What will I do without you, Giuriato?"*

A short while later both Suissé and her new friend joined the Weepers.

"I have told my friend that we were on our way to the Benito exhibition," she said. "I have insisted she join us, and assured her you will be more civilized than that oaf Giuriato."

The woman was introduced.

Her name, she said, was Francesca V. Artists, Francesca said, were her favorite people. She regretted her late acquaintance Giuriato was not an artist, but was instead a putrid worm working in the bowels of the civil service. If Giuriato, she said, had possessed the good luck of being born an artist and not a putrid worm in the bowels of the civil service, he would undoubtedly have been a much more agreeable person, and much less the diabolical toad he had now proved himself to be. For ten years she had acceded to the toad's every request each Tuesday and Friday afternoons, with no recompense whatsoever, not even so much as these red shoes on her feet or ever a smile on his face. But only lies and more lies and one broken promise after another. For that putrid worm she had forsaken home and family and a fine career in the space travels industry — and now look at her — moaning for the putrid worm when with a little luck her heart could be radiant with good thoughts of a salutary world where everyone was besieged with happiness at every turn.

She said this, walking along with Suissé and the old Weepers across the piazza by the fountain where she paused and pitched out her chest in competition with the nipples of the Seven Naked Wonders of the Underworld.

A cheer went up through the whole of the piazza. Strangers rushed up to dance with her. At the windows men and women clapped. The Giuriato woman was again divinely beautiful.

A pigeon clucked over the stones. A poem was unfolded.

>*Forgive me.*
>*G.*

The group hurried on, laughing.

Bon, bon, bon! All the way up the cobblestones of Via Veneziano, they sang.

*T*he retired banker Plevano stood in the doorway of his gadget shop, watching them go. Across the street he saw Signora Pietro, old Weeper Pietro's wife, buying herself a new umbrella colored in the fashionable Matissian style. A few minutes later, under the excellent new umbrella, she scuttled by.

Plevano bowed. "Where are you off to now, Signora, in the lovely rain?" Plevano asked.

"I sniff! I rummage! I seek!" the old woman said.

Plevano recognized these words. The old signora never knew when it was raining, but she knew each line of Puccini's *Tosca*.

>*No space without form.*
>*No form without being.*
>*No being without history.*

At Galleria Svengali on Via Veneziano a large, angry crowd had assembled. Policemen on foot and on horseback patrolled the area, alert for any disorder that exceeded the nation's harmonious relationship with mayhem and common disorder. The gallery's glass windows lay shattered upon the cobblestones. A nun stood on a bucket by the gallery entrance, snapping photographs. Journalists darted here and there. Television cameras were everywhere, from as far away as Rome and Messina and Trieste.

The noising mob was shouting for the artist Benito to show his face. Unknown to them, Benito was not present. He was at his house in the hills, behind his easel, painting a picture of the lemon orchard against which his daughter executed unending cartwheels.

The diminutive gallery proprietor Svengali stood in the doorway, armed with a silver walking stick, fending off those attempting entrance with lit torches. The state of his suit revealed that he had been pelted with numerous rotten fruits. Nearby, in a boxer's pose, stood the artist Fruhöffer, Benito's wife and his child's mother, dripping blood from her nose.

"You do not deserve art," she was shouting to the clamoring rabble. "You deserve only your own ugly lives!"

The crowd responded in similar kind.

"The Holy Virgin," someone shouted, "was not present at The Last Supper!"

"Someone had to cook the meal," shouted back the mad Austrian.

From the darkened gallery a police official emerged. In the transparent sack he carried could be seen the chopper which had been lodged in the Savior's brow.

"We have fingerprinted the weapon," the official said, addressing the assembly. "The guilty will be charged. Justice will be served."

But the mob did not want such simple justice. The artist Benito had committed a sacrilege. Benito was a non-believer, a trouble-maker, a bohemian, as all artists were. They defied convention and hindered the march of orderly civilization, these artists. They led lives of debauchery. They respected nothing. Benito's work should be burnt and the artist be made to rot forever in jail.

But then — then here came along the cobblestones of Via Veneziano the old Weepers. Old Pietro, Old Pettifoggi, Old Belicoso, and Old Marinetti, all hobbling along on tortuous canes and crutches.

The crowd fell away, some offering apology. The Weepers were respectable; in some quarters they were revered. They attended church. Their mothers, just to mention this, were among the oldest people in Vicenza. They had lived here all their lives. They painted inexpensive pictures of noble horses and dogs and pretty serpents and sweet miniatures on silk or velvet that one could present on birthdays to one's sweetheart or parents. They painted what one could recognize. Everyone knew the Weepers. They were a safe, harmless bunch.

"Sorry, sorry," their friends said to them. "You know of course, in our talk of the rabid artist, of the depraved artistic temperament, we did not mean to include you."

The Weepers at first said nothing. They hobbled with equanimity through the agitated mob. They hobbled together up to the Galleria Svengali's very door. Here, they turned; they faced the mob.

One after another, they spoke.

The Weepers, they said, would guard Benito's painting with their lives. To destroy his work, they said, you must first destroy us.

*F*or the next few minutes after Plevano's exchange with old Signora Pietro the ex-banker had busied himself. He had set out a folding table on the stones outside his gadget store. Over the table top he spread a blue jeweler's cloth. On the cloth he set a white vase filled with tulips arranged in a Matissian manner. He set upon the cloth also a tall handblown glass. On the rim of the glass he perched one blue and one yellow bird. From a silver goblet he filled the glass with water. Then he reentered the gadget store, emerging — in elegant tuxedo — with two white wicker chairs, their cushions done up in a fabric reminiscent of Matisse. A moment later his wife Carla appeared as a vision of splendor over the cobblestones, a Matissian flower adorning her hair. She sat down.

Plevano kissed her hand; he poured champagne.

He addressed, in a gentlemanly tone, the two birds perched on the glass.

"Drink," he said.

The birds drank.

"Sing," he said.

The music of the little birds carried out over the piazza and up every Vicenza street.

Fuori, Satana, fuori! sang the one bird
Away with thee, Satan, away!
Dami i colori! sang the other bird.
Give me my paints!

Through the whole of Vicenza, into every shop and through every open window, soared the music of the operatic birds.

It was this music that the protesting mob at Galleria Svengali now heard.

They fell silent. They listened to the great singing birds, whose voices sounded so very identical to that of the great Freni and the great Pavorotti.

There now appeared out of Galleria Svengali the boy who had last been seen playing with a blue boat at the fountain of the Seven Naked Wonders of the Underworld. The boy carried bobbing by his head a gleaming silver tray on which were borne tall tulip glasses filled with champagne. The boy was dressed now in a black tuxedo, his black shoes highly polished. In a side pocket could be seen the little boat he would go and play with later.

On the gallery roof top Benito and Fruhöffer's child, in flowing silks, performed endless cartwheels.

The boy passed with his tray among the assemblage. They accepted with enthusiasm Svengali's champagne. In a matter of minutes their inflamed tempers dissipated; they dropped their nasty choppers into the street. The nun snapping pictures stepped down from her pail. The police relaxed. They too had champagne.

Soon everyone's voice joined in with those of the singing birds.

Go on talking to me as you talked before, they sang.

The sound of your voice is so sweet...

United and wandering in exile, our love through all the world will spread harmony of colour...

....armonie di canti diffondem.

"*C'est fini,*" said Suissé, the garrulous painter's muse.

With those words she flung her yellow hat high into the heavens and her body followed after it.

FAZZINI MUST HAVE YOU EVER AT HER SIDE

One evening in winter just after dark, Fazzini's son by a previous marriage, a mere child, hardly more than six, now living with his famous mother, was seen racing across Vicenza.

His friends, spotting him, called out, "Marco, Marco, where are you going so fast?' — but the boy flung himself along, taking no time to reply, inasmuch as his racing was indeed borne of emergency and panic and the direst need.

He burst into his father's house just as the latter was sitting down to dinner. "Father, father," the boy said, "come quickly, for our mother is saying she will do away with herself."

The father at once leapt up from the table and now there were two Fazzinis racing across Vicenza, their foot-race borne of direst emergency, and no time in their running to reply to the curious bystanders on Vicenza's streets who called out, "Hey, you two stallions, why are you racing so, why don't you slow down and live, take time to enjoy yourselves?"

Between gulps of breath, oh, racing so fast, the father asked his son, "Your dear mother, the most precious of women, the happiest of women, why is she wanting to do away with herself?"

To which the hurrying boy replied, "Papa, papa, how you do astound me! Do you not remember that my darling mother is always unhappiest when she is completing a painting, and papa, papa, she may already have completed her painting and be yet this very second on the very brink of doing away with herself, so let's hurry, dear papa, and save this chatter for the more reposed moment."

So there they were yet again, racing — how many times in a single year to speed back and forth across the city to the woman who was about to do herself in, as she was ever about to do on those frequent and heart-numbing occasions when the one painting was nearing completion and the next not yet begun, and never perhaps to be begun, because with one painting done the artist so rarely could see herself setting down to begin another, and thus her life would be over, since what reason could she have to go on drawing human breath when she had not the smallest conception of what canvas she might next turn to — no, and never would again, for her brain was dead and her body dying also.

This she would say to the boy, her face and hands dripping paint, her brush hand furiously at work on the all-but-completed painting: "Oh my dearest boy, my most acutely enamored son, my sweetest heart, although I love you dearly and can not bear the thought of being parted from you, you who mean everything to me! But what am I without my painting, this poisonous art, this worm that drinks my blood? I am nothing, a no one, a meaningless cipher in life's treadmill, a nonentity and a groaner, a sniveller, a hack, bad-mooded and ill-tempered and totally unrecognizable even as a human being! Without my painting I will be no good to you as a mother and I will despair and my despair will ruin your life, my dearest son, as it has ruined so many others, not to exclude your loving father, oh goodbye my darling, though for the moment I live, I work, I paint in this fever, but come and kiss me, do, there, there's a sweet boy, do forgive me!"

So everyone in Vicenza who saw the first Marco and his son the second Marco running so fast looked up at the stars, and said to one another, "Well, my goodness, that Francesca, she must be about to finish her new painting."

So, then:

Quickly as one could speak the words, father and son burst into the painter's studio, those old and creaking paint-bespattered rooms high on the hill, with the warped doors, the creaking floor, the crooked walls, the ragged ceiling where a thousand spiders had spun their webs since time immemorial, but boasting high, clean windows which admitted good light even in cruelest winter, with a view from these windows of the Villa of the Famous Dwarfs who were known themselves to cavort about in a frenzy and hide their heads in agony whenever the painter Francesca was about to pronounce "Fini" to her new painting and splash on the wild signature which only another spider could decipher . . .

Why, yes, father Marco and son Marco, as alike in their jitters as the yolks from two eggs, sweat dripping from their eyes, their hearts pounding, their eyes bulging, entering —

Entering to see the dear artist at work so intensely with her paints and brushes in that smallest pocket down in the painting's infamous right corner that she scarcely could take time out to lift her eyes in acknowledgement of them, her hair a tangle of fiery vermilion and ochre and russet hues that might have been taken for ancient blood, that might have been sludge washed into her scalp from primordial rock, her brow furrowed in deepest concentration, her smock a sea of stains, and muttering to herself, "The light, the light, oh, for the presence of unremitting light!"— because daylight had indeed waned and here she was working now from the mere, intermittent, all but inconsequential illumination that a single cigarette could provide. Oh, *puff-puff*, the brief orange glow, paint paint, *puff-puff*, another quick stroke, brush work down in that tight, meanest little final corner, the painter squinting, *puff-puff*, her teeth gnawing first one and then the other lip, *puff-puff*, the curling ash, the brief glow of light, the quickest stab of paint, her rapt, tortured face but inches from the canvas . . .

Then, *Voila! Holy Moses! Jumping Jehoshaphat!* — a great shout from the artist (*"I'm done, done, fini, fini, fait accompli!" Skaal! Prosit! To my health!*) — and the paint brushes pitched across the room, a foot kicking aside the mountain of cigarette butts, wading through ash, a carpet of wrenched tubes, nubbed brushes, tin cans, discarded rags, as a hand clutches a wine bottle, as the artist swigs, the artist next clawing at her hair, burying her face momentarily within her frock's stiffened folds, muttering incantation to herself before flinging a massive new canvas onto her easel, that canvas sized, primed, ready. Then . . .

Only then lifting an astonished face to her wide-eyed visitors, that face lit with sudden, transforming radiance by the most heart-warming cheer, now exclaiming to this most-excellent duo of Marco Fazzinis, "Darlings, my treasures, in the nick of time! The very nick! My best painting ever, oh my lovelies, a work of genius with no known comparison —now, *now, shoo! shoo! Away from me, you gnats!* — those other immortals must step aside! Michelangelo, Masaccio, Masolino, Parmigianino, step aside! Oh, but not you, my darlings, come and hold me, let me embrace you, oh let me kiss your faces, and after the kisses, champagne, more champagne, champagne until we drop, my wonders, but one sip only for me, one only, and a quick brush of my teeth to extract from my jaws this vile taste that benumbs my mouth, perhaps afterwards a second sip, a third, and then it's onwards to my next work, my sweet stallions, because I am in the grip of delirious fever and must keep on, *on on on!* with no time out for dinner or the conventional human intercourse between closest friends, or even to properly greet you, my darlings, how nice of you to drop in and what on earth would become of me if I did not have you ever at my side?

HOT

*D*rink this water, Emmitt told me. This was after sixteen hours, the baby not yet coming. After I'd renounced my joys, together with all else.

Drink this.

I was still in the habit of doing what he said. Not all the time, but the practice lingered. I drank what he offered, and all but shot from the table. That's how it felt. It was Napoleon Five Star he'd given me. I don't know how he'd got the bottle into the delivery room. He can, that's all I know.

I learned a lot about his thoughts on motherhood during this ordeal, and what value he put on the human race. Alcohol can maim a baby. Smoke, too, and he was blowing that over my face. Had my daughter been born with withered limbs and a head big as his own, he wouldn't have cared. Nor would I have, at that time.

We had both been so bad.

That I was going through with it at all was a big surprise.

Though Mom's was the bigger quandary. It meant I had a hold on him stronger than her own. We were then still at those crossroads. All those red eyes.

My mind wasn't all there. That's why I was having such a hard time. For my money, the worst pain was in having Emmitt in the room with me. He didn't want to be, but some decency remained. Dirt under his nails, filthy cuffs. Bloodshot eyes. All that language. And my mother pacing the hall. Doing push-ups, I was told.

But she came and went. He would disappear too, he would go out and comfort her. I told the nurse, yes, I can imagine what form that comfort takes.

When he came back in I could see her lipstick smeared over his face. His shirt-tail out. He bent over me, blew smoke over my face.

"Just checking," he said.

I could smell their sweat on him.

I knew the fool I looked, on that table with my beggar's belly, my splayed legs. Even your feet look ridiculous in a situation like that.

"You don't want this child, do you?" the doctor said.

"Do you?" I said.

No, I didn't want it for myself, or the baby's self, not at that moment, but I wanted it for the revenge. What was inside me was mine and Emmitt's, and my mother could never have that. She could have her own with him, not yet over the hill, but never have what I had with him first. She knew it too. That's why she was prowling the halls, standing on her head.

I painted on lipstick.

I said to everyone, "Do something about this hair. I'll die if I didn't run a comb through my hair."

"Does that crazy woman out there belong to anyone in here?" another nurse asked.

"She belongs to him," I said, hooking my thumb Emmitt's way. He was rubbing my lower back and the heel of his hand almost shoved through my spine.

He drifted over to the window. I snapped shut my little compact, imitation silver.

"Go ahead," I said. "Jump."

"Dry up," he said.

"You couldn't even walk the white line," I told him, thinking of the cop in the cruiser that night who had made him walk it, while I scrambled to get my dress back on.

My heart was broken anyhow, these persecutions formed no set-back. When the doctor said push, what I thought of was Emmitt sawing away above me. All those times. Or me sawing at him. "My cup overfloweth." That's what he always said.

A pig can shoot a pint of semen, I thought. Pints of the stuff, in a single hour.

"Quit thinking," said the nurse. "How much thinking does it take to push?"

"Yeah," Emmitt said, laughing. "Push."

The doctor was in and out. Gone one minute, back the next. I'd open my eyes and his gloved fist would be inside me.

"Prep her," he told someone.

"Doctor, she's been prepped," someone said.

"Make Emmitt do it," I said. "I want him to do it."

I cried loudly, hoarse through to my feet. I was crying up and down myself. I was one big bucket of crybaby, until the next pain hit. Lightning bolts.

"Drink this," someone said.

"No, I won't," I said. "How crazy do you think I am?"

In the rush, I had left home without the new robe I'd bought by selling fudge. All the other women had sixty-dollar perms. They wore new shoes, shuffling down the hallway.

These gifts hadn't improved their dispositions the slightest.

A pan was placed between my spread legs and Emmitt lathered, his eyes set way back. His tongue hanging. Mint Julep, I thought. I yanked his hand up and sucked four of his fingers into my mouth.

"Looky there," he said, tipping the pan. "Now you've gone and wet yourself."

I went on sucking, my eyes closed. Keep talking, I thought. Lay on your sweet words. Mom would poke her head through the door, see him shaving my cubby-hole clean, and never be the same again for the whole of her remaining years.

"Scandalous," the nurse said. "What do you mean to name the child?"

"Cognac," Emmitt said, and produced the bottle out of his pocket. Slugging away.

He shaved me beautifully. How many others had he shaved?

"Stop bawling," the doctor said. "Push, goddamit. How did you get these scars on your elbows?"

Some time had passed.

"Where's Emmitt?" I asked.

"Gone back to the motel. He did a slink out the back way. He's horsemeat."

The nurse piped in.

"She's well-rid of that flake. I go to the washroom, he's asking me out."

"You don't don't know anything," I said. "Emmitt's got virtues miles deep."

I had in mind his eyes, blue as gas flames.

I knew I was lost.

I was lost, inside my own head.

I saw a two-lane road, and me walking it, pushing the baby in a blue stroller. I would push her uphill and downhill. I would have my hitching thumb out. I would call her Imogene. Soon I'd be seventeen. I would learn to read road maps. I'm strong and can work. I'll be crazy about her, like she was catnip.

THE SIX BLIND BOYS
OF SANTA OCURO

The señora's second husband died suddenly, falling from a rooftop. Earlier, for a brief time, she had been married to the Colonel. The day after the husband's death the Colonel returned to her house. Within the very first hour of his arrival he took the señora to her bed. He was done with hypocrisy and the cant of the brainless many, he told her. She would be wise to do so as well, he said, for the country was entering a new era and one could choose either to be the wheel or to be among those many the wheel would trod over. He entreated her to cast off the faded nightgown she had worn through nine years of ridiculous marriage. Go away and burn the rag, he told her, and return to me naked and eager.

The señora did so. She poured wine from a Murani jug and they drank the wine and she straddled the Colonel. Yes, the Colonel said angrily. Nine years married to a man who was a toad and a blockhead and a villain.

The woman wept to hear these terrible remarks weighed against her dead husband. She thrust her hips more powerfully above him and smiled to see sweat beading his brow and his fists and eyes clenching.

The dead husband's family was arriving on the morrow, she said. Servants had been preparing food all day; the entire village would have to be fed.

Put chains over the door, the Colonel told her. Station your servants at the gate. Have them turn away everyone.

"I have seen many people die," the Colonel said. "More than a few have been transported to paradise by my own hands. Look here the blood," he said — cackling merrily when by some trick the light showed his hands stained red. "One more now matters no more to me than the snap of these fingers. Better yet that the most recent should have been your worthless husband."

He said this and other such calumny into the widow's ears, abed on her white pillows, through the whole of that first night, swaying above her with a violence that she remembered of old and which she likened unto a cunning vengeance the two of them together were affecting upon a malodorous world.

In the morning the widow awakened feeling more refreshed and vigorous than she had in years. She summoned the servants to her chambers and gave instructions to the aghast and trembling group.

"Lock the doors. Chain the gate. Let no one enter."

The servants blinked disbelief at the sight of their mistress with her hair tangled, her shoulders bruised, her mouth twisting in rancor at any mention of her departed husband. The naked Colonel glared at them from her rumpled bed, the blade of his saber swishing about and his nasty cigar smoke billowing in the love-soaked air.

Later that morning all in the village could see the Colonel taking the air on the widow's balcony, smoking his cigar. Soon the señora joined him, the two drinking champagne in near-nudity as they surveyed the ripening groves and village rooftops.

A man from the funeral house arrived, intending to show his coffins.

The priest arrived.

Flower vendors came.

All were turned away.

A small boy, said to be the Colonel's son, stood at the gate a long time, calling, *"Papa, Papa, Papa!"* In the end, he too went away.

Two sorrowing peasants, in the company of a policeman, gained brief entrance. The peasants stood looking down at their naked feet on the tiles as the policeman expounded on their woes.

A small child, he explained, had gone missing.

The policeman showed the widow a photograph of the missing girl, in which she stood holding hands with the dead husband.

"Go away," the widow said.

She called her servants to come with mop and pail to clean that spot on her tiles where the peasants had stood.

A bone merchant arrived to ask if he could purchase the dead husband's bones.

Carriages clattered to a stop beneath the trees outside the señora's main gate and the dead man's mother and father, his many sisters and brothers, together with scores of others of diverse affinity, alighted and moved about for some time in agitated, noisy demonstration.

The Colonel stood on the balcony, shouting obscenities at this group.

Women in black plodded along the señora's walls from dawn until dust, reciting the rosary.

The Colonel's wife, a girl of sixteen, ran shrieking up and down the village streets from dawn until sunset. She ripped off all of her clothes and tore at her hair, screaming the señora's name.

A search for the missing girl, underway throughout the village, revealed nothing.

She last had been seen in the dead husband's company.

One shoe, said to be hers, was later discovered on the rooftop where the dead husband had met his doom.

In the evenings the widow's house was lit and passers-by on the street and people in their houses on the surrounding hills were filled with dread, to see the disreputable pair dancing together behind the windows.

Another police official arrived. He informed the Colonel and the señora that the undertaker had removed the husband's corpse from his establishment and placed it on a chair in the middle of the street. Dogs were taking an interest in the body and the villagers did not know why God was punishing them this way. Water would turn sour, blood would stream from the church ceiling, and strange malignancy overtake the children. Sight of the dead man propped up in the chair in the street, he said, unnerved his men who had the unfortunate duty of guarding the dead man in his chair, and there was much talk, and traffic was having to be rerouted.

"Great calamity," he told them, "will come to us all, if the matter is not soon corrected."

The Colonel strode out upon the balcony and looked down over the rooftops and groves and patches of garden at the dead husband propped up in his chair outside the funeral house on Calle de la Noche de la mil Lunas. He smacked his lips together and called out dire insults to the dead husband; he then returned to the señor, beaming a renewed splendor.

"The dogs are indeed interested," he said.

The despairing policeman inquired of the widow if she had any instructions.

"My dead husband's bones mean nothing to me," the señora said. "Let the dogs and the vultures have him."

The Colonel rattled his saber in the police captain's face.

"Burn him," he said.

So it was agreed.

The priest returned a second and a third time to the señora's house, but was turned away.

The widow dispatched her servants and the corpse was roped to his chair and chair and corpse were transported by cart to the cemetery on the hill.

Twigs were set afire, and finally huge limbs and a plethora of rubbish and bric-a-brac, and when cinders were flaring over the village the cart was pushed into the blaze. Cart, chair, and corpse burned through the whole of that day and night.

A heavy rain fell the next morning and continued without letup through the day. At night it fell harder, and then harder yet, and the villagers crossed themselves and smacked their children silent and recited the rosary and remained indoors.

Gravestones tumbled over and slid about in the muck in the cemetery on the hill and rivers of mud poured down every street. But it was said the dead man's bones were still intact and sitting upright in the unscarred, impervious chair.

Each evening the Colonel and his mistress strolled the balcony, embraced and coupled in full sight there, from time to time pausing to fire the Colonel's pistol at movement in the trees.

All the widow's servants had departed.

Days passed.

The group known as the Six Blind Boys of Santa Ocuro arrived in the village and set up to play in the plaza's pavilion. It irritated them to find the streets empty and no dignitaries to greet them. It puzzled them that village señoritas were not pulling at their elbows amid peels of laughter and vague or brazen hints at secret assignations once the concert ended. The unnatural silence of the place unnerved them. The Six Blind Boys of Santa Ocuro considered it outrageous that their hosts had not spread straw about to disguise the muck, or thought to sweep away the vast array of debris corrupting the stage. This would have been the decent thing to do. Affairs in this village were not well conducted. Apparently people in this village believed esteemed visitors should see to such business themselves.

At eight o'clock precisely they took up their instruments and played. They played and sang with their customary fire, complaining to themselves from time to time that the villagers here were a strangely silent lot.

They did not know that their audience consisted of a few starving dogs and the dead man whose white bones now sat upright in the uncharred chair on the granite base of an old memorial at the plaza's centre.

The Six Blind Boys from Santa Ocuro played their two full hours.

*E*venings, these days, a chatter of young girls stroll the plaza in the one direction. Young boys stroll the opposite direction, hissing impertinences. Their keepers eye the youthful passage with mean suspicion; they miss nothing. Small children flit noisily here and there. Babies doze within the black rebozos of silent grandmothers. Old men in decaying serapes play chess on the white-washed benches consigned to the area. Dogs nose the uneven stones.

The dead husband's bleached bones sit high in his chair.

A black wrought-iron fence has been installed around the flood-lit bones. Carnations in copious number adorn the granite base. Love birds nest in the skull.

The priest clasps his beads, and nods, nods, nods.
He smiles to each passing party.
"God be with you, Father."
"And God be with you."
"God love you, Father."
"And God love you, my child."
And God love you.

ST. PETE
AND THE CHAMBER OF HORRORS

*D*eGood's Chamber of Horrors in St. Petersburg was located next door to the mayor's house, a Mr. Crispen. Droves of tourists, and locals, too, came to witness its many wonders during the weeks following its opening, and everyone agreed DeGood had a winner. Most thought there would be a good deal of carry-over for the town. The two quick-fly eateries would make a comeback, the service station and the grocery store would reopen and prosper, and maybe the old motel down the road would have to file the rust from its No Vacancy sign.

God knows the little town needed this, because the GE plant had been closed for fifteen years, the Oats outfit had long since moved to Mexico, and all the young people were getting out of St. Pete as fast as they could.

Not that the mayor wasn't doing his job. Crispen worked extraordinarily hard at it, and you could hardly fault him for having so little success. St. Pete was no longer beautiful, by any means; its water table was low, its power supply erratic; it had no airport, bus, or train service; its labor force was unenlightened, and the absence of any highway, or even a paved county road, made the town all but inaccessible. Sea and mountain were far away, and the nearest metropolis a good day's drive. Until DeGood's Chamber of Horrors opened, you could sit on your porch any given day without ever seeing a face you hadn't seen almost every day since the day you were born.

Crispen often went north, with contracts in his pockets, seeking new industries and offering every land or tax incentive anyone could devise. Those businesses that he did succeed in luring seemed all but invisible. They hired no one and rarely required even a building. Now and then a mail-order hut would go up inside a chain fence, with maybe a guard dog roaming at night, but that was largely the extent of St. Pete's forays into the good times. An astonishing number of post office boxes had been rented, so many that any local person wanting one was out of luck. Global Printing did the occasional handbill or certificate advertising condominiums for sale, or prime "estate" land, and TV's or cars someone far away had won, but after that any benefit accruing to the town was strictly a product of the unanchored mind.

The printer at Global said that these jobs he did on his old hand-cranker press mostly seemed to be suggesting that this St. Pete was that other St. Pete over in Florida. Everything was ordered by phone and dispatched to the post office boxes and he had yet to see a human face. He'd talked to Crispen about this, but all Crispen ever said was, "Do a better job and the world will be wearing out your door mat."

As the unemployment rate in St. Pete hung at about ninety per cent, the printer was glad to get what jobs he could.

So everyone was ecstatic when Crispen returned from one of his northern trips and announced that the DeGood Company of East St. Louis and Chicago would be taking over the old Harrowood Place and converting it to their purposes. No expense spared.

"It's a big company, huh?"

"One of the biggest."

"And what is to be their payroll?"

"Payroll?"

"How many will they be hiring?"

"Not many to start with. Two or three. A minimum ten by the end of the year. Then the sky!"

"How'd you get the shiner?"

Crispen had returned from this trip with the entire left side of his face behind bandages. His right eye was discolored and puffy, and the left had the strong gleam of glass. He carried one arm as if it had been broken, and no one had noticed before the bad limp in his left leg.

He had been gone three months and many in St. Pete figured he wouldn't be returning. The town council had even had the printer from Globe, who had a mathematical mind, come in and run a secret audit of the books.

Some of the young people in town had been taking a close look at the mayor's house in the dark of night, willing to bet that the mayor might have a few articles inside that would fetch top dollar. This element had been deeply disappointed by his return.

They would have gone in already, and taken what they wanted and smashed up the place, but for the sounds that emanated from within. Some had said it sounded to them like a choking parrot. Others said it was a wild animal — of some size — with its leg caught in a trap. One of their lot maintained the fool had simply left his radio on, thinking to scare off burglars. As if *they* could be deceived by such a childish ruse. All the same, none was willing to enter the house.

So they crossed the mayor's lawn to the Harrowood house and wrecked it instead. This was something they did two or three times each year, though never with much enthusiasm. The Harrowood house had hardly anything inside, or outside either, left to be wrecked. Old Mrs. Harrowood had seen to that decades ago, when she came home one day from her mission work and found her husband hanging from the clothesline. He was wearing her favorite dress.

The sight had embittered her immensely. She had wanted to hang him herself, though not from her clothesline. A row of eucalypti in fresh bloom ran alongside the clothesline, and to her mind this made the scene of her husband hanging look altogether too pretty. With a little Brylcream in his hair, and his own clothes exchanged for hers, the picture of him hanging could have been featured on the cover of *Country Living.*

So she had gone inside the house and ripped it apart room by room, and afterwards had attacked the exterior.

"This DeGood fella," the townspeople inquired of the mayor. "They mean to restore the place to its former dignity, huh?"

"No expense spared."

"He's a big-shot, then? This DeGood?"

"The biggest."

"What sold such a tycoon on St. Pete? You didn't promise free water and mineral rights, did you?"

"Nothing like that. Sentimentality did it."

"Sin — what was that?"

"He got his start in the other St. Pete. I guess he figured it would be fun to round out his career in another place of the same name."

"He's old, then?"

"*He is.* But he's got a lot of young sons. Comes from a big family."

"So . . . so," they said. "Tell us about your wounds. Some big bruiser of a husband come after you? You were out chasing a woman, on company time? Is that what happened?"

They put this question to the mayor all right, though they knew better than to press him. He was in a bad fix — looked like he'd been run over by a truck — but you didn't want to rub up against Crispen's wrong side. A few people in St. Pete had, and you didn't see these people around any more.

So they bantered with him, ducking their heads this way and that, and poking him on his good arm, to show him they were only kidding.

In any event, whether you liked Crispen's way of doing things or not, he'd brought this new industry to town. He'd cracked the wedge. Found daylight. A few more industries like this one, and little St. Pete might very well be humming.

"So," they said. "This DeGood. What kind of horrors is he thinking of having in the place? Nothing indecent, or beyond the pale, we hope."

"He has his eye on The Spider Child."

"Spy? — Say what?"

"The Spider Child. The wonder of all Europe. Looks like a child, behaves like a spider. You want a freak, he's the one you go after."

"Sounds good."

"A Miss Carlotta DeLisle will be managing the place."

"Carlotta? Miss? She sounds pretty dishy."

"Oh, she's a world-class act, Miss Carlotta DeLisle. Top of the Mart. She will put this burg on the map."

The townspeople — the men anyway — went away from this interview imagining themselves in the arms of this doubtlessly flamboyant creature, and hoping somehow that her presence might bring some boom to the real estate situation. At the moment, scarcely a house in town was worth so much as its taxes, and *any* relief on this front would be highly appreciated. The women folk went away thinking this Carlotta DeLisle sounded rather snooty. She would likely have long pointy fingers painted red, and lounge about in *Hustler* attire, and try to steal all their husbands. If so, more power to her.

The whole town, that is to say, was curious.

They were even happier, and more curious, when work started on the old Harrowood house, and a few fix-it-up people in town had to dust off their tools and actually go to work.

This was in fact such a novel sight in St. Pete that the school board put back the school's opening time each day, by one hour, in order to allow the children the pleasure of seeing their parents, with lunch pails swinging and their baseball caps worn at a cocky angle, troop off to their labors.

The weeks passed, and matters were moving along at a good clip.

A few of the old walls at the Harrowood house could be saved, they determined, and the brick work on the chimneys was solid. A patch-up job could be done on the wiring, so long as the incoming residents practiced a rudimentary caution. The well was dry; that was a problem. Did Mr. DeGood, or Miss Carlotta DeLisle, want a new one dug? Well, the fix-it-up forces would just await their instructions; there never had been any plumbing, but the old outhouse in back could be propped up, and maybe some lime dumped into the two-seater. Anything fancier, and someone would have to make a supply run to the metropolis. Few home owners in St. Pete had gone in for the flush toilet.

Lord knows, though, what might be done with the amazing objects that had been found in the basement. Boxes and boxes. Were those bones? Where on earth had so many bones come from, and which of those old-timers had been the collector? Not Mr. Harrowood, certainly, because that strange gentleman had not once in the whole of his adult years been known to venture past his front gate. Mrs. Harrowood, on the other hand, had roved far and wide in her mission work, and had often been seen ushering groups of young boys into the house. Were these bones, then, the bones of those children? They were certainly not *dog* bones, or the bones of any known domesticated creature, and they did roughly correspond to a child's size. In many cases they had unearthed full and complete skeletons, minus the skulls. So, yes, likely that was the story.

Boxes and boxes, and trunks stacked to the ceiling, and others beneath the floor boards, all stacked with bones, and, finally, thousands of plain paper sacks from the old Kroger's Store, each filled with small human skulls.

The question put to the mayor was, What do we do now? And what will Mr. DeGood and Miss Carlotta Delisle think of us if they find out they have invested in a place where upwards of a thousand children have gone to their untimely rewards? Did you see the size of those cooking pots we found? Have you seen the ten thousand mason jars filled with that strange lard?

"Now don't go off on a tangent," Crispen told this lot. "I am sure Mr. DeGood and Miss Carlotta DeLisle are sophisticated people with experience of this world, who will not give one whit of concern to this little localized mystery. Go on digging and hammering and don't think about it. Anything you find that can't be used just haul away to the town dump."

"By the way," these representatives asked him. "When is this DeLisle woman coming to town? You don't have a picture, do you?"

"Come on," the mayor said. "Back to work. You are not being paid just to stand around."

"Pay?"

It had been a mistake for Crispen to use this word. None of the workers had been paid yet, and the weeks were rushing by. Their children had no shoes, liens were being attached to their abodes, their cars sat up rusting on blocks because the gas station had refused them credit, and the St. Pete bank wouldn't lend them another cent. They had run up huge bills at the grocery, and bigger ones at St. Pete's two quick-fly eateries, all in anticipation of their first big fat pay cheque, and — pardon — they wanted to know now when Mr. DeGood's greenbacks might be forthcoming.

Crispen told them not to fly off the handle. Rome wasn't built in a day, he said. Tuck in the belt a little tighter, the way he had done.

This did not satisfy them.

"All right, I'll tell you," he said. "Mr. DeGood's cash flow is at the moment less than fluid. His funds are tied up in off-shore oil rigs off Haiti. Some deal he had with Poppa Doc. His greenbacks are held in banks in the Bahamas. Paper work, you see. Extensive paper work, getting these greenbacks released. Similarly, the case in Zurich. His Columbian business is experiencing some squeeze. Last week, for instance, his potato crops in that country were bombed from the air by zealous rivals. His sons have proved untrustworthy. Trouble in the family, I am saying. Plus, he has been hit by unexpected developments from within the federal government. A few harmless indictments. Old tax matters. One of his closest associates showed up the other day in the boot of a car parked at O'Hare. Something about Mr. DeGood's fingerprints being found in the car, and on a tire iron, although that's up in the air.

"But not to worry. The money will be forthcoming, perhaps by week's end. I understand he is sending it in by nightbag."

Nightbag? At mention of this word, the mouths of Crispen's petitioners dropped open. The thought of all the money owed them floating about in a nightbag — what on earth was a nightbag? — quite exhilarated them. Some saw in their minds millions of dollars tucked away in a big sack borne by wonderful wings; others could not see their money at all, not in a bag; they could see, however, reams and reams of beautiful greenbacks raining down from the heavens, tumbling all about their heads.

They went back to their work happily, and at the end of the day's work went on a wildly extravagant shopping spree through St. Pete's tumble-down core.

Miss Carlotta Delisle came to St. Pete in August, a month before the Chamber of Horrors was to open, and went directly to Mayor Crispen's house.

Mr. DeGood passed through St. Pete as well, or so it was rumored. Some said they saw his face peeking from behind drawn shades in the mayor's upstairs windows. A large fellow with a pig's face was seen nightly on guard by the front door. For sure, a long, wide, dusty automobile with real-leather interior and mud flaps, had sat out of sight for three days in the mayor's garage.

Miss Carlotta DeLisle was seen twice, alone in the mayor's garden. She seemed always to be wearing the same rain coat, and nothing else. She was shoeless both times. Leaves and brush gave texture to a bouffantish stack of blue hair. She looked to be on the frail side. Her age, amazingly, was guessed to be in excess of one hundred. Reliable witnesses alleged that she was, at the maximum, no more than three feet tall. She was remarkably bent, even for a woman of her considerable years. When seen, she was staring up apparently at a rank of vultures perched over her head on webby tree limbs. St. Pete had been invaded by hundreds of these birds since the first work began on the Harrowood house. You could see these birds every day, in every nearby tree, watching and waiting.

"God knows," the people said, "what they do at night."

Miss Carlotta DeLisle was carrying empty gin bottles in her two hands, and presumably was thinking about throwing them at these vultures. In any case, she flung out both her arms simultaneously, the bottles tumbled flimsily into air, and the next second she did the same, dropping flat on her face in the grass.

She did not get up. It she did, it was not until long after sundown, for the whole gang of workers next door had their eyes on her every minute.

This happened *twice*, exactly as described.

St. Pete was not impressed with the news.

They were running out of patience with DeGood, with the Horror's manageress, and with their long-time mayor, Crispen.

Crispen had come to St. Pete as a young man. What did they know about him other than that?

The St. Pete council decided again that they'd have the printer come in and run another secret — this time exhaustive — audit of the town books.

They were relieved somewhat to discover that Crispen had not spent a single penny, at any time during the past several years, on garbage, gutters, education, water treatment, health, parking, police affairs, jail up-keep, the Main Street Rape Center, the fire brigade, roads, lighting, parks and parklands, the Half-way Hut For Repeat Offenders, zoning enforcement, or on juvenile rehabilitation (that had been a big pitch of his during the last mayoralty race).

He had paid, out of the public purse, for vast quantities of printed matter of an unspecified nature; he had paid for six post office boxes rented in his own name; he had drawn reimbursement cheques for thirteen official trips to East St. Louis and Chicago, all apparently designed to lure industry to St. Pete. The town had also paid for one official trip to Leavenworth State Penitentiary, lasting nine days.

The town had also paid his salary, of course.

It had given him a bonus of six thousand dollars back in January, together with seven thousand in June, that no one on the Council could quite recall authorizing.

The town had footed the bill for a lavish reception no one remembered attending.

There were gaming bills paid to casinos in Atlantic City and Windsor.

He had signed a rather questionable contract for a landfill or nuclear waste site east of the town, paying out some fifty thousand dollars to a company whose name on the document was illegible.

"Nothing really extraordinary," as one councillor put it. "Nothing you can sink your teeth into."

No smoking gun.

All the same, they were now wary.

It was suggested to Crispen, at an in-camera session, that he might want to take a stress-break.

Oh!

Crispen studied the faces, and decided this might be wise.

Worse luck, a whole spate of bad news was breaking each day, deeply hurting the image of the town and despoiling its good name.

The two quick-fly eateries on Main Street, and the one service station, declared bankruptcy.

Ye Olde Pool Hall & Snooker Bar, which had enjoyed regal Saturday nights, went belly-up.

The Tammy Wynette Show was cancelled. She had thought this St. Pete was that other St. Pete.

The cable TV people, beaming their signal in from the metropolis, decided to cut their losses.

The Great Atlantic and Pacific Telephone Company turned over their local business to Sprint. Sprint did not do business in St. Pete.

The Monkey Ward catalog store closed its doors.The bank was now open only from two until five, every other Wednesday.

The Feed Store became a cut-rate cigarette emporium, and the drug store seemed unable to get its annual delivery of goods.

The Christian Brothers Tabernacle on Main Street was holding shoe sales.

The Baptist Church on Main Street held a Virgins' Night, and two thousand young women from the surrounding area, together with three young men scarred by acne, declared their intention, before Christ, to remain in that state until marriage.

Statistics showed that not one person in St. Pete had married during the past nine years.

The state disclosed that the median death age in St. Pete was 47, lowest in the nation.

Something called Outwards Migration was highest.

St. Pete held the record for presence of vultures, beating out Deadwood Gulch, Colorado, by a wide margin.

More than a few aged busybody parents were stealing into town to ask sinister questions about the Harrowood bones and to root about in the town dump. The gang of rowdies who had wanted to break into the mayor's house, sons and daughters of the pillars of the community, in a series of curious accidents, drove five cars into the old gravel pit at the end of Main Street, and seventeen of their members perished.

Town water smelt of lye.

The sewage treatment plant was being forced to shut down for six months, following an unscheduled visit by foreign officials.

All terrible news, and to halt the leak in the dam St. Pete required a strong and aggressive mayor.

The town again approached their best candidate, Crispen. "I'll do it," Crispen said. "There are too many nay-sayers around here. What we need is the positive outlook. For instance, don't forget we've still got DeGood's Chamber of Horrors. The grand opening has been moved up to next week. Go home, sleep, take it easy. St. Pete has never been in better shape. We are entering a new, dynamic, modern age.

"By the way," he said, "we landed that Spider Child."

"Spy? — Say what?"

"You remember. That guy with the baby face, who eats flies and climbs walls."

Many of the older people in St. Pete felt homesick for the good old days when Mrs. Harrowood had ruled this neck of the woods, and cows and pigs and the occasional bloody boy had aimlessly roamed the streets.

When the Chamber of Horror finally had its grand opening, townspeople were elated. It astonished them to discover so many luxury automobiles wedged along Main Street, most of them bearing East St. Louis or Chicago license tags.

The men emerging from these cars flashed diamond rings from their every pinkie, and their young, bosomy companions wore shoes with heels so high they hobbled along the sidewalks like enfeebled mountain goats.

The locals watched with intense delight as these tourists trooped one by one into the restored Harrowood House, and plunked down their admission money, rarely bothering to wait for change.

At the end of the first day, some in town swore that one-hundred dollar bills were just floating about the grounds.

These tourists liked what they saw in there, too, because they stayed inside the whole of the first three days.

Then there were gunshots — part of the show, the locals assumed — and a few of the gentlemen did at last stagger out. Others emerged on the run and dragged these people to their cars, and the cars shot away under the squeal and smoke of burning rubber.

DeGood himself came outside with ten or twelve of his friends. They stared awhile at the vultures perched on the overhead wires, and in the trees, and on the rooftops. Then they marched in soldierly formation over to the mayor's house.

They had come equipped with drink, it seemed, and any manner of other party goods, and a number of the highheeled women proved to be songbirds; it became quite roisterous over there.

If you had been present at this affair, you would have been taken aback to see the tycoon DeGood advance upon Miss Carlotta DeLisle snoring in her chair, kneel before her, and lower his head into her lap. It would have amazed you to see his tears flow, and to hear him say, "Mama, Mama."

"Mama, the deck is clean. Our family is intact and secure for another hundred years. We have rubbed out the divisive element."

You would not have known what this meant.

Nor would matters have been clarified when you observed Mayor Crispen tip-toe into this family assembly, and drop two pistols and a sawed-off shotgun into Miss Carlotta DeLisle's lap, together with a suitcase brimming over with money.

You would have scratched your head.

It would have further astonished you to see the woman's reaction to this homage. She screamed out names of people you had never heard of, and beat her breasts with her fists, and cried such lamentable woe that you would have believed her possessed. She whipped DeGood's head still at rest in her lap, pulled at his hair, and all but ripped his head from his neck. You would have thought she was acting exactly as a mother might, faced with a death in the family.

Finally, one of the high-heeled women brought her something to drink.

*I*n the weeks since The Horror opened — that is what it was called now — nearly everyone in town has somehow scraped together the fee. Some of the more affluent St. Petes have visited the place any number of times.

It lives up to its billing, they say.

The DeGood fella has put in a small airport outside of town, and every midnight his company planes circle St. Pete, blink their lights, and settle quietly down. The landings hardly disturb anyone.

Business is booming at the quick-fly eateries and a new hot-spot has opened; here the whole town congregates each evening, to see the songbirds in their high heels sing, dance, and disrobe.

At the moment there is little mixing between the locals and the DeGood people, but the mayor says all this will sort itself out in good time.

Stabbings and shootings have increased. Crispen reminds everyone this is the price one pays.

The vultures have become a huge problem.

But St. Pete is seeing a number of new faces. You can see these people crouched in their automobiles in the Hot Spot parking lot, whispering into their car radios. Big vans with an Elmer's Plumbing logo on the sides park each night outside the mayor's house and the Harrowood place, their roofs bedecked with tired vultures.

It amazes the locals to think their little town is being promoted and talked about in places they have never heard of. Some secretly wish Crispen, in his early days, had not destroyed the town's fine old Bow String Bridge, or allowed the demolishment of the many fine old Colonial houses that once upon a time graced St. Pete's narrow brick streets and pathways. They wish he had not bulldozed the many ancient smithy shops, and old Inns, or filled in and laid concrete over the nice meandering streams, or taken dynamite to row upon row of stately trees.

St. Pete, some old codgers claim, could have been another Williamsburg. After all, the town has a rightful claim on history; as any text will tell you, Old St. Pete was one of the very first permanent settlements in the New World.

Now it has its Chamber of Horrors, though, and a prosperity few want to criticize.

It has its Spider Child performing daily in The Horror. This baby-faced, half-human creature has the uncanny ability to wrinkle itself up into a form hardly larger than the human head. It can scoot quickly this way and that, on eight hairy legs, exactly the way a spider can. You should hear the guffaws that erupt when someone throws it a bug, or the silence that falls when it speaks: "I am so happy to be in St. Pete. St. Pete is my kind of town." Its squeaky voice shivers the spine.

The Spider Child's understanding of the basic sciences is a wonder to behold. It can climb walls, and scoot upside down on any ceiling. From its buttocks-hole, or from its mouth, it can produce all but invisible strands, these of considerable strength, and do so in a minute, even as you watch. It can weave powerful nets over anything or anyone not moving, and scoot into a crevice or corner, and from that space level its fierce gaze upon you.

You would go weak in the knees, to see it.

You would feel your face heating.

Of all the many wonders at the Chamber of Horrors, the Spider Child is the clear sensation.

Word has it, if you can believe Crispen, that it has now struck up a relationship with some undisclosed party. They intend to put their roots down in St. Pete, and raise a family.

As the mayor says, soon we shall be seeing little spider children running everywhere.

If the vultures don't do it — bring glory to St. Pete — the Spider People will.

THE HOUSE
OF THE SLEEPING DRUNKARDS

*T*he old man was down on the floor crying, saying how hard his life was. It had been hard before his accident, he said, when he had his legs — it had been God's own hell — but now it was harder. Now it was unbearable.

He moaned and moaned.

Cissy Bains said, "Somebody give him a biscuit."

But we had eaten all the biscuits. We had consumed all the licker too. Not one drop was in any of the bottles.

"You'll have to git more," Cissy Bains said. "He can't git through the night without his licker biscuit."

"Can't," we said. "It's a blizzard out there and the car is broke down."

"Is there any lye?" the old man asked. "Ain't there any old sterno can about? Me and lye or sterno can git along just fine."

He moaned and moaned.

We were all moaning. We all needed a drink bad.

Cissy popped out of the door and a minute later we saw her crawling under the car. The snow was churning, all but hiding her and the car, but we saw she had a bucket with her and knew she meant draining antifreeze out of the radiator.

"It's too rusty," we told her when she dragged herself in. "There are depths to which we will not sink."

"Fine," she said. "That means more for me and him."

We gave the liquid in her bucket a good long close look. It was near to black. It was all lumpy.

"That there rusty antifreeze will kill you," we said.

"Worse didn't," said Cissy.

"Let's git to it," the old man said.

We got busy and cooked up a new plate of biscuits.

"Make one of them biscuits a cheese biscuit," Cissy Bains said. "A sprinkle of cheeses in that biscuit will really have him snapping his gums."

So we made a cheese biscuit and poured the antifreeze over it.

The old man was moaning and moaning. We were all moaning.

"Put that biscuit on a nice saucer," Cissy said. "He may be old and no account, I won't have him treated like no dog."

"Yessir," the old man was saying. "It was God's own hell before I lost me my legs, but now it's got a heap-site blacker. You children have lost all respect."

We gave him his biscuit.

"That there car block's going to crack in the cold," we said. "It ain't going to hold up through the night, not in this ungodly freeze. We are going to be stuck out here forever, without one single drink between us."

"Stop moaning," said Cissy Bains. "Look on the bright side. We got a whole night of drinking and rowdyism to look forward to, and if we die it won't be absence of drink that killed us. Shove me over one of them biscuits."

So we shoved over the plate. The biscuits were right blackened and the smell knocked right down to your stomach.

But the old man was moaning.

"I can't eat me this biscuit," he said. "It reminds me too much of my accident and how life is so horrible."

Then we remembered how the old man had been a garage mechanic in his wild youth and how it was his life had turned.

"Do as I aim to do," said Cissy Bains. "Just look up to the ceiling as you swallow it whole. That way the fumes git sooner inside your gullet where they can do the faster good."

But the old man's face was a map of tears.

"If I hadn't been drinking that foul day," he said, "I'd have me my legs now and I'd be sitting up there at the table with the rest of you."

We agreed with him on this, though Cissy Bains pointed out the trolley he was sitting on was the best money could buy.

"Drink is the ruination of us all," the old man said.

"Hey, now," we said. "Old man, you are going too far. You can't blame all our woes, or the whole of the world's woes, on good strong drink."

But the old man went on with his blubbering.

We were getting right concerned.

He scooted round and around on his trolley, smacking the floor with his fists and acting, Cissy Bains said, exactly like an idiot.

"I am never touching me another drop," the old man proclaimed. "I have see the light. Drink has condemned me to my everlasting hell."

Cissy Bains said, "What bedlam, a body can't hear herself think."

We each broke off a little nibble of biscuit and nibbled on that.

The old man's old hound dog had slunkered in out of the freezing cold. It had lapped out its great tongue and gulped down the old man's biscuit.

Now it was down under the table twitching and retching.

"Look at that dog," we said.

After a minute or two the dog stopped twitching and died.

"Look at that dog," we said.

"See!" the old man shouted. "That there is your living proof of licker the killer, as I am here to tell you."

He dragged up the old hound in his arms and moaned over it.

We all moaned. It had been a good old dog, more like a brother.

So we dumped our plate of rusty biscuits and told stories of this and that heroic deed the dog had performed over the full span of its perfect lifetime, and thus we pass that night without one drop of licker entering out gullets.

I tell you, mother, there was never a sorrier time spent by your fellow human beings than was that evening we spent that evening.

Comes spring, the old man was out on the grave site among the pines, moaning over his dead dog.

We'd had to carry him out there in our arms and now we'd have to carry him back again.

We were wondering if it was worth it.

The old man was saying this old dog had been dearer to him than nearabouts any human being on the whole face of the planet.

Cissy Bains said, "You old fool, where does that leave me?"

She said, "If you care more about that old dog than you care about me after all I have done for you then I don't hardly care if I keel over on this very spot and never see sunshine again."

She keeled over.

She said, "With two bodies in that hole to fill it up wouldn't take near as much dirt."

She said, "I have devoted the whole of my life to the care of that old cripple and now he tells me he liked that old dog better than me."

We said, "Oh Cissy Bains, shut up!"

The old man said, "It's a heap-sorry day when a man can not mourn his old dog."

We left Cissy Bains and the old man on the hillside and slunkered back to the house.

"God, I need me a drink," we said.

We went in and had one, it fresh-drawn in the jug.

We picked us some collard greens out in the field and we cooked them flat and then we set down to table.

"Did that old dog ever have a name?" we asked.

"No, it never had no name."

We thought hard and long and that turnabout.

"Where'd that old dog come from anyhow?" we asked.

"It just limped in one day."

"Then it ain't as though it was family, is it now?"

"No. No, it ain't as though that dog was like a real brother."

We left a filling of greens for Cissy Bains and the water they'd cooked in for the old man, because he could eat that, then we thought about licker again and maybe catching some shuteye.

It was getting on towards darkness.

Cissy Bains and the old man were out hollering on the hillside, so there went our shuteye.

The old car set out on its blocks in the high weeds, going nowhere.

We'd had us a full long day, mother, full of family woe.

Come home soonest, mother, dearest, and deliver us from evil, for thine is the kingdom.

APOLOGY
FOR NOT GETTING BACK TO YOU
SOONER

Went to see the professor today. The professor said, What happened to you? Suffer a stroke? Can't you hold your head up?

He had me confused. I didn't know whether he was talking about that minute alone or about every minute of my life leading up to that minute.

I tried lifting my head, tried getting a bead on him, but he was up too high. I'd get my eye-level up to his chin, then give out. Energywise, I would give out. Energywise, it was not my day.

Has it ever occurred to you, he said, that possibly you're in the wrong place? That possibly an institution of higher education is not the place for you? You look kind of old for it anyhow.

I didn't say anything. I figured maybe he had me there. Maybe I had been a bit headstrong in coming here.

Possibly you should have stayed in your own baili-wick, he said. Been content, I mean. You ever thought of that?

I had never thought of that.

Where are you from? he said. How'd a fellow like you come by these strange ideas?

I propped up my head on my knuckles and spoke to his necktie.

I'm from Chigocar, I said.

Chigocar?

My head swayed a bit. My knuckles were tired.

Little Rock, I said. Some kind of rock. Or Clearwater. Some kind of water. I was in Puckett, Maine, for a year. I'm from all over.

This was the longest speech I'd ever made. My mouth had gone dry.

What I had meant to say was, the gist of it was, careerwise, that getting here had been a long haul. That I had picked myself up by my own bootstraps.

I tried popping a Tic-Tac in my mouth but the Tic-Tacs kept rolling. I had a lapful of loose Tic-Tacs.

Cinnamon flavored.

Are you a Vet? he asked.

A Vet? He had me there. A Vet of what?

All you Vietnam Vets are the same, he said. You think you're *merde* on the membrane. Conceptually speaking, you think the world owes you a hog dog.

I got a finger up in my ear and gave it a good twist. The professor had me feeling knock-kneed. I didn't know whether I was coming or going.

He eyed me a minute, then got up and left the room. Then he came back in with a big jug and poured water over a few dead plants on his window sill. One was a hydrodermia. Hydrosomething-or-other.

I'd had a dead one just like it my year in Puckett, Maine.

I'd been hell on wheels my year in Puckett, Maine.

Do you even know what course you're enrolled in? he said.

He had ants crawling up and down the wall to his hydrodermia.

Neat-O, I thought.

Is it my Image Development 101 you're in? he asked. Or is it my 402 or my 328? Have you any idea?

I stayed quiet. Could be it was bingo on any one of these but I wasn't going out on a limb.

Or maybe it's my Creative Development Lab, he said. You older chaps enroll pretty heavily in that. You are in Education, I take it.

Dead-on. This guy was smart.

He let out a big laugh. He knew he'd scored. He got a big kick out of himself.

Those ants went right on marching.

You guys slay me, he said. You guys tickle my udders.

He rearranged the air pillow in his chair and sat back down. It was a ring pillow, open in the middle.

I wished I had one.

Anyway, Mr. Popadoupalas, he said, what do you want? Why have you called on me? If you want to complain about your marks, then we've got proper procedures. If you're here to tell me you're ready to buckle down, burn the midnight oil, then let's hear it. Lay it on me.

Popadoupalas? I said. Where'd you get the idea I was Popadoupalas?

His face shot out over the desk. He glided in real low, bringing his eyes right up close to mine. He had a moustache the size of a baseball bat. He wore a jacket about nine sizes too big.

I had him there. On the dress front I was miles ahead of the professor. I was wearing my spiked boots and a glitzy T-shirt that said I was the Father of Jazz.

In the wardrobe department I don't fool around.

He was still staring. He had this pen in his hand, which he kept tapping against his teeth.

You're not Popadoupalas? he said. Then who the bejesus are you?

He had me there. I knew all right. I just couldn't dredge it up.

He leaned back, clasping his hands over his belly.

I too slid down a bit. The old seat-back felt pretty good along my backbone.

You are in my class, aren't you? he said. I know I've seen you somewhere. Now that I look you over I can see you're not Popadoupalas. But Popadoupalas, well, all I've ever seen of him is the top of his head. His shoe soles. Why can't you students hold up your heads? It really isn't that hard.

This was embarrassing. My head had plopped way down. I could hardly get it off my chest. Fact is, I was feeling a mite dopey. Worn out. These hot afternoons, the droning sunshine, they'll really stamp out a guy's pep.

Why do you keep twitching? he asked.

I guess I had been twitching. I was beginning to wonder if I had come to the right office. This professor with the baseball bat moustache didn't look familiar enough somehow.

I wished I could wheel back and take another gander at the nameplate on his door.

That Popadoupalas, he said. He's giving me a hard time. I wish you *were* Popadoupalas. I'd give you a piece of my mind.

I found this interesting. Popadoupalas was the Big Man on Campus. He was a ball of fire, old Popadoupalas, so I'd heard.

I'd met this co-ed once, in the Dope House. She'd gone out with Popadoupalas. Wow! she'd said. That Popadoupalas steams up my eyeballs.

I could have taken that co-ed home. She said I could. But my coat sleeve kept catching on my hand. Time I had that coat on she'd gone off with someone else. Maybe Popadoupalas.

You got to strike like lightning to catch these co-eds.

You're sure you're not Popadoupalas? the professor said. He was peering at me again. His brows had gone up. You've got his same way of not saying much. His same way of hiding his thoughts. Verbally speaking, you're him to a T.

Goalwise, I gave some thought to what it might be like to be Popadoupalas. Popadoupalas would have co-eds all over him.

Here, take this handkerchief, the professor said. You're drooling. By God, why must you students drool?

I watched the ants climbing his wall. One rank went up empty-handed while the other rank came down loaded with dead hydrodermia.

I wished I could be them ants.

They had made a trail right over my boots.

What's that? the professor said. Your dog died?

Then he smacked his brow. He was getting excited.

Are you Grunger? he said. I bet my supper you're Grunger. You're the guy been making those calls to my wife.

I was willing to swear I wasn't anybody named Grunger. Calling his wife?

The professor stood up. He was wearing this brass rodeo buckle which had a picture of a horse jumping a rail fence.

You'd better streamline your folkways, Grunger, he said. Now get out of my office, or I'm calling Security.

Funny thing. Until that moment it had slipped my mind that I was one of his colleagues.

Dean of the Faculty, for Christ's sake.

It was what I had come to talk to him about: security.

You bother her again, he said, I'm calling the law.

I went out to the parking lot and sat in my car a long time in the rain.

It *looked* like my car.

It *looked* like my parking lot.

Hard to know *what* to do.

Not quite sure *which* way was home.

Was it rain?

I felt like crying.

So I did cry.

I cried about making those phone calls, and about not making those phone calls.

I cried for the whole of humanity.

If I cried, I thought, really pitifully, some nice person would come in and sit with me. She'd dry my face. She'd hold my hand. She'd lean me on her chest. She'd pat my shoulder. She'd run her fingers through my hair. Later on, we would marry. We'd have one or two of those — what do you call them? — children.

RSVP

We cooked a pig and fourteen people took sick. The wife said pig was wrong, we should have cooked a stallion. I looked at the stallion, and figured otherwise. Yet fourteen people took sick, eighteen if you count the brothers, so could be the wife was right. Could be she is on to something.

The fourteen people who took sick have today received a questionnaire. Where do you think we went wrong? At what point did you begin to feel sick? Is it possible that your illness had to do with our menu? What was the status of your health prior to your arrival? Were our actions, once you fell ill, all that might be expected? Would you come again and how soon?

The wife hopes the responses will be in before this weekend, since this weekend we plan an even larger party. The invitations have gone out. We've hired Ted Oliver to sing and bring his band. Ted Oliver's band is a wonderful band, the finest available. Ted Oliver's musicians come attired in white shoes and funky leather. As the wife says, you can't go wrong with Ted Oliver.

The brothers are coming, that's for sure.

The pig was smoked. Maybe it was the smoke. Whatever the case, we went to considerable trouble, smoking that pig. This weekend we shall not serve smoked pig, even if it is not the same pig. We are laying cucumber sandwiches by, just in case. My wife will dance. She is an extraordinary dancer, especially when backed by Ted Oliver. I think we can assure everyone a good time. We will have hot tubs on the premises as well.

My wife figures twelve. I figure eight. We shall compromise on the tubs, just as we did on the Ted Oliver band.

Last week she tried to get the Ted Oliver band, but they were on the road. That was unfortunate because, as the wife says, last week's music was definitely not up to scratch. She hardly danced at all. For long periods she moped as though confronting a blizzard.

Then everyone took sick.

This week the brothers will be passing out their usual leaflets.

Maybe the stallion. I'm still looking him over. But not smoked. I put my foot down there.

We hope you will join us. Actually, everyone we know is invited.

Know, too, that we have a backup plan in the event it showers.

Frankly, on this one, we are leaving no stone unturned.

PLAY GREENSLEEVES

Now here was a couple who did not get along. You spent a minute in this pair's company, you'd know this pair did not get along. If ever there was such a pair, this was this pair.

Okay, she has moved to Florida, we are all safe.

He is gone, too, but where he is gone is up to . . . to someone else to say. He died. Which is what prompts this accounting, his death.

Oodles of money the guy leaves behind. Let's just say, for *him* money was the thing. Let's say *she* agreed.

Didn't I say it? They were a pair.

Pre the Sunshine State move she begins thinking *frugality*. He can't take it with him where he's gone, but she can, all the way to Florida.

"*What!*" she says. "Spend all my dough on *that!* You have got to be insane!"

Who she is saying this to is the undertaker in the funeral home.

Her guy's been dead maybe six hours. The guy she lived with all those — how many? — forty-three years.

She says: "You think just because I'm a woman grieving you can *soak* me? You think could be I didn't peruse Jessica Mitford's graveyard book? Think again, buster!"

What she's pointing at as she says this is this casket the guy is showing her. He's got this little cloth, he keeps polishing, polishing. Buffing up the goods.

"Look at yourself," he says. "You can see yourself in the shine."

You can, but is she looking?

She knows a thing or two about dust; boy, does she ever.

"Four thousand smackers!" she says. "Hell's bells, man, I could fly the Concorde to Paris for what you're asking."

The undertaker guy murmurs what it is that undertakers facing such tightwads murmur. People who won't shell out a few extra bucks for the loved ones, are they ever a pill.

"You'll notice the pure brass fittings," he says.

"Is that silk?" she says. "Is that a silk pillow? Why is it so tiny? My husband, you know, hated *fancy.* You put sauce on a dish he'd run screaming from the dining room. Now you want me to put his head on *that pillow?*"

The guy is polishing, polishing.

So she decides it's time she took the bull by the horns.

"Have I said I wanted my Harry buried naked?" she says. "Have I told you I wanted you to squeeze the ring off his finger? Did I not spring for new shoes? Did I request a special rate on your embalming fluid? No. I am not *cheap!* Suit, okay, new shoes, okay, the fluid, okay, but if you think I'm parting with four thousand bucks for that lousy box, then you're nuts."

"Grow up," she says. "You undertaker guy ought to *grow up!* Show me something else."

So now she's shopping the joint.

"What's *this?*" she says. "How *much?*"

The undertaker's eyes go bug-eyed.

"Madame?" he says. "Madame? *That,* my good woman, is a child's coffin."

"So?" she says. "Harry *liked* children. He *liked* the infants especially. Although in my opinion he liked them only because we never had any. But, yes, about the only beings on this earth he did like were *infants.* So let's not hem and haw. Quote me a price."

"Madame," the undertaker guy says. "Madame, leave us not be silly."

"Cut to the nitty-gritty," she says. "How much?"

The guy then saying, "Madame, please! Your husband won't *fit!* He simply won't *fit!*"

"Oh, he'll fit," she says. "Harry was a louse and I ought to have slit his throat a thousand times, but he never had any trouble fitting in, wherever he went. He fit too well, if you ask me. The bastard could charm the legs off a snake, he wanted to. So don't talk to me about fit. He'll *fit!* Spare me the details, but you just see that he does."

So the guy caves in.

Why not? Who these days has any respect for their recently-departed.

Now she's out of there, the deal concluded.

She walks out into sunshine, feeling pretty pleased with herself. She's managed, she's survived. The worst is over.

"Off to Florida tomorrow," she says.

This to a guy in a greasy coat, trying to panhandle her.

"A free woman at last," she says.

The guy, the panhandler, gives her the finger.

She doesn't see it, moving so fast, though if she had it wouldn't have made a dent in her hide. If she saw it, she'd have given the finger back, with maybe a little speech about how the dumb shit ought to do something worthwhile with his life.

"Go out," she'd have said, "and get yourself a job. Show some responsibility. Society doesn't owe you jerks nothing, buddy. I certainly don't."

She'd have said that. She's probably saying it this minute, to some guy down in Florida.

I told you at the start she wasn't nice.

REPRIEVE

*D*eath saw me waiting by the road, and when he was upon me I jumped up with a smile, saying in full merriment, "Hail, good fellow, and a happy day to you, and many more, or my name be not Seamus Roomie!" Whereupon, Death's features heightened a trifle, his cheeks blushed, and he said to me: "Why are you waiting? Get along now and behave yourself, Seamus Roomie, and I shall see you another evening." And thus, he spurred his charge onwards, raising a great dust, though I did not tarry, but raced back to my house and home, where everyone was muffled in grief, and come to see Seamus Roomie asleep in his casket. But these mourners sang out in astonishment when they saw me, and encircled my neck, saying, "Seamus Roomie, as I live and breathe. You have conquered death, now sit yourself down here prettily and drink and eat all these fun things your wake is providing." So I lived long and plentifully, and Death has yet to call me a second time.

THE WOMAN
WITH THE ELECTRIFIED HEART

*T*o continue.

She was born with it.

Deep purple and roughly textured, this skin over Baby's heart. Like beets stewed in a pot. And the flesh so hot. Always so hot.

Pity the poor forlorn mite.

Baby's parents viewed the discoloration as some kind of vile birthmark, or signature, God had imprinted upon the child, in revenge for sins deeply embedded in their own mean existence. This they acknowledged with stolid ceremony twice daily at meal times and each evening shortly after sunset, when wicks had been dowsed and household members knelt raw-kneed by their bedsides: oh, Father, punish us. Oh, Father, forgive us. Oh, Father, save us. Oh, Father, let Baby's heart be pure, though her skin be sour as beast's tongue in rain-barrel.

Mother wanted the child to bear the name Naomi, but Father viewed the naming otherwise: Ruth would be her name. Jehovah's book clearly favored Ruth, among the few females worthy of mention. Such a froth of rabble, he would say. Whore and whore-mongerer heaped into the same basket. Snakes, all. Be sure, and how can a woman ever live down the callous infamy?

"Her naming, sire."

With so many Ruth's now occupying the world one more mayhaps would receive scant notice. Such anonymity would benefit the child, he averred. Praise God, she's plain; that will keep her as well.

Oh, Father, torment us.

Drape blackened cloth over hearth and mantel.

Favor us with cup upon cup of your pestilence.

Humble us until our shame steams every window.

Let us cough vermilion.

Salt Lake authority issued stern opinion:

Look to your faith, Christian.

Take ye your Fatted Calf and hang the quarry leg-high from your foremost chimney. Set pot to catch the mouth's drippings and smooth this rendering thrice daily over your new-born's afflicted bosom.

Pray to your very innermost innards.

The Salt's out of touch, said some in the local congregation. They hold none's true but them.

Aye. They'se pork has gone rancid. High time we undid the affiliation.

A poor man, in these parts, possessed but one wife. The baby's father had two, others more; the practice was not uncommon among those in these webbed highlands who shared their sect's bewildering podge of beliefs: dollops passed down over centuries, others created spark and spur. "Catch as catch can, brethren. Shoulder the wheel."

These highland peaks were ever misty. Angels bathing in milky pool, they sometimes said. Pilgrims, on march to paradise, in beclouded assembly. The valleys, too, were often shrouded in fog. It was a land on its way to becoming something else, their leaders preached, though none alive now to hear their voices would be alive to witness the coming cataclysm. Oceans asplit, mountains at quake. "Yea. You will be dead and gone to Glory. If your hearts be true. God is merciful. Praise God."

Abelard Sharman, press forward.

Eloise and Isaiah Muschig, lately of Ohio, press forward.

Auntie Stone, with the snuff stick hidden in your sleeve, press forward.

Them who are obedient in the new resurrecting, step forward.

*H*er second mother the child called Auntie, as was proper. It was Auntie's wizened breast she first suckled, and that name, when she learned speech, first to pour, in the manner of treacle, from her lips. Auntie Stone openly scoffed at the blood parents' fears as to the meaning behind the child's ill-hued chest. Many of this sect's beliefs she accepted unblushingly; as to certain other matters, she kept her own ragged council. "Snuff? No-t'ing wrong with snuff." A woman's tread, so it was give out, must be light; she must lean upon every manly shoulder. Or give that appearance. "That does not mean, child, that her must be foolish. Niccht! Listen to Auntie." Nighttime, she would whisper so to the child. "I got him, your daddy, second-wedded, which saved me from the poor house."

She chortled, holding her mouth close-by Baby's ear. "I put out me had a wedge of property, with good water. I bartered it him, yea, and he took me unto his blanket. Like Boaz done your namesake. I honeyed me bones. Niccht! Tell me it is wrong, an old woman to honey she bones?"

Frequently, while in the bed they shared, Auntie Stone settled her ancient, bewhiskered face over the child's scarlet chest, convinced that over time this practice would cure the deafness in her ears, ease the cataracts' crippling invasion on her sight. Certainly, it would stave off the runny nose, which had been an affliction borne all her whole life. She was losing her hair, too, and the last of her teeth, but wanting Delilah tresses and a strong gnaw were more than she dared ask.

"I like the heat," she would say, touching her lips to the baby's skin. "Red-hot stove warms Auntie no better, child, than your good heart. Ooo! 'Tis skillet-hot! Now don't you go squirming, overmuch, through the night."

Mornings, long before first light, the child a soft bundle harbored on her shoulder, Auntie Stone stood on planks at the back door, among a gaunt horizon of trees, rattling spoon over washboard or breadpan as she shouted laboriously into the dark:

"Wake up, wake up! All sleepyjacks, press forward!"

The baby waked with a jolt of limbs and a raucous cry.

"Hush," Auntie Stone said. The gnarlish face instantly found repose. "Hush, divinist one. Niccht! Compose thy wee self."

The echo of clanging pans, the baby's faint, errant cry, died away upon shelf after shelf of undulating mountain-top.

Wind music. Oh, there's many a chicanery in these hills. They will be hearing this child's cry into the next century, Auntie thought. Though me can scarce hear it meself.

Mind your spittle, now.

Later on, the cocks crowing, and serenade of similar cacophony up and down the smoky range, through the next half hour.

Muschig. The Muschig roosters, Auntie Stone observed, three miles away as the crow flies — never straight — were always last to greet the dawn.

Something in their feed, people said.

Them Muschigs breathe a different air. Newcomers, ye know. Come from Ohio, ye know. With their dusty wagon load and trailed by a sweep of forty bedraggled goats.

Dawn's light swelling inch by inch, lancing the bloated clouds.

"It is God's sky, yea," Auntie Stone would say. "And His plan. But you steer your own destiny, Mistress. Accept little else as it is give out by them in the business." By them in the business to tell you your business, she meant. She was thinking snuff. It galled her, this churchly abomination of the dipper's gold.

Husband's shadow loomed oppressively over them.

"God's morning to you," the forbidding patriarch would say. "Ply the table, woman. We've much to get done this day."

"Aye, my Lord. As with every other."

*A*untie was twice the age of her husband, who was old himself: she was ancient, scarred, and bent, and her induction into the family nest had been an act of pure generosity, kindness. Godliness. Such was the news the family gave out.

"Rubbish," declared Auntie Stone, working her snuff stick about her gums. "It were for me dink of property, and the good water."

*D*uring the third week of the baby's life, church dignitaries called at the Healy place and viewed with malevolent suspicion the infant's flaming chest. Heads wagging, hands knotted behind their backs, these bleak creatures in their black raiment trod importantly upon the grass. Eventually to issue grave pronouncement.

"'Tis Satan's fire-box."

"Aye. Fir-box. So 'tis."

"'Tis the ruby merchant's left-over buckets of coal."

"Aye. That fixes cause. Now to cure."

They meditated through the long hour, calling for an early dinner of their hosts' best viands, and afterwards summoning from their mule's bag their many books, or looking to such treatises as might have been composed in the very air.

"Amputation's the thing."

"Aye."

"Sever small finger of the left hand. 'Tis nearest the heart. T'will drain the fire's essence and smother Lucifer's rabid flame."

"Aye. Secure the hand. Fetch axe, together with sharpest chisel. One stroke only, to snip the member clean. Have pot of salted water on boil, standing by. Afterwards, bury the nub. Deep. Under slab of heaviest rock, lest it take the shape of fury and return to haunt us."

"Aye. Praise Jehovah. 'Tis a fine job the church has done this day."

So the baby's digit was set for removal, while Auntie Stone paced the tree-line, screeching her ingratitude from every bush.

"Niccht! Niccht! Murderous pot-belly fiends!"

Mother held the child's wrist to table, as was her duty. A smallish block of cherrywood displayed the isolated finger. Father, with seeming relish, wielded the chisel. Upraised his woodchopper's axe.

The sky was darkening; it was getting on towards nightfall now

"Don't dither, Brother Healy."

"Aye. And see to it ye don't lock stare with the vixen's widish eyes."

Then all fell mute.

The wood-block split and Brother Healy's chisel went on through, to split a board in the very table; it snitched away near the whole of three of the child's fingers.

"So much the better. Aye?"

"Aye. T'was our Master's intention."

"T'was her fate."

"Aye. T'was. Now administer Balm of David to the screaming infant and let her sleep."

The women, save Auntie Stone, set to, cleansing away the heavy wash of blood.

Some little had stained father's attire; he saw in this bad omen and harumphed his dissatisfaction at the impertinence.

*E*vening, and dogs at howl through the hills. Bitter cold now. Lamp-lit windows fading in this valley one by one. Auntie Stone in the far hen house is fast at work. Her hands have the shakes. She wishes her old eyes could see. She is at work with her needles, under dim candlelight. Flicker, flicker. She's thankful this minute that her ears are largely deaf. She's grateful there's this blow of strong, chilling wind. None will venture out this night; wind will erase the child's helpless cries. But she wishes these old palsied hands of hers didn't shake. She wishes these old eyes might momentarily unweb. "Niccht! Niccht! Don't hate ye old auntie, me love." She's biting her lower lip as she works. She's straining her eyes. Her mouth's dry.There's more bleeding than she would wish. Her own heart shares the child's pain. The candle blows out and she works on, by feel alone, in the dark. Them with their divine authority, she thinks. Them with their toad-pudding for brains. "Had me me druthers," she says. "Had me me druthers, I'd lame each of them sordid fiends. Screw up ye face, child. Screech out ye rage and never mind ye old Auntie's got she own belly full." Howl. Howl.

She's stitching to the child's fourth finger some little nub of flesh she'd secretly picked up, midst all the scurry, from the ogre's yard. "Fate. Shaw! T'was fate, we'd all carry broomstick between our legs. T'was fate, I'd be merry prankster aflit hill to hill."

Nor was the child's curing, once her nubs were at heal, yet complete.

Each day at high noon she was secured to a slab bench positioned in the Healy yard, and set out to cook in the sun for one hour. This was the solution of the sect's elder's council, after a second visit. Mix peroxide of water, together with a potion of vinegar from our tubs. Let all who love her dribble said remedy over her chest, from a clean rag of bolting cloth boiled in goat's milk of the first yielding.

These learned men did not establish a calendar termination for the treatment. The family, in confusion over the matter, but reluctant to appeal for enlightenment, carried on the punishment full into winter, until snow piled high about the slab bench, the baby mewing her displeasure with every desperate syllable.

Waaaaaaaaaa! Waaaaaaaaaaaaaaaa!

These cries endless.

It was observed that although the falling snow might cover the baby's limbs and obscure for a while her face and stomach, the drops melted, disappeared, the instant they touched her chest.

Peroxide was without effect.

The father worked far afield, of weekdays, and on the Sabbath saw that he was occupied elsewhere; he had refused ever to touch the child, having decided the stain on the child's chest now clearly bore the like resemblance of Satan's hand. You could see, he said, the palm-print. You could see the long womanly nails. You could see his grinning face in the mottled skin. He spoke of dropping her into seed bag and throwing the body into engorged river, the way he did the periodic plague of pup-dogs. But the Lord rewarded patience; he was earning with this tolerance his plentitude in the Hereafter.

Mother Healy wrung her hands, yanked the goat teats viciously, and prayed more vigilantly. Mother and father were at odds: which of them carried the greater guilt? On which side, and how far back, the heinous crime? She scoured the child's chest with dilution of vinegar and lye, to scrub away Satan's likeness. Bleach. Bleach the skin raw. She'd pour on boiling water, peel the flesh with paring knife, it won't a sin. Some she'd heard of up here had done worse. The Muschig bunch, rumor had it, had had baby born with no eyes and hid her away. Kept it in root cellar, word had it. But the Muschigs kept their mischief to home, she'd give them that much. They won't gadabout slackards spending their time poking nose where nose won't wanted, like many she could name.

Scrub, scrub.

Heat from Baby's skin was as like embered fire.

Punish us, my Lord.

Auntie Stone watched, devoutly watched, and snatched the child to safety the minute the imposed hour elapsed; other than as assigned timekeeper, it was made clear to her that she had no say in the matter.

Auntie's mind had been fetched by the gleaners: all were in agreement on this front. Marriage to such a good man as Brother Healy had loosened her hold on reality. Her brain's a cowpat, her husband said. And my diviner's rod has yet to find the hag's alleged water.

Auntie cackled. She hooted. She thumped the floor with her walking stick. "Oh, there's water aplenty. There's water to bestir oceans, ye can but find it."

Daily, she was made to draw maps on little scraps of paper or to compose tiddly scratchings in the yard: "Look here, sire. Here. Ye wand's held too tight in the hand. It can't git she no action." Chortle, chortle.

The question was one hotly debated throughout the local parlors and kitchens: would God, a just God, admit lunatics into his heaven? She used snuff; what could you expect from such a woman? She needs lashing. Seat her fork-legged above a smoking chimney.

Yet, Auntie Stone, to her own manner of thinking, was in her glory.

Consider:

Runny nose, after a few month's proximity to the child's warmish breathing, was already an affliction all but forgotten. Her vision remained blurry, the cataracts sore and ugly, burlish grotesquery where lids should be, but she had set no great store by those hopes from the beginning. God's mercy was never a thing she had seen

in abundance. By the same token, though she showed herself unchanged, ever cupping a hand to this or that ear any
time a person spoke within her presence, and haranguing
them with her own querulous, stark inquiry — "*Say what?
Say who?*" — it seemed to her there now was sound in her
left ear. Some little pitter-pat. Ants' feet at move inside the
tender canals. In that ear which, because of her arthritic
and rheumatic pains, she found it most possible to press
nightly upon the child's bold, hot heart.

She knew it a bold heart now.

She saw no devil's image. What rubbish. The Healys
had a backwards frame to their nature was her surmise.
Though they think they walk on water. She smeared
scented bear grease over the skin, to counter the idjit
mother's doltish concoctions.

At prayer time — except in the evenings when
alone with the baby, and on her knees — Auntie Stone
effected a certain speech impediment, so that she might
not be impeded in bringing her news to God and her
savior, while at the same time keeping these Healys in
ignorance as to her blessings, together with their cause.

She would hobble with the baby, or by herself sometimes, to a running brook fed by a spring that sprayed
water into air as from a fountain — in a hideaway thicket grown over with fern and lacy Bride's Moss, and hon-
eysuckle, thank ye Lord — a tortuous distance up from
the house, and listen to clean, icy water at flow over the
stones. *Her* brook. Aye. *Her* water. Let the husbandman
prowl this property through the long day, shouting his
displeasure, citing disharmony of fellowship with his
wizard's wand."Idjit man. Reprobate. Maimer of me
baby's sweet, wee hand."

Hard winter now, the child a year and some into
life, predictions to the contrary.

Auntie's ruint, child. Lets us sit us down.

Him with his wavery diviner's rod, but me, child,
still with me water. He was good to Baby, good to
Auntie, her might could repent she ways.

Hush, now.

Auntie Stone could hear it. She could hear the flow of
water, soft and distant and, yes, hardly there, in this ear

which had been dead for years and years. Since that time when someone — she no longer remembered her suspicions about the identity of the party in question, or the circumstances giving rise to such demented behavior — had cracked a steel pipe across her head. "Auntie a young sprout, then, and innocent of the world's wicked ways." It had been dark, she had been walking barefoot upon a dirt road going though a mountain pass not far from here.

"By them Muschig fields, me pretty. By wherein they've lit down. Strange events come to pass anytime you got Muschig, or Ohio, in the picture. Mark me words."

A shape had slung itself up from a ditch, from somewhere, nowhere, with this pipe, and clanged her in the head. Or perhaps it had been a rock. Rock or pipe, she could feel it to this day.

She had known no sound in her ears since that moment. She had been thirteen. Or maybe twenty. She didn't remember.

But long before she took to wearing these high-top men's boots, her seven-fold layer of undergarments, and her bonnets. Long before she'd come to know the deep pleasures of snuff.

"Oh, olden days."

This story she related to the child, in a somber, even voice none else in her new family, or few others beyond it, had ever heard.

"Man With A Rock," she shouted. "Press forward!"

And laughed at herself, and at the baby's rapt face, for this was new, too: this way of instilling humor upon a thing, which was a feature in herself she had thought long eroded. This desire to talk about it, and to a mere infant, looking back at her goggle-eyed.

And laughed at this laughter also, for heaven knows these were sounds uncustomary to her throat. It hurt. She would have to practice. Practice, she thought, with the baby.

Us will neither of us get precious little of laughter's heather, otherwise.

Here. I wash ye in this spring water. It's cold? Oh, yes, don't me hands know it.

She set the child within a pocket of mossy stones, and the child played.

They stayed by the brook, this one day, through the fall of darkness, and on the way home no man lunged from that darkness, to straddle Auntie Stone and pin her legs. How uncanny. For never until now had darkness fallen, without her seeing there the loathsome ogre. Which is why, she told the child, me rattles pot and pan, of a morning. To set the ogre scurrying.

She had memorized the placement of stones in this brook, and it seemed to her that she could pinpoint the different sounds arising from each stone as the water rippled over them.

Auntie Stone had entered life, and endured it, with more than one disfigurement, and such scorching as defaced Ruth's flesh, in Auntie's view, was not worth the tallying, among the vast miseries of the world. "Neither here in our mountains," she told the child, "nor elsewhere in the universe, where infidels are said to believe God resides in tree stumps, in marshy bog, and frog-leg Saviors sit mossy-eyed and naked in the boughs. Hush, child. Listen. Behold ye the bounty. And ye will mayhaps prosper."

One spring morning some seasons later the girl was informed that her duty hereafter would include a special and privileged chore; she was to collect, at the stroke of dawn, eggs from the henhouses, and from other such diverse and untoward spot as the fowl may have chosen to drop them. None must elude her, and no shell suffer her clumsiness.

Ruth at cold dawn in the henhouse, surrounded by squawking fowl: holding in her hands her first collected egg. The egg was freshly laid, and warm, though not so warm as her hands. Her heart beat rapidly. She closed the door. The darkness comforted the chickens and they quickly settled. The heat inside her chest beat almost as some severe pain. Her eyes were closed; her small hands cupped the egg. Her heart fluttered; she could feel heat coursing through her veins. Her hands sweated. One minute passed. Then two. The egg became too hot for her hands. She let it rest in the folds of the long black gown she was made to wear.

She peered out between the slats. No one about. All serene.

She seated herself, picked up a small stone from the ground, and cracked the shell; she peeled away the shell, and bit into the soft yoke, and slowly, blissfully, ate the egg which the heat of her hands, the heat of her heart, had so deliciously cooked.

Oh, wonder!

Oh, such a rapturous egg!

Next time me must remember bring packet of salt.

Now one more egg me hands to cook three minutes, for me sweet Auntie.

She counted off the seconds, scrunching up her eyes. The egg heated. It was cooking. Oh, divine egg.

She holds the egg inside her cradled hands. She clenches her eyes tight. She feels her hands warming fast. Her mouth goes dry. The egg warms. She silently counts the seconds. How many seconds in a minute? At the count of ten she begins again. She can count no higher than ten. One, seven, nine, thirteen, ten. Start over. Start over for Auntie. Three, eight, four, thirteen, ten. Mama, mama, don't whoop me. Whoop that Muschig, up the tree.

The egg cooks.

Oh, divine egg.

The cock is crowing again. Always late, that foolish cock. It is full light now.

She scratches up chicken droppings over her leavings, scurries away with her gift for Auntie Stone. Contentedly precedes with her chores.

She was six years old.

The year was 19 —

*M*ove along now. A spring day.

Spring is the time for weddings in these highland

folds, among those sharing the Healy beliefs. Mary married Joseph, did she not, in the spring? Celebration is desirable after the long winter. We are all starved, are we not, for new faces? Fetch the brooms, open every window. Turn every mattress. Mind your feet now. Move, move, girl, can't ye move? Shake a leg. Air, air, we must have air in this house, we must air out each nook and cranny. Set out our black iron pots in the yard, and bring the water to mean boil. Bubble, bubble. Lay on the wood, lay it on. Fetch boiling stick, don't skimp on the lye soap. Fetch your bedding, fetch your longjohns, scurry back here with each tablecloth, doily, and curtain.

Clean your house top to bottom. Rake the yard. Prune your orchard trees, repair your fencing, dig the new outhouse, shovel the coop floors, see to the leaning barn. Don't dawdle now. No seat for slowpokes in Gloryland. Cut your hair, your toenails, brush up on your manners, clean your ears. Good, good, yes, you will pass. You're fit and ready.

Now go and fetch yourself a bride.

Plant the seed, Brother.

Aaron Muschig, lately of Ohio, step forward.

Ruth Healy, of the crippled hand, step forward.

Let all who would oppose this union shut their mouths.

*R*uth Healy is thirteen years old. Old enough, and a good bargain: she comes with water in her dowry. If Aaron Muschig is the good diviner he can find it, after all others have failed. Ruth Healy is pretty as a sunbeam, her innocence is ashine as the morning dew. Jay-bird tall, skinny as your clothesline, but going to be a powerful helpmate, once a bit of fat adheres to her bones. Feed her and she'll thrive. Never ye mind the girl's disfigured hand. Her prideful manner, her disdainful gaze, her slouching disregard for the Holy Book.

*A*untie Stone rocks in her rocker on the Healy porch. She is ancient now, there is weariness in her bones.

She's curved like limbered pine, scarcely four feet tall, and indeed a frail bird to behold. But Ruth loves her. Ruth can not bear to leave her. She can not bear the thought of going to live as wife to Aaron Muschig. Them scalawag Muschigs, ugh. May his buggy upwheel itself on the jackknife road. Let vultures pick his bones. Yes, and the bones of all who have had a hand arranging this travesty.

Auntie Stone's voice snaps with the creaks of the rocker. No one can understand a word she says, save Ruth Healy. She talks nonsense, they say. Be such a relief when she dies.

And she will die, Ruth thinks, without me here to tend her. She will dribble away. No one even to see she has from time to time a fresh snuff stick. Or snuff itself, for that matter.

Auntie Stone seethes with fury, spitting out her words, and only Ruth knows what she is saying.

Get your poppa's shotgun. Steal up to the barn-loft door. You'll have good sighting from that spot. Pick that Muschig weasel off the minute his buggy rounds the curve. Do it meself, me had the strent.

Don't ye tell him the whereabouts of my water.

Never never never. Promise me, child.

I promise, Auntie. I'll run a pitchfork through his belly the instant he tries touching me.

Aye. Ye take after ye old Auntie. He'll not trim you down to the Muschig size. Him to find he's bitten off more than he can chew, but has hold of what can chew on him.

Auntie Stone is approaching one hundred, is the surmise, and good only for rocking. Ruth Healy, thirteen, stands behind the rocking chair, giving Auntie a strong push now and again. Rock, rock. Rock and burn. You take your first breath on this earth with a degree of expectation. They can beat it out of you like dust out of a blanket. But expectation holds.

It survives. *Not this. Surely, not this.*

They are both looking up the road, listening for the rattle of Aaron Muschig's buggy, or wagon, or whatever shiftless transport he has arranged.

Auntie Stone hits her spit-can dead-on. Smear your loins with excrement, she says. That'll keep his nose afar.

I won't never sleep, Auntie. Not never.

Smear dog's vomit over your honey-patch. Smear it nightly.

I will Auntie. I'll dip, too. I'll spit snuff up his nose.

Aye. And never, never lead the jackel to Auntie's water.

Aaron Muschig, the czar. Already he has two wives. And a sister some say is used as a third. Ruth Muschig will be lowest on the picking post. Pity the poor forlorn mite.

Do ye hear it? Is he coming, child?

I'm lost, Auntie. I'm done for.

MORE YOU MAY NOT EXPECT
FROM RUNTÉ

*L*ately Runté's neighbors have been leaving food
parcels at his door: vegetables from the nutrition station, sanctioned replicas of the real thing — potatoes,
leeks, choy. His neighbors like Runté. He worries them.
Over the past year Runté has lost weight; now he is skin
and bones, hollow-eyed, haunted. He looks and smells
old. Perhaps the smell is explained by Runté's work.
Perhaps not. All the same, it bothers these neighbors
when Runté's eyes will not meet theirs. They see him
slouching along in the rain, unprotected, and their
hearts lurch; there is something frightening about Runté,
about what has happened to him.

He is polite, friendly — certainly he is that — but he
has lost his bounce, the zest for life that such a short
while ago characterized him. The old residents of his
district are always saying to him, "Runté, please! Be so
kind. Look after yourself."

Children like Runté, too. If they bruise a knee and
the choice for comfort rests between Runté or parents
assigned to care for these children, it is Runté to whom
they run. They bring him their government-mandated
toys, saying, "Fix this for me, Runté. Then will you play
with me?"

Runté says to them, "It can't be fixed. It never
worked." That is one reason children like Runté. He's a
straight-shooter; he isn't ever saluting the flag. They
come up to Runté standing in the rain, they pat his
shoulders, saying, "Ah, Runté, don't be sad."

Some in Runté's circle believe it is simply the rain
that has got him down. Each week or two Control
Central issues announcements: the cause has been determined, a solution is imminent — but it has been raining
every day and night now for more than a year. A grey
drizzle, constant, the air ever clouded — misty, forbidding, cheerless.

Every roof in the city leaks; even in Runté's privileged neighborhood, walls, ceilings, are decaying. Nothing ever dries. The air, everything, feels clammy. Floors buckle, worms of a tenacious new variety multiply in the bedding, in the carpets, in one's very clothing.

Control Central — Universal, the Unicenter, the system's government — boasts that it has mastered weather, seasons, the sun. It has the temperature under control: a constant 56 degrees Fahrenheit through two decades. Just enough to make one shiver.

The rain, however, defeats the Control scientists. It even baffles Dr. Lamarze, the infamous traitor and saboteur. In broadsides which find their way into the city, Dr. Lamarze surmises that the eternal rain is not unrelated to the phenomenon of an eternal temperature; in tampering with one aspect of nature the scientists created havoc with the other. What was to have been Universal's model city, Lethe-on-the-river, has become its shame. Dr. Lamarze's tracts come with his usual slogan: Expect More From Your Universe.

Citizens acknowledge the traitor's jibe is appropriate. Thank God someone, even if it's the traitor, can still make one smile. Last week, for instance, a dog was reported running loose in the city. Everyone was horrified, they dared not step outdoors. A few such creatures survive in the uplands beyond the city walls, though their sighting is rare. An emergency was declared, the militia was called out. When the dog was finally captured, it was found to have been a product of Dr. Lamarze's laboratory. Or so the government at first said. The next day it reversed itself: thanks to the quick response of the Unicenter, the stalwart work of the militia, disorder, widespread disease, had been averted.

This made the people laugh a second time. Everyone in the city is sick. They are always wet, they are always cold, always coughing. Everyone goes around sneezing germs on everyone else.

After a year of rain people here scarcely recall a time when it did not rain. Control in fact discourages one from such useless rumination. The past, according to current doctrine, is irrelevant, meaningless, without essence.

History is repellent, evil. The span of one's own personal experience is itself specious. Nostalgia, memory, refuge in the codes of previous eras, has no play in the social fabric. Only through concentration upon the here and now will the future be secured.

Obsession with the past undermines both the individual and the corporate body. Scientific study of the ancients is forbidden, punishable by exile or death. Every day one hears of those who have paid the price. Which is another reason the ransom on Dr. Lamarze is so high. Before he became the turncoat, the doctor was this system's most applauded specialist in the study of antiquity, the phenomenology of time and being.

As for the rain, official announcements appear daily from Control. On any street corner you have only to punch a button. The recorded year's rainfall, their specialists declare, has not exceeded the normal. Clear skies are forecast for the near future. But the next day this view will be reversed: an emergency situation exists; the very city is in peril. It is sinking, it is crumbling. On any given day hotlines are created, to which one is obliged to report potential disasters, the critical situation, catastrophe — erosion, mudslides, the like. Corrective measures will be ordered immediately.

A day later such hotlines are declared inoperative; they have been dismantled, they were an unnecessary precaution. Their establishment was a gross mismanagement of public funds. The proper officials have been chastised, dismissed, exiled. Such irresponsibility, says Central, will not be tolerated in the model city.

But where is Control Central? Dr. Lamarze's handbills claim the Unicenter itself no longer exists, that Universal itself has crumbled, that these conflicting directives which arrive daily are being beamed from satellite worlds impervious to this system's needs — that it is a matter of bureaucratic buttons pressing bureaucratic buttons. Those truly responsible have fled, rich and untouchable, to far away galaxies created solely for and by their kind. Yet that can not be. One way or another the city functions. The temperature remains a reliable 56 degrees, just enough to make you shiver; service has declined, certainly, but the basic amenities — in reduced form most surely — remain available. Learning stations are open, shops continue to show their wares, entertainment is not lacking. The courts still dispense justice, security forces abound, family licensing centers still interview new applicants, place children, and dispense accommodation; people still work and receive voucher compensation. Tax continues to be collected and administered. Universal's books are balanced, deficits unthinkable.

As for problems associated with the rain, workers patrol the city in anonymous convoy, providing temporary relief. Control Central, responsible for the environment, for banking, dwelling, the flow of goods, the management of lands and seas — the assurance of happiness — is living up to its mandate; it is, it says, more than meeting the model city's current and long-term requirements.

Yet buildings collapse. Hillside estates, factories, streets, entire areas slide into oblivion. Public transport, except for renegade, lawless jinrikshas operated by illegal immigrants, has by and large disappeared. Certain areas of the city are rumored no longer to be inhabitable. Dr. Lamarze's anarchist sheets often contain panascopes depicting this or that neighborhood in rubble, corpses unattended and rotting, maggots breeding. UniHealth can not reach these suburban outposts; security forces do not dare.

Expect More, Lamarze the revolutionary says, From Your Universe.

If only there was occasional change in the rain's drizzle, the affliction might be bearable. The raging downpour, say, accompanied by hurricane winds, followed by a slackening. The flash of lightning, thunder's rumble, the intermittent blizzard. But, no, there is only the endless drizzle, day after day. If only the skies would admit an occasional ray of sunlight, the firmament admit a star's sparkle, then one's hopes might be quickened, the heart cease its remorseful pounding.

So it is this only, some of Runté's neighbors say, which has affected him. The stress of the here and now. Model City life. Certainly poor Runté is to be pitied, but is he alone? Are we not all suffering?

Robert Runté, it should be said, is largely unaware that he excites these novel concerns. He has sunken cheeks and hollow eyes and these eyes stare out at him from the monitoring plate when he executes his morning shave. Alas, alas, he says. Not that the gaunt look astonishes him; he sees this same look everywhere he goes. Everyone in the model city, even the children, has these drawn faces.

No, not everyone.

This morning Runté answered a summons at his door. A beautiful woman greeted him. "Forgive me," she said. "I only wanted to look into your eyes."

She was wearing yellow knee boots, rain dripping around her from a red umbrella. How long had it been, Runté wondered, since he had seen a beautiful woman, a red umbrella?

The sewer grate outside Runté's door had clogged up again. Gutters were overflowing. A pool of water covers the street's ancient cobblestones, riding up over the landing at Runté's door. Water ripples down the long hallway, courses inside every room. It has been this way for the whole of the year, the mean level at times rising an inch or two, at times receding. Which must indicate, to Runté's way of thinking, that the rain's eternal drizzle is less steady than it appears. It has peak periods, he suspects, in the night when people are sleeping. If they sleep, for Runté does not himself sleep, or never easily.

The beautiful woman looked at Runté and for once Runté did not drop his eyes.

If he had not been made nervous by the unexpected call, if surprise had not shaken him, Runté would have invited the woman inside. He wished afterwards he had done so. A long time has passed since Runté has felt the quickening his body experienced when the woman looked at him. Runté is lonely. He can not recall any special person, man or woman, who ever existed in his life, although surely there must once have been such a person. He is forty-three years old; he has normal needs, urges, dreams. He can remember feeling desire even if the memory of that desire's outcome has deserted him. He knows, for instance, at age eighteen that he applied for a family warrant at one or another licensing center, because such was, is now, mandatory. Memory of the person applying with him — the mate UniMating ordained be paired with him — has been erased. Her name, what became of her, how they fared, what offspring they contributed to the Nurturing Wards, eludes him. By emptying one's mind of the past, so Control maintains, society can better focus on the present, better lay the groundwork for future epochs. But a strange pattern of aimlessness ensues — Runté has come to believe — when one's past is deleted, subverted, denied: in the dearth, the mind devises stratagems to off-set the loss; one improvises, day dreams, seeks harmony between the artificial and the true. Lethe, the model city, he often feels, is a sprawling clinic for the insane. Perhaps the entire galaxy is; perhaps everywhere one can go it is like this.

That Unicenter abets their antimemory policy Runté is convinced. Chemicals designed to achieve that effect are infused into the tasteless foods, into the very water, the wines, the sweetened soporifics, one ingests. Thus the choy, the potatoes, the various foods left at Runté's door by concerned friends remain uneaten. In time, they rot, they smell, they decompose into vile liquids just as some maintain real foods once did. When Runté thinks of it he discards the dripping waste under stealth of night. For nourishment he consumes only the pills purloined from his workplace, Office 12.

"Thank you," the beautiful woman said. "I — "

But then workers riding their anonymous convoy of thunderous machines passed down Runté's street, on their way to some disaster, washing up enormous waves over his own and the woman's boots. Pranksters everywhere have placed up signs: Mind the Wake. The noise of these huge machines is incredible, their very weight, most believe, adding to the damage their employment is meant to alleviate.

So Runté could not hear the woman's words. He was confused in the first place that a person of her distinction should have sought him out. He could not stop looking at the amazing red umbrella, the yellow boots, her perfect face.

But what the woman said next he heard with full clarity.

"Dr. Lamarze," she said, "sends his regards."

The woman's smile enraptured him. He could not recall ever witnessing such a smile. But the Lamarze name on her lips was terrifying. Universal's spies were everywhere. Your next-door neighbor may be in their employ. If discovered perusing one of his documents, for merely speaking the Lamarze name aloud, one can be taken away for questioning, tortured, incarcerated — never seen again.

Yet here this beautiful woman was, without a care, saying to him that Dr. Lamarze was aware of his situation with regard to Office 12.

"Aware of . . . ?"

Runté's mind refused to function.

"Yes," the woman said. "Dr. Lamarze wants you to know that he is knowledgeable of your contribution through Office 12. I am to tell you that he finds your labor admirable."

Runté paled. His hands shook. If the sworn adversary of Universal knew of his methods at Office 12, then perhaps so did everyone.

The woman took his hand. "I have frightened you. I am sorry." She looked into his eyes. "I am keeping you from your work. But we shall see each other again I am sure."

She smiled anew. She tilted her umbrella, looking up at the rain. Runté was fascinated. All this while he had been standing with her beneath the umbrella. He could feel her warmth, smell her scent.

"Expect More From The Universe," she said.

Then she was striding away through the grey, incessant rain.

He went to work. Office 12, so much to do. Office 12 is corrupt, no doubt about it; money exchanges hands, certainly. Runté is but one clerk among many working the Death Desks, not everyone expresses a preference for Runté; they trust the greased palm more than they trust Runté; but word has got around about Runté, the bleeding heart, Runté, the do-gooder, the soft touch. Always his corridor is stacked twenty, thirty deep.

That evening when he returned home from Office 12 Runté found on his doorstep a bird in a cage. When Runté lifted the cage the bird, asleep, lifted its head from beneath a yellow wing.

"Are you mine?" it sang.

Though it looked like an actual bird, and bore Universal's certification of authenticity, Runté recognized it as a mechanical creature from Dr. Lamarze's laboratory. Dr. Lamarze's birds were prized objects, extremely rare: with the wave of one's hand, the blink of one's eye, the Lamarze birds could erupt into fabulous song. The birds in official production, ever malfunctioning, were capable of performing only uncomplicated tunes of a patriotic nature; the repertory of Dr. Lamarze's birds included music in all languages, dialects within a language; their music embraced any period or style. Moreover, the Lamarze birds could fly. It was believed by some that they even nested, migrated between galaxies, mated and reproduced themselves.

For decades Control Central had been in search of Dr. Lamarze's clandestine laboratory. Often the government announced the doctor's capture, sometimes his death, and for a few days, weeks, nothing would be heard in disproof of this. The news would be accepted and the people secretly mourn. Then another of the doctor's inventions would appear. These at times were frivolous creations — spurious, done on a whim. Unthinkably silly. Balloons that belched, a pepper shaker with contents that scurried about like ants, self-polishing shoes that walked by themselves. But more often than not his objects were rudimentary, practical, useful. Necessary. These Control after an interval claimed as products from their own laboratories. The iron, for instance, which could press clothes flat while simultaneously removing dampness. A mildew or fungus eradicator which one could spray from a cylinder. Pumps that converted water into air.

He invented dangerous objects said to undermine society: apples on actual trees, beans that hung from vines, a white liquid he called milk.

Earlier in the year, the doctor had terrified the city when he released upon it thousands of clucking birdlike creatures, each with two witless eyes, with skinny, scaly legs, a beak, an obscene tail. They were harmless, he said, as old or older than the human race. Chickens, they were called. Take one home, keep it in your yard. It will lay something called an egg. You may eat this egg.

Occasionally the doctor created strangely beautiful objects of disturbing gravity. A while ago in Lethe's main square a white sculpture had suddenly appeared. Massive, taller than Universal's synthetic trees that the rain has long since reduced to sodden lumps. Michelangelo's "David," he called this piece. Art, his pamphlets said it was. Florence, Italy, the earth, 1501-1504. But who was this Michelangelo, this David, where was this earth? Had beings actually lived in a year so long ago? From all over the city people flocked by the thousands to see the spectacle. Heedless of the rain, they endlessly speculated upon the figure's imposing form. What did it *do*? What purpose could it possibly serve? What was Dr. Lamarze's *point*?

All the same, they were moved. "Look at that head," they said — "that sloping back, the gigantic hands, the legs, the huge feet. Look at the rain dripping from the shrivelled penis." Transfixed, in awe, they were unable to remove their eyes from the beautiful form. Incomprehensibly, they laughed, they wept. Time and time again they returned to marvel, to ponder, to appreciate. So this was art. Here was history. Well, well. Then how could history be so entirely repugnant? Splattering upon David's head and shoulders, cascading down the long back, even the abysmal rain looked beautiful.

The militia cleared the square. Machines were called in to destroy the work. But Lamarze had made his David impregnable. It resisted the crane's tugging, pulverization by earth-moving equipment, explosives. Control decided it would cover the monstrosity with dirt; it would turn the square into a giant potato field. Amazingly, protesters defied this decision; they organized. Their bodies, hundreds deep, formed a human chain around the work. Michelangelo's "David," Florence, Italy, 1501-1504, the people had decided, must be saved. The militia attacked. Citizens killed by the score. Hundreds imprisoned, exiled. The model city's model square indeed became a potato field. But the rain washes away Control's synthetic earth. Potato and mud, silt, the plant's resilient vines, clog the sewers. The heart of the city becomes day by day more the putrid swamp.

Runté, to improve his mood, chose something lightly operatic. The current fashion. But the bird shook her head. She paced the cage, rustling her yellow wings, impatient with him. "Then perform what you like," Runté said. "Surprise me." The cage lit up; the evening's program was announced: Ekadakoo's *Other Worlds*, from the Jacqueline Period, 5000 B.C. Dire and heavy, as somber as Runté's humor.

The music was beautiful, even so, and despite the rain, the mist that would creep into his rooms to further dampen everything inside, Runté opened every window. He wanted the bird's concert to be shared with his neighbors. He would take the risk.

One by one Runté's neighbors opened their windows; at first scarcely an inch or so, then fully. A woman who once had worked in Office 9, administering the city's Workjoy Program For The Unstable, waved at him. Runté waved back. The woman was fifty-six — intelligent, robust, a generous and tolerant soul. At age fifty she had made her compulsive pilgrimage to the termination warren that was Office 12. She had the good fortune to be routed to Runté's desk. On the Control Center books, if such books were not annually shredded, she would be listed as terminated.

Through the turbid drizzle Runté observed her lips mouthing the bird's song. Drink the Letheian waters, the bird sang. Enter oblivion.

Runté released the bird from its cage and carried it out onto the covered balcony; let the entire city hear its song.

Drink the Letheian waters.

Let the river of forgetfulness be yours.

Rainwater gushed along the street. In low-lying sections of the city, where residents had been forced to take to boats, Runté could see through the rain a half-dozen high-rise apartment complexes in slow disintegration.

The people there stayed on; they had no other place to go.

It was late. Lights in neighboring windows were fading. Nearly all the people in these nearby buildings were older people. Past fifty. Runté had saved them. He, too, was a traitor.

It seemed to Runté, looking out into the eternal rain, that the rain was falling harder. Dr. Lamarze has predicted one day there will be colossal rains. The deluge will come. Universal's model city, the universe itself, will fade into history. It will fade into the nothingness of the past.

Runté rubbed his eyes, wondering whether this was so. Likely his sense of a quickening rain is delusion cast up by insomnia, his fractured mind, the stress factor at Office 12. At office 12 clerks of Runté's level assist their clients in arriving at a tranquil state of mind. The clients have no memory of any depth, why should they resist? Two minutes, then, to fulfill this obligation. In the meantime, the clerk has set out on a blue, sterile cloth a single pill. A glass of water, or Universal liqueur, should the client choose. The unconscious client is sped away to the hosing room. After cleansing comes surgery. In surgery organs are scanned and functioning ones removed. Rush these organs to rehabilitation chambers in the Hatchery. Every system has its hatcheries; how otherwise could civilization continue, prosper, enrich itself?

Runté saw, walking towards him down his street, the beautiful woman in the red umbrella. Where the water was less deep, he could make out her yellow boots. Once she stopped, leaned a thin arm against a wall — emptied the boots. When she neared he saw that she too was waving; she was calling to him.

Come with me, she said. All is lost here. But there are other worlds. Other model cities are being conceived this very minute. Come. The doctor is waiting. We must go.

She may have said these words. In the drizzling rain, Runté wasn't sure; it very well could be that his mind invented them.

All the same she is there, looking up at him. The red umbrella pitched back, the rain on her face.

On the street she takes his hand. They go.

Far away now, in the falling rain, can be seen the bird's yellow wings rising in the rainy night.

It may be that the woman holding his hand is another of the doctor's astonishing machines. Her hand is warm. Runté smells her scent. All will be understood in time.

THE BELL

*M*y neighbor Joe, not the name you know him by, tells me that as a boy he hated home. He hated each of the various houses in which he from time to time lived, each of the gravel streets those houses sat upon — hated the whole of the vile town. If this was home, he wanted no part of home.

He remembers most clearly, Joe says, the two upstairs rooms he lived in during most of the years of World War II.

He remembers a bell.

The bell's reason for being was neither ornamental nor aesthetic. It was not there to summon servants.

The bell was suspended by a cord from a window in the rear room. It was there to summon help, in the event Joe's father returned.

His father did not live any longer in this town. He lived in Norfolk, two hours away. It was not known what he did there.

The one rule, or law, that existed in Joe's home was that the father not be allowed in the house.

If the man did somehow gain entrance and Joe's mother said no to him, no on any account, he would be enraged, especially if he were drunk, which he would be; he would break down the door and beat them all to death.

The *them* included Joe, his older brother and sister, and their mother.

Several times already he had come close.

Each of them knew with certainty that one day he would return. It was crucial, therefore, that a means be devised whereby they might summon the law.

Hence, the bell.

They had no phone themselves, and were never likely to, but the woman next door did, and a promise was secured from this person that she would get the police running at the first ringing of this bell, whatever the hour.

She did not accept this assignment readily. She had seen the man in action and knew that she could easily become one of his victims.

In that town at this time people locked their doors and put out their lights early. A knock on any one's door after eight o'clock was all but unheard of.

Their father would come at night when he could not be seen. He would come after the town's two taverns had closed, provided, Joe's mother said, that none of the tarts who hung out let him take them home.

So long as he had his tarts everyone except the tarts would be safe.

Their two upstairs rooms had but a single entry and exit. If he got in, they would not get out.

Entry was gained by a door off the front porch.

The children, little Joe among them, were trained to race for the bell at the first sound of footsteps on the porch. If creeping was heard on the stairs, it already was too late.

"Practice," Joe's mother said. "We must practice."

She was speaking of the bell.

Joe was about four at the beginning of this period. His brother was six. His sister was eight.

His brother and sister had suffered under their father's hands a good deal more than Joe had. They had the quicker memory.

All four of them remembered the most recent incident. They were all tied to a bed. He was beating them with his belt.

Joe says that he remembers he very much wanted to be the person giving the alarm. But the others could run faster than he could; when rehearsing, he always was last to reach the bell.

It terrified him to see his mother running, his brother and sister running, and Joe chasing at their heels, because he would be the party his father first snatched up, and the one first to die under his knife or belt or fists.

Joe and his brother slept together on a narrow cot in the rear room, the kitchen. The sister slept with their mother in the other room, on the double bed where they not long ago had been tied.

How many times, drifting off to sleep, did they hear him? How often did Joe wake to see his brother, trembling in his pyjamas, standing by the window in the dark, ready to yank the cord?

Or the four of them, crowded together, silent and listening, trying to decide what sound it was they had heard, or if they had heard a sound — a creak on the stairs; stealthy footsteps on the porch — and whether they should not this instant be ringing the bell.

This, Joe says, was home.

"You'll forgive me," he says, "for not having romantic attachment to this idea of home."

In those days the older children and their mother willingly discussed the man's propensity for violence.

Later on, this would not be the case. Later on, which in this instance means these days, Joe's sister can not bear to hear her father's name mentioned. She collapses on the spot, or races away in tears.

He did return home from time to time; rumors would reach their mother: how he had got into this or that fight, a scrape with this or that woman — some nastiness at one of the taverns.

Once, Joe saw his father's picture in the paper. It was not the picture of anyone he recognized, though the caption contained his name. The headline said:

AREA MAN CHARGED WITH ASSAULT.

What most surprised Joe was how normal he looked.

In the spring of 1944 Joe's mother took up briefly with a man named Tracy Bibb. That is to say, she went for an occasional walk with him. Once in a while, she sat with Tracy Bibb in her kitchen. Once, she went with him to a dance. She came home from that dance with a bloody mouth and blood in her hair; she had to be helped up the stairs. Afterwards, she and her daughter locked themselves away in the bathroom, and remained there a long time whispering to each other.

Joe remembers his brother standing in his pyjamas on their side of the locked door, endlessly asking, "What happened? What's going on?"

— Who did that to you? Was it Tracy Bibb?

The sister kept telling them to shut up and go to bed.

Sooner or later, Joe guesses, they all did.

But it was not an easy sleep. Either Tracy Bibb, or their father, meant to break down the door, climb the stairs, and kill them while they slept. So Joe's brother lengthened the cord running from the window to the bell, and slept that night with the cord tied to his arm.

The news came at daylight, with someone pounding on the downstairs door.

Tracy Bibb was trussed up on the front steps, with rags stuffed in his mouth. A note was pinned to his clothes.

The note said: *This is what happens to your boyfriends.*

It said: *I can have you anytime I want.*

A ladder leaned against the side of the house. Their father had climbed the ladder during the night and removed the clapper from the bell.

So that, Joe says, was home.

When his father died, years ago, a pauper and a drunk in Norfolk, Joe's brother drove there, claimed the body, and brought it home.

This is not a deed either his mother or sister, he says, are ever to know.

"He was the meanest man who ever lived," the brother says, "and ruined all our lives. But it still seemed important to me that he be buried at home."

IF WE MAY NOT SAVE THE LIVING
LET US SAVE THE DEAD

Near nightfall a man showed up wounded in the head. He was dying.

"I will operate," said a voice. The voice belonged to a Jew wearing ragged trousers.

"Heat my tools," this little doctor said.

The patient was pallid; we had to hold him up. He had stopped breathing.

"Strap him down," the doctor said.

The door rattled; people were trying to get in.

"Give us food," cried the people at the door. "Give us water. We are dying."

The light was bad in the room; we could barely see what the doctor was doing. In the corner lay a pile of rags. He seemed to be cleaning his hands.

"Where would we get water?" someone said. "Where would we get food?"

But the people still rattled the door. "It always seems so much better on the other side," a woman said. "What the closed door signifies is promise."

For us the door held no promise. It was a door we had already passed through.

The doctor was sharpening his tools.

"False promise," the woman said, "is better than nothing."

We looked at the woman. We wondered where she had come from. Although her mouth had not opened she had spoken.

The dead man on the table had been dead about two minutes now. His body had turned blue from the cold.

We were all blue but he was bluest.

The door rattled.

"Food!" the people shouted. "Water!"

What is food? we thought. What is water?

The doctor had rolled back his sleeves; he was already operating.

It was so dark now that we could not see each other.

"Come closer," the doctor said to the woman who had spoken about doors and their promises.

"Turn up the wattage," the little Jew said to her. "I can't see."

The woman lowered her face within inches of the patient. She was extremely light-skinned. None of us knew where she had come from. We had never seen her before. She was dressed peculiarly. We wondered if she had slipped inside when we were not looking.

"More light!" shouted the doctor.

The woman slid her war coat from her shoulders. Beneath the coat she was naked.

The room brightened ever so fractionally.

"Fine," said the little Jew doctor. "Keep it simple."

All we could see of events taking place over the table was the woman's glowing skin, the patient's bleeding head, the doctor's hands flitting one way and another in the shadows.

The people at the door had gone. They would be seeking another door to rattle for their food and water.

The doctor dropped something into a pan. It gave a metallic ring. It was a bullet from the patient's brain.

"Silence!" someone said. "I want silence."

The silence, it seemed to us, went on for an eternity.

It seemed to us the voice calling for silence belonged to the patient on the table. It seemed to us his eyes were open. It seemed to us that he was staring fixedly at the woman, as though he knew her from some place. But where that place was was not a place that would fix itself in the brain.

Time was out of joint; a part of his mind was among the stars.

We were having the same problem.

Then — it was all over so quickly — the patient was sitting up. The Jew was wrapping the patient's head in strips torn from the bundle of rags in the corner.

"Next!" the doctor shouted. "Hurry!"

The need for speed was obvious. The woman was shivering. Her flesh glowed less now. Her color was pallid.

It was getting dark again.

We crowded up to the table. About sixty of us all at once tried climbing upon it.

"Sort it out among yourselves!" the little Jew doctor shouted. "Let's have order!"

His hands were under his arms; he was trying to warm them. He was such a small doctor he had to stand on a box at the table.

We looked to the woman. We saw her eyes searching our faces, first one of us and then the other. She seemed to be trying to decide where she had seen us before, or whether she had.

It was how all of us had looked at the Jew when he first had said, "I am a doctor."

It was how we had looked at each other.

Which of us climbed upon the table would be the woman's decision. We were content with that. It was not a decision we could make ourselves.

We waited for her to peel the blue finger.

But her flesh had lost its luster. She was dying.

We had to hold her up.

She was no longer breathing.

We moved her onto the table.

"More light!" shouted the doctor.

We stripped ourselves. We flung our rags into the corner.

Ever so fractionally, the room brightened.

The doctor's hands flitted one way and another.

The door rattled. The people were back again.

"Food!" they shouted. "Water! You will not fool us this time with your empty promises!"

We were passing among ourselves the woman's war coat.

It seemed to us we would survive if only we could touch it.

ADVENTURES IN FAIRYLAND

Once upon a time there was a child who was given everything she wanted. She had only to ask and she would receive. If she wanted snails for lunch she was given snails and if she wanted to eat an old shoe, then she was given an old shoe. One day the child beat her fists on her head and drummed her feet against the floor, saying, "I want a horse, I want a horse!" But the child was not given a horse. Months went by and still the child was not given a horse; the child drummed her feet against the earth and beat her fists on her head, and sometimes even yanked out her hair.

"I want a horse, I want a horse!"

So the child was given a horse.

Even so, the child cried. "I wanted a *black* horse," the child cried.

"A *black* horse?"

"Why, yes indeedy-deed-deed, a *black* horse."

So the white horse was returned to the horse dealer and exchanged for the blackest horse anyone had ever seen.

The child was so happy she danced in circles on the grass and flew from tree limb to tree limb, but then she cried. "How can I mount this horse?" she cried. "Surely I must have a magic chair!"

So a magic chair was secured and once again the child danced in circles on the grass, saying to anyone who would listen, "What a perfect horse, what a perfect chair!"

The child hopped onto the chair and hopped from the chair onto the horse's back and said "Giddyup" to the horse, but the horse stayed exactly where it was.

"*Giddyup, giddyup!*" said the child, but the horse stayed exactly where it was.

Someone even swatted the horse on its big rear-end, but the horse this time looked even more like a statue, remaining exactly where it was.

"Feed it an apple," someone said, and the horse was fed an apple, then everyone had to chase the horse around

Oh!

the yard, so much did the horse seem to want another apple, and also a pear, a banana, a peach. Not to mention a full bucket of oats and its head in the water trough.

Then the child hopped onto her chair and onto the horse's back and strapped on her magic chair and said, "Now let's go!"

There they went, fast as you could see.

Another day, the child said to the horse, "What is your name? I am so tired of calling you 'horse'."

But the horse did not speak. It shook its withers and pawed the earth, but it did not say a single word.

This horse, apparently, was a non-speaking horse.

"My goodness," said the child. "Surely the horse must have a name."

"Call it whatever name you want it to have," the child was told.

"That's madness," said the child. "I can't give this horse any name except its own name."

So the horse dealer was telephoned and inquiries made as to the horse's proper name. "We call it Good Horse," said the dealer. "That's all we've ever called it around here."

"Was it a good horse?"

"It was an excellent horse. To tell you the truth, it was something of a magic horse."

"Then why don't we call it Magic Horse?"

"You *could,* I suppose," said the dealer. "But probably it just thinks of itself as a *good* horse, and that is how it wants to be called."

The child went out for another glorious ride on the horse. She rode the horse all over town. The child rode the horse up over hills and down many valleys and through a residence of grassy meadows. When she returned home the child was asked how she liked her horse.

"It is a good horse," the child said.

"Is it a magic horse?"

"No, it is a plain, regular horse. It gallops, it eats tufts of grass — it does exactly what a regular horse does."

"But it is a *good* horse?"

"It is a very good horse."

"So why don't you call it Good Horse?" she was asked.

"Because that is a terrible name," said the child. "How would I like it if I were called Good Child? I would hate that name. I would hate it so much I'd become the worst child ever. I don't doubt for a second I would."

Just as this discussion was taking place, it began raining. Then the heavens thundered and lightning roared and everyone taking part in the discussion became drenched.

"Why don't you call the horse Thunder?" it was suggested. "Do you think that is a good name?"

The child thought this over for some many minutes. Then she said aloud, "Thunder?"

The horse, looking at her, pitched back its head. It shook that head from side to side, and rippled its withers and pawed the ground until it was up to its knees in bad temper.

The child considered the horse's odd behavior for a good many minutes. She shifted her head on her shoulders this way and that and finally she nodded.

"Thunder," the child said. "The horse clearly dislikes the name, but I like it and it is my horse. The name has a certain *je ne sais quoi,* so I shall call this horse Thunder."

"You are being a bad child," the child was told. "You are being the worst child ever."

The horse reared on its hind legs and clamped the child's hair in its teeth and pulled the child's hair, some of it right out of her head.

"You are both being bad," they were told. "You are both being the worst ever."

"I am going riding now," said the child. "Out of my way!"

She hopped onto her magic chair and from there onto the horse's back, then arranged her magic chair behind her. Then off she went riding.

When she called the horse Thunder the horse ran like thunder, so frightening the child that she stopped calling the horse Thunder except when extremely agitated and when on her worst behavior. When she called the horse Good Horse the horse was a most excellent horse and riding companion.

So the horse became known as Good Horse, which was the name it had been known by for the whole of its days on earth. The child went riding every day, all day and all over. She rode up hill and down hill and across swollen rivers and until her every limb ached and her bottom felt like a sausage. Wherever she rode she found herself having to answer countless questions from curious citizens, such as, Where did you get that fine chair? What does that horse eat? Where does that horse sleep? Has that horse ever thrown you?

This last question utterly amazed the child. The child thought it a most perplexing question. She looked at her interlocutor in wonder, saying, "Why would my own horse throw me? What an extraordinary idea! I think some wizard must have stolen every ounce of your brains."

That very afternoon the horse approached a wire fence, halted, pitched its hind legs into the air, and somersaulted the child over the fence into the thickest briar patch imaginable.

In the briar patch was a Tar Body. The child said, I have never spoken this wish aloud, but one thing I have always wanted, next to wanting a horse, is a tarred old sticky Tar Body.

Tar Body was crying. It said it had been in the briar patch unwanted for nearly a million years. It said, "What do you mean, *old?*" It said, "What do you mean, *sticky?*" It said, "I have waited ages for someone to rescue me from oblivion. From my bad start in life and from life's heinous racial practices. Do you want to take me home?"

Tar Body and the child hopped onto the chair and from the chair onto the waiting horse. They rode and rode. They rode until the very sun high in the heavens said, "What a long day? Why don't all of you go home, so I can find my repose for the night?"

The child said, "Oh, sun, why are you always disappearing? Are you sleepy? I would be a happy child if just one day you would stay awake all night because then I could do the same."

At which point the moon said, "You are the most surly child I have ever seen. Look at that Tar Body. Look at that horse. Because they are not nearly so witless as you are, they are perfectly happy to go home, to have a nice bedtime story read to them, and to go to sleep so that in the morning they can happily arise from their beds and eat their pudding."

The child looked at Tar Body and the horse in utter surprise. "Do you eat pudding?" she said. "My goodness, you are fellow pudding lovers? What kind of pudding? For myself the only pudding worth eating is chocolate pudding."

Tar Body expressed the view that this was indeed, among Tar Bodies, the preferred pudding. It was right up there with eating tar or mud, or both simultaneously.

The horse said nothing because apparently it was a non-speaking horse.

It pawed the ground however and neighed so mightily that a thousand animals piped up from their nests and from their lairs in the ground and even in the tree tops and under mulching leaves, all of them saying the same thing, which was — "Would someone please shut up that horse? We need our beauty sleep."

So the child and Tar Body and the horse went home and that night Tar Body slept with the child and the horse slept standing up by the window inside the child's room because it was too tired even to think of sitting.

In the morning Tar Body and the child were so alike one could not tell them apart. Even the bed they had slept on looked like it was made of tar, and everything in the room Tar Body had touched looked like sticky tar.

The child was made to take a long bath. The long bath was a bath which lasted an eternity. She was scrubbed with brushes made from sharp wire bristles and all the hair on her head had to be chopped off. She emerged so wrinkled from the bath that she looked exactly like her grandfather, who was two hundred years old and one of the people seeing to it that she took a proper bath and scrubbed herself mercilessly.

For much of this time Tar Body was up on the roof, repairing rain holes that had appeared around the chimney.

The child was probably cleaner than she had ever been in her life. Se was probably the cleanest child anyone in that house had ever seen.

When she emerged from her bath, everyone in the house screamed out in the loudest voice, including Tar Body, "Who on earth is that clean person? Will she give us a kiss? Will she tell us how she has worked this wonderful miracle?"

Her first words when she emerged from the bath, however, were as follows: "I want that Tar Body retarred. Then I want him to be made less sticky."

This was done.

Tar Body was dressed in a suit of shiny clothes that made him look very much like a stick of licorice candy.

Except for his little white teeth and his short neck and pug nose, and his great round eyes and black squishy feet, he hardly looked any more like Tar Body. He looked like a dapper licorice prince on his way to the fair.

At that point the retarred and suited Tar Body made a long speech.

"I want it known," said Tar Body, "that you have made a serious error in divining my gender. I am a female Tar Body and wish to be attired in dress appropriate to the same. I want a dress that comes to my ankles and a wide-brimmed hat with countless feathers and a string of finest beads strung around my neck and tall boots that will come to my navel."

So they had to dress Tar Body all over again and although Tar Body was a delight to look at in her splendid new clothes, everyone else in the house was miserable because they looked more like Tar Body than they looked like themselves and the whole day one person or another had to sit in the tub and rub the body raw with sharp wire brushes and cut off all their hair, until they looked like themselves again.

Then the child said, "Now let's have no more dithering. Now let us eat chocolate pudding and pancakes and drink our breakfast juices and eat our vegetables so we can live forever."

The horse was summoned, and Tar Body, the horse, and the child ate a sumptuous breakfast.

Then the child and the divinely-attired Tar Body went for another endless ride on the horse which had eaten all the pudding it could hold and was clearly in a good mood because not once did it throw them.

They made a strange sight, the child and divinely-attired Tar Body in the magic chair riding through the countryside.

They had numerous exciting adventures. Once they found wolves huffing and puffing, trying to blow down houses occupied by three little pigs, and they chased the wolves all the way into another kingdom. Then they came back and had tea in each of the three little pigs' three little houses, the pigs of course being elated.

They came across another nasty wolf pretending to be a beautiful young girl's grandmother — better to eat you with, my dear, it was constantly saying — and this ferocious wolf they chased all the way to Hades. Then they came back and ate wonderful cookies with the beautiful girl and her grandmother.

"You are so sweet I could kiss you," the grandmother said, and kissed all three of them, but when she kissed Tar Body they became so stuck together the one became the other.

That was another great adventure because the grandmother of course had to soak in the bath the longest time, and work at her skin with wire bristles and to have all her hair cut off and her toenails too because she was tarred all over.

During this while Tar Body was again on the roof repairing rain holes by jumping and dancing and rolling all over.

The horse sat on a three-legged chair in the kitchen, eating buckets and buckets of pudding, topped off with gingerbread truffles, followed by oceans of water.

Then the child and Tar Body rode up the road on the horse's back to another house lived in by three bears, where someone named Goldilocks had slept in each of the bears' three beds, which was such a good idea, they thought, that the three of them slept in each of the three beds, making such a mess of things that when the three bears came home they flew into such a terrible rage that all three, and Goldilocks as well, were pitched without warning to the floor.

We like things *neat!* the three bears said, growling and venting their rage without the least show of mercy.

So they had to make things *neat* before the bears would let them have any pudding.

Then Tar Body had to go up and repair every leak in the roofing and Baby Bear had to have endless rides on the horse's back and the child had to wash every dish and utensil.

Next, news came that Jack was up the beanstalk having a raging battle with the giant, but when they arrived at the beanstalk they found Jack had everything well in hand.

So they left him to his labors, leaving him, however, for his delectation, a giant bowl of pudding.

Later on, they knocked awhile at the door of the house of the woman who lived in a shoe, but it turned out she had built herself another house high on a hill, which was a house that had so many rooms you could go from one room to another forever without ever being in the same room twice, and all of that just on the first floor.

This was where she had put all her many children, some of whom now had their own children and kept them in shoeboxes under the bed.

The house had a fine new roof and for once Tar Body was not obliged to make any repairs.

The whole gigantic house was up on stilts that looked exactly like chicken legs and each morning at dawn the house made a crowing sound exactly like that of a big rooster. Whereupon, scores of children burst from the house, collecting thousands of chicken eggs.

Then Jack came running, saying the giant had fallen from the bean stalk and opened a giant crack in his head, and had at once to be rushed to the hospital.

So the giant was fitted to the horse's back in the magic chair, and off they went racing clippidy-clop, the giant moaning and thrashing and passing wicked remarks about Jack the whole while.

The giant was a truly terrible creature, the ogre of ogres. In the giant world everyone not a giant was a slave of the giants, kept in chains and fed not even so much as bread and water. Worse yet, the giants exerted giant influence over the other one hundred and sixty kingdoms in the giant world, and if one of those kingdoms did something the giants didn't like the giants strode in and made them eat crow.

But at the hospital the giant cried without end while the crack in his brains was being mended with ceiling plaster. He was an ogre who was a terribly cry-baby. To calm him, Tar Body had to go in and hold his hands and tell him stories that curdled his brow with their horrors. "If you had been where I have been and seen what I have seen," said Tar Body, "you would have good reason for your socially inept and backwards behavior. But as you have not, there is no excuse for your sordid practice. The first thing you must do when you return to your castle is civilize every giant in your kingdom. You must restore civil rights to your lowest urchin, and elect Tar Babies to positions of authority in your every institution."

"I promise," said the giant, profusely tearful and repentant.

The child came in and drove a wooden peg into his skull's soft ceiling plaster, so that when the plaster hardened the peg would always be there so that each time the giant saw it he would remember and heed this valuable lesson.

Afterwards, the giant was made to soak a long time in a bath of vinegary water, from which he emerged so shrunken and insignificant that you had to look twice even to see him.

On the way back through the forest the child, Tar Body, and the horse experienced nasty episode upon episode with wicked witches too numerous to recount here in this simple narrative.

Suffice it to say on that score that a thousand princesses were rescued and restored to their own story, as for instance the beautiful princess whose beautiful foot fit the glass slipper, who missed her midnight carriage home from the ball and had to ride the magic chair on the horse's back to her wicked sisters, unfortunately clutching Tar Body the whole distance so that her beautiful foot looked exactly like Tar Body's and probably would never again fit into a glass slipper as long as she lived.

But before they parted from this princess they went in and chopped off all the wicked sisters' hair and issued a stern discourse on sisterly love, on household management, and manners.

A wooden boy with a long nose came prancing along their path, but the child, Tar Body, and the horse were napping by the side of the road, exhausted by their many adventures, and did not have to listen to the boy's fabulous lies.

While they were on the road word came from the other kingdom that the wolves the child had chased there were causing nothing but trouble.

"You had better come and take these troublesome wolves back where they belong," said the king's messenger.

So off the child and Tar Body flew on the horse's back to the troubled kingdom.

The first thing they saw were a thousand people assembled at the border. These people were in a frightful mood. They said to the child, "Just look what those bad wolves have done. Ours used to be such a pretty kingdom, and now because of you we have to live in a place as ugly as the ugliest junk yard."

The child said, "Let me talk to those troublesome befurred and fangy creatures."

Instantly, every wolf in the land gathered before her.

"You would not let us huff and puff," cried the wolves, "as is our rightful and proper behavior. You would not let us eat the three plump little pigs!" cried the wolves. "You would not let us eat the nice old grandmother or the nice young girl who told us we had such beautiful eyes and such beautiful teeth. So we have cast off our carnivorous yearnings and turned ourselves into chalk-faced vegetarians. We only eat carrots now, and broccoli, and tomatoes, and green peas, and lettuce in the lettuce patch. For dessert nothing satisfies us so much as eating field after field of pretty flowers."

"*Yes!!*" cried the assembled people. "They have chomped on every zinnia and buttercup, every rose and snapdragon! They have even consumed every dandelion growing wild in a field."

The child then understood why the kingdom was so ugly. No sooner did a flower bloom than was that flower being devoured by the vegetarian wolves.

Not a blossom remained in the kingdom, either in greenhouse, in window box, or garden.

The child said, "Why don't you eat pudding?"

The wolves cried out as one: "Eating pudding is not natural to a wolf, not by your chinny-chin-chin. Eating pudding is anathema to us. Whoever heard of a wolf eating pudding? Our image would suffer terribly. No one would view the wolf with any respect at all if we spent our lives wolfing down like a pig your ridiculous pudding."

The child was at her wit's end. She threw up her hands in despair and resignation and said all her good work and Tar Body's good work and Good Horse's good work had, forsooth and alas, come to nothing.

Tar Body and the child conferred for a long time, biting their lips and rejecting a whole hodge-podge of unthinkably bad ideas.

"You should eat tar and mud," cried Tar Body, "as I have done for two thousand years, and see how you like that!"

"Ugh!" said the wolves. "What an outlandish suggestion!"

Finally, the child clapped her hands and gave a speech from Good Horse's high back, standing tall and radiant on her tippie-toes in the magic chair.

"Okay," said the child. "Flower growers, go back to your flower growing. You of the wolf world go back to your huffing and puffing. All of you, go back to what you were originally doing. I and Tar Body and the horse will no longer interfere and the pigs and the people in the gingerbread houses will just have to get themselves vicious watch dogs and generally look to their own security."

So all the wolves crowded onto the horse's back, along with Tar Body and the child and her magic chair, and they rode back to their old kingdom, all chattering away endlessly and with boundless mirth and excitement while lapping at each other.

But when they got home not one of them could dismount nor could the Tar Body be seen. Tar Body was somewhere in the middle of the pack of wolves, yelling its head off, and all the wolves were stuck together, looking so much like Tar Babies that anyone could see theirs was a terrible predicament.

"This is a frightful situation," said the child. "Now you will all have to have a long bath, and go at your skin with wire bristles, and all your fur must be cut off with the sharpest hedge-clippers."

So this they did and in the end the wolves looked so much unlike wolves that even the little pigs showed up and hooted with laughter.

"Don't they look silly," said the pigs. "Wouldn't they look ridiculous, huffing and puffing?"

The wolves paid not the slightest attention to these laughing pigs. They were very pleased with how they looked, and especially were excited by the wonders of their bone structure, their sinewy muscles, their long skinny legs and sleek tails, and their big ears as tough as the finest shoe leather. Anyway, they knew that when their fur grew back they would be more beautiful than ever.

They had also decided they would beautify their doors and their windows with pot upon pot of beautiful flowers, and any wolf who ate these flowers would be made to scrub each and every chimney in the wolf kingdom.

Then the sun waned, saying it was sleepy, so sleepy, and the moon came out and told everyone that if they did not go home at once the night would be made so black their eyes would pop from their heads and every tree on the road would bump into them.

So the child hopped up on her chair to the horse's back and the Tar Body did the same and the child said, "Giddyup, Good Horse," and the horse trudged back home, as tired as could be, with all of their heads nodding.

"This is a wonderful life," said the child to her parents. "I could live like this forever."

"Well, that is fine and dandy," said the child's parents, "but now please go to sleep and no more talking. Rest up and dream good dreams and in the morning you will be ready for brave new adventures."

"Where do I sleep?" asked Tar Body. "Why is no one looking after me?"

She still wore her wide-brimmed hat with its many feathers, her boots that came to her navel, her glittering bead necklace, and looked so spectacular that already that day she had turned down five hundred offers of marriage from five hundred woodcutters, stone masons, poets or preachers, including Jack at his beanstalk on his knees delivering a promise of eternal worship.

"Hush," Tar Body was told. "Hush, and put on these nice new pyjamas, and sleep in this nice new Tar Bed by the stove."

At this remark the horse, which had been eating every window shade in the house and eyeing the poinsettias, let out a terrible neigh.

"Neigh, neigh," the horse said. "Tar Body can't sleep by the stove. If Tar Body sleeps by the stove, come morning she will no longer be a Tar Body. She will have lost all her elegance. She will be no better than a puddle of sticky stuff you spread over rainholes on your roof. Mercy me, what am I to do with you people! Let's show a little responsibility here. Yes, a little mature thought, I would say, is very much in order."

All this the horse said so suddenly and with such authority no one could believe their ears.

The child was so excited she fell from the bed. She was so excited she was pulling her hair and dancing as though in frolic with a fiddle. She leapt up from the floor, examining this horse with utter amazement.

"Did I hear that horse speak?" asked the child. "Or was that horse speaking a figment of my imagination?"

The horse executed a formal curtsy, such as one might see in the courts of ancient kings and queens or at a monthly meeting of the Knights of the Round Table.

The horse looked every inch the noble steed stepped from the illuminated pages depicting the famous pilgrimages and quests of fabled antiquity.

The horse said, "By your leave, Governor. Who ever heard of a horse that couldn't talk? Of course I can talk. I can talk a mile a minute. I can talk until my words pile up and fill every corner."

And the horse went on talking until his words filled every crevice, every nook and corner of the child's already crowded room. The horse's speech covered every inch of floor and stacked up to the ceiling and when the room was full of words the child and the Tar Body would have been buried alive by so many words had they not in the nick of time escaped by the window.

And still the horse went on talking. The horse's words filled the entire night air, until the very trees and every bush went running for some other country. The words pushed into every room of every house and up over every rooftop and through the clouds and up into the very heavens until even the very moon was being pushed this way and that, and the very man in the moon, and green cheese on the moon were being pressed flat by the horse's unrelenting flow of speech. Words, words, words everywhere. Filling every space until no space was left over.

On the other side of the world the sun heard the horse's words, and here on this side the three little pigs, the grandmother in her gingerbread house, the bears in theirs, the cavorting wolves without fur, they all said in a mighty chorus, "Someone shut up that horse! Someone muffle that stallion! Someone please, please do something to curb the ceaseless speech of that blabbermouth horse before the whole world sinks from the weight."

"You can talk!" the child kept saying. "At last I have a talking horse! What a good horse, Hooray, hooray!"

"I don't see why you are so surprised," said Tar Body. "That horse of yours has been talking to me every minute."

"Bless my soul!" said the child.

"Yes," said Tar Body. "Started of, it was talking Latin, talking Greek, then before I know it that black horse is talking soul, talking be-bop, talking rap — talking anything you could name."

"Well, my goodness," said the child. "And me all that while in the dark!"

So the child and the horse and Tar Body too all stayed up all night talking until the very world tumbled from the weight of so many words. Words, words everywhere, filling each nook and cranny and smallest hole in the wall. So many words up in the heavens even the falling stars can't fall. Sentences whirling this way and that, like huge schools of fish or whirling comets. People having to run and duck and weave and hide behind boulders.

Talk, talk, my how that horse could talk.

Half the people and animals and insects ended up standing on their heads and the others did not know where they stood — but all of them were endlessly shouting, "Enough! Enough! Put a lid on it, horse!"

It turned out the horse knew every language known to humankind, and numerous other unknown languages, plus horse languages and Tar Body languages and every language not yet invented. It had attitudes on any subject anyone could mention and was in fact famous for its attitudes, as for instance on how to rear a child. "Like, for instance," the horse said, "not giving a child everything it wanted."

"Be quiet!" said the child. "What kind of attitude is that? That is the most astounding attitude I have ever heard, especially coming from a horse."

The horse had opinions about how to keep a Tar Body from sticking to everything, as well as how to cure snakebite, why horseradish was called by that name, what you did to help someone who suddenly went blue in the face, where beneath the rainbow gold was buried, why it was necessary to have an occasional bath, why horsehair sofas were a rotten idea, what to do about wolves puffing at pigs' doors, why you must never pour salt on a bird's tail, how to prevent measles in a child, what to do when parents misbehaved and — oh, a thousand useful things.

Plus, it turned out the horse was well-versed in the higher mathematics, in philosophy, in astronomy, musicology, the arts and crafts — in every knowledgeable endeavor known to man or beast or the spirit world. The horse was only too pleased to lecture the child and Tar Body on some little piece of Einstein's theory of relativity which they did not understand, to elaborate upon prevailing economic theories, explain the origins of the universe, give in excruciating detail a lecture on Darwinism, diagram with its hoof in the dirt the principals of mechanical engineering, reveal how best to combat the menace of horse flies, how stars were formed and why they disintegrated, and where babies came from — oh, a thousand such things.

There was scarcely not a thing the horse did not know, and when it did not know a thing it knew precisely where to go to find the answer or who it was one should ask. The horse told the child the pursuit of knowledge was a pleasurable and rewarding experience, as was the pursuit of excellence in almost any form. Improving the mind was even better than eating pudding, the horse said; even better than ice cream, but not better than love, the horse said, "because there is nothing better than love, absolutely nothing, yes, absolutely."

When the horse said this last all the bellowing people on earth, in whatever topsy-turvy position they were found, and all the animals and insects, and also the moon and the man in the moon and the sun on the other side of the world suddenly fell silent and picked up their ears because all of the other endless words from the horse's mouth simply disappeared, simply slid away and were not there any more.

It was like all the other trillions of words filling the universe all at once vanished so that this one sentence from the horse's mouth could be heard.

One after the other every living thing in the universe said, "What did he say? What was that he said?"

Suddenly the heavens were empty of words, and the earth was empty of words, and everyone could breathe easily again, and again had room for their elbows, their arms and legs, and in fact they felt a freedom such as they had not felt in all the time they could remember. Tears were pouring from the eyes of these people, from the insects and animals — from everyone, so moved were they by the horse's words.

Now they wanted to hear the horse talk more. They wanted the horse to talk itself hoarse and say again what they thought it was that the horse had just said. That bit it had said about the pursuit of excellence, the excitement of learning new ideas, about love and — well, they wanted to hear again practically every thing of importance the horse had said.

A great clamor went up from them, billions of voices saying, "Hey, horse! Yes, you! What was that you said? Would you please repeat that last little bit you were saying?"

But the horse was indeed hoarse by this time and although it stretched its long neck and opened its mouth wider than it ever had before, not a single word could it speak. It was tongue-tied. It was so fatigued from its speechifying that its tongue hung from its mouth.

Yet everyone was waiting. Not a peep was to be heard throughout the universe, and you felt the whole world would perish and tumble off into the void if the people, the animals, the birds and insects and even the lowest caterpillar could not hear again what it was about love and loving one another that they thought they had heard the horse say.

You could hear a pin drop anywhere in the universe, that's how quiet the universe was.

So the child looked at the silent horse. The child looked at the Tar Body and both looked at the horse, but the horse just closed its eyes and went to sleep standing up, in just that awkward and surprising way a horse will.

"My goodness," the child said. "What a time to fall asleep! What has got into my horse, that it wants to be sleeping now?"

Tar Body said to the child, "I am just a Tar Body, who is going to listen to me? If anyone is going to tell those creatures out there what it was the horse said, then I guess it will have to be you."

"Me?" said the child. "I am but a mere child. I am but a mere slip of a small girl, with such a small squeaky voice, who is going to listen to me?"

The child listened to the silence a long time, and a long time the silence listened back.

Then the child said, "Okay, I will do it. I will repeat what the horse said, but only this one time, because I am sleepy too. And, really, someone else ought to have this job."

"No," said Tar Body. "I think it is probably best, certainly more familiar — more easy to take — coming from a child."

So the child picked up her magic chair and climbed with it up to the roof top where she lived. She stood on her tip-toes on the magic chair, looking out over the whole of the starry night and sensing in her every heart-beat the millions of living things all looking back.

This is what the child said.

"All of you out there. Here is a child who from birth was given everything she wanted, including a talking horse. Now my horse has spoken and first you wanted him to shut up, then you wanted him to repeat himself. Here is what I think. I think you are just pretending you did not hear what my horse said about love, that you now want to hear repeated. You are thinking that what my horse said went through one of your ears and out the other, and now you have nothing between those ears. You want what my horse said on the subject to remain between your ears. But I don't believe you. Tar Body does not believe you. My sleeping horse does not believe you.

"What I think is that you will have to do the work yourselves. You will just have to figure out for your-selves what Good Horse was saying. You will have to think long and hard on the matter and come up with your own good ideas.

"In the meantime, it has been a long day, and I for one am going to sleep now. I'm going to sleep my head off and wake refreshed in the morning so that Tar Body and I and the horse can go on with all our adventures in life.

"I am going to love all of you, however, and do my best to keep you at least as happy as I am.

"I trust you will return the favor.

"Maybe that is all my horse was saying.

"Think about it, anyway.

"So good night and so long. Hasta la vista, as my horse would say. Many happy returns until we see you on our next adventure."

Then the child went inside and got in bed, pulling her covers up over her face, she was that exhausted from her speechifying, and feeling humiliated that she had not done a more inspiring job.

Tar Body and the horse, they too slept.

The rest of the universe stayed up the whole night, thinking deep thoughts, tossing and turning. Trying with all their might to figure out what on earth it was the child had said the horse had said, one party saying he had said the one thing and the other party saying he had said the other and one saying it meant one thing and the other saying it meant something different, but all of them thinking, "Well, maybe we can spruce up our act a little bit. Maybe we can enhance a little the *look* of the place, because one of these days the Noble Trio would be coming down our road, doing their good deeds, and it would be a deep embarrassment if that amazing child, that sticky Tar Body, and that talking horse did not think well of us. If they did not see us in a good light and know that we at least are trying to be every bit as good and kind as they are.

THE GUACAMOLE GAME

A NOVELLA

*T*wenty years they had been playing the game. She made the guacamole, he mixed the masa, deep-fried the tortillas, they played the game.

Name?

Thomas J. Pabst.

J?

Sorry. James.

Occupation?

Bricklayer. You mean now?

Yes, now, Thomas James Pabst.

Bricklayer. This month it's bricklayer.

Age?

Age, I'm . . ..

Count it on your fingers, Thomas James Pabst.

Forty-seven. Eight? I am forty-seven.

Thomas James Pabst is forty-seven?

Right. Make that forty-nine. Dock me one hundred.

His first docking, getting a free ride on the J, they would pause to dip the chips into the guacamole, munch the dip, sip the drinks.

Get another scorecard if the other one is full, assure themselves that the pens are in good working order.

Then get back to the game.

Address?

Address, you know my address.

The address, please, of Thomas James Pabst and kindly dock yourself five hundred points for delay of game.

Shit! 209 Saints Road, Estuary, Ontario, Canada, Zip NOB 1PO.

You lose, Thomas James Pabst.

What do you mean, lose? I only said —

You said, 'shit', Thomas James Pabst, in an explosive voice. So you lose. Mark that another ten thousand in my favor for the one-minute game.

Shit!

Yes, you said that. Again? Want to play again?

*H*e always wanted to play again. It infuriated him that she beat him, beat him nearly every time, often within a minute of starting. So they would refreshen the drinks, eat a little guacamole, and play again.

Ninety-nine games out of the hundred, she skunked him. You could say that and it would be true, but when she lost it would be a whopper. Her losing would be such a whopping big loss that they would be back again nearly even.

This afternoon, for instance, start of the game, he was fifty million points in the hole. She was feeling safe. She could not see any way at all, any way in hell, she said to herself, he would ever again make the comeback. The fifty million he was in the hole meant he had the dishes to wash three times a day for the rest of their lives, the grass to mow over the next thirty summers, every door knob in the house to polish through the next lifetime, every window to clean until he was an old man. The floors to scrub, the laundry to wash, the house to paint, even a roof job.

Fifty million represented a lot of labor.

He would be working as her slave forever.

She should have been content with that. She should have said, That's it, no more of this game, what else is there left for me to win?

But, no, the cat left her tongue, she was bloated on guacamole, into her third drink when she found herself saying, "Want to play again?"

That was her big mistake, proposing to re-establish the conflict, re-open the fray, when she was, one, pissed off generally, and, two, so pissed off at her daughter that already twice today she had slammed the door in her face.

In the bitch's face! How she put it in her own mind: *Twice today in the bitch's face and if she shows up a third time, watch out!*

Name?

Vivian Darling-Pabst.

That is your full and entire name?

Vivian *Samantha* Darling-Pabst.

Kindly dock yourself one hundred points.

She did so.

Known as Vivian Darling?

Yes.

Age?

Forty-seven.

Income?

Today, not one penny. Last week, four hundred and sixty dollars. Last month, thirty-two five. How far back do you want me to go?

Never mind. Marital Status?

Not single.

Does that mean married, Vivian Darling?

Yes. Married.

To?

Thomas J. for James Pabst.

Children?

She should have seen it coming. Right there she should have seen the line he would take, and invented a legitimate means for withdrawing from the game without penalty. She should right there have said the house was on fire, that an attack of appendicitis was killing her, that she had just seen two goons going through the neighbor's window. Anything to get herself out of the game.

But she had seen the little crack of mirth on his lips when he said "Children?" in what he assumed was a bland, naively-innocent voice but which was so blatantly obvious that she was not fooled for a minute. Quite the contrary. She was flooded with such disdain and contempt for his abilities with this game that she hesitated only for the merest second.

Yes, children.

How many among the living?

Two.

The name, please, of the youngest-born of this pair.

Christina Dolores Heiss.

Her age?

Twenty-six.

Residing?

Estuary, Ontario.

The marital status, please, of this daughter?

Or, right there with that question, pulled up the drawbridge. In the least, have argued for the docking of more points on his scoresheet, since the daughter's *name* very clearly, if erroneously, suggested the daughter's marital status.

In transition, she said.

That answer is not acceptable. Please dock yourself one hundred points.

She fumed, but did so. The game did not allow one to be vague in one's responses.

Again, the marital status of this daughter, Christina Dolores Heiss?

My daughter Christina is presently engaged in the process of divorcing her first and so far only husband.

The income of this daughter in the current fiscal year?

I don't know.

Please hazard a guess at this daughter's income.

Here Vivian took the offensive. She was becoming more and more displeased with the smirk that was surfacing on his face. She did not like it either that his drink was nearly full, while she had drained hers.

You know very well, she told him, that guesses are disallowed except under extreme circumstances in very well-defined game situations. This is not one of those moments. So kindly dock yourself five hundred points.

He smiled, very agreeably doing so.

It surprised her that he did not argue the matter. Had he cared to, a strong case could have been made for his *hazard a guess* question. That he did not do so was only another indication of how poorly he played the game.

She felt almost sorry for him. He was in the heel fifty million and every extra one hundred points docked meant one more doorknob he would have to polish, yet one more time he would have to polish her car, shine her shoes, clean the refrigerator.

All the same, she was perspiring. She knew she was, had felt herself in the hot-seat, and should have stopped the game right there. That was one of the rules. If at any point you wanted to calmly refuse — equanimity, calmness, being the crucial issue here — to answer a question you could do so and there was nothing the other party could do but accept it. Or if someone knocked at the door, the phone rang, an emergency developed, the game could be stopped on a no-fault basis.

The rules stated that you signalled this by drumming your heels six times in rapid succession on the floor.

She did not drum her shoes.

Ready? he said.

She nodded.

Your estimate, Vivian Samantha Darling-Pabst, of your daughter's annual income this past year based on personal knowledge of the house she occupies, the furniture in that house, the grounds, the neighborhood, how she keeps it up, the car she drives, the clothes she wears, the —

Which daughter?

His eyebrows went up. Without his asking her to do so she docked herself one thousand points. It was patently clear which daughter was being asked about.

She should have let him lose his way in the interminable question and she would have been off the hook.

The game rule was that you could weave your question down a thousand roads, snake down a thousand alleys, lump in as many clauses as your wit allowed, but in the end you were to restrict yourself to the single question.

That was another reason he was fifty million in the hole: he had a fondness for the compound question.

I would estimate the annual income of this daughter this past year to be in the vicinity of $14,668.

She knew the precise figure. Thomas James Pabst did this daughter's tax statement and each year he told her.

After or before taxes? he next asked.

After.

Cheating or reporting accurately?

Cheating.

Earned how?

Waitressing.

Education?

Nil.

Was that a joke, Vivian Darling-Pabst? If so, it was a costly one. Kindly dock your account the required amount since you very well know your daughter is college educated.

A lie told in a jokey vein only cost half-a-million. She did not begrudge this half-million.

How long has this daughter, Christina Dolores Heiss, resided at her present address?

One year.

Be more precise, please, or dock yourself one thousand points.

All *right!* My daughter has resided at her present address seven months and twenty-eight days.

Kindly dock yourself five thousand points for the snippy tone employed in your 'All *right!*'

To signal a delay in the game all that was required was that you elevate your right arm and pull it up and down as though you were yanking an invisible cord that in the old days would have summoned a servant.

Now he was the servant.

She so signalled.

She went into the kitchen and poured herself another glass of white wine.

He used the moment to feed himself over the guacamole bowl. His own drink was virtually untouched.

She then used the bathroom, the small one off the kitchen.

For a long time she washed her face in cold water. She looked at her face and said to her eyes in the mirror, "I know exactly where the son of a bitch is going."

While in there she gave close inspection of his handiwork. The toilet bowl sparkled. The chrome knob was shiny. Even the rust in the holding tank had been removed. The tiles gleamed. There was no mildew in the shower corners. When she turned on the fan it no longer rattled. The blue guest towels with the lace trims were freshly washed and precisely folded. The basket of fancy soaps in the shape of sea shells had been dusted.

She climbed up on the toilet bowl to inspect the sill in the small window. The sill was free of grime.

The sky through that window was blue.

But blue skies would not save his puny butt.

She got down, examining the mirror for any trace of sludge.

No sludge

About forty thousand points, she thought, in this one small room alone.

This made her feel *much* better.

Returning to the sitting area, she saw that he had not moved except to all but empty the guacamole bowl. He had not made enough chips.

He looked at her expectantly, but she did not yet return to her seat. It surprised her that her wine glass was on empty. She topped it up.

Then they got back to the game.

It amazed her that he sprung so quickly to the chase. His question caught her with a mouthful of wine.

In the past one month how often have you seen this daughter?

Right here she should have drummed her feet six times on the floor. She should have drummed her feet, stood up, refreshened her drink, and told him to get busy working off his fifty million points.

She didn't. Later, she would wonder why. She would decide that the reason she had remained in the game was because all the questions he posed were questions she had already posed to herself — never mind that the answers ever on the tip of her tongue were not game-winning replies. Analyzing the game later, she would tell herself that at least some good had come out of it. His cleverness, astuteness, adroitness, elevated him somewhat in her mind. She had got herself believing he must be pretty dumb, even stupid, to be fifty million in the hole. A slave. Yes, he must be pretty stupid, she had come to think, and should she really be married to a stupid person?

But all that was later.

Tonight he was playing the game well. He likely would have said he was narrowing in, honing in for the kill, but in fact he was not probing any corners she had not gone herself. So she was confident she could keep her poise. She was not about to allow herself to be ambushed.

Time! he said. He had been looking at the clock.

Still the son of a bitch had not touched his drink.

She debated asking him to repeat the question. It was allowed, but at a cost of one thousand points.

She looked at the scorecard. This particular game was still very much hers.

If he did not repeat the same question *he* would lose a thousand points. She had probably made a quarter of her points through this tactic alone, because the son of a bitch never could remember his question.

She decided to risk it.

I pray thee, kind knight, to repeat the question.

That was the form the game required.

In this past month how often have you seen Christina Dolores Heiss?

She docked herself one thousand.

Twice today I saw her when I slammed the door in her face.

Hard?

Yes, hard.

You did not see her yesterday?

Not at all.

The past week?

Not at all.

Nor at any time over the past month until today when you twice slammed the door in her face?

She hesitated.

If one answered an opponent's question with a lie and the opponent could prove the answer a lie, then one lost a million points. It was thus a requirement that one have a good idea what information the opponent possessed. A week ago she had seen her daughter quite by accident in the No Frills Supermarket parking lot, her daughter carrying a bag of groceries in her arms, getting into a man's car. Did he know this? Did he know she had then seen her daughter slide across the seat and kiss the unknown man on the mouth?

She was pretty sure her daughter had not seen her.

She was damned sure she had not mentioned this sighting to Thomas James Pabst.

Your time is up. Answer, please, or default.

According to the rules she had sixty seconds to prepare her response. Normally he did not bother himself, but tonight he was watching the clock.

I wish to buy more time from the bank, she said.

One was allowed to buy up to two minutes extra time at a cost of ten thousand points per minute.

She bought one minute.

At this he let out a bark that in his mind represented laughter, then got up and went to the kitchen where he plopped an ice cube, nothing else, into his drink.

Yes, she thought, he is on the button tonight.

He came back with uncooked tortillas for the dip.

She was looking for traps. She had seen her daughter, the grocery bag, the man, the man's car. In her purse now was the car's license plate number. It had been a red car, quite ratty. The man had not been one of her daughter's old boy friends before she married. So far as she knew Thomas James Pabst had not talked to his daughter the whole of this week. You could not say they were notably close. In fact, in recent times he had not been speaking to his daughter either. Even so, there was no advantage in risking a million points. That was a lot of door knobs.

Time! he said. His mouth was full of guacamole, which was disgusting, and that he was jabbing his finger at the clock, more so.

To your question have I seen my daughter in the past stated period beyond the two episodes today when I slammed the door in her face, my answer is no.

He was instantly on his feet. A slab of guacamole flew across the room, landing on the garden window, slithering down one of his very clean panes.

Liar! he said. *Knave, I impeach thee!*

In the accepted fashion.

In the entire years that they had been playing this game, he had rarely had the opportunity to shout these lines. Whereas, she had done so frequently.

She was amazed. But she was not stunned.

She quickly lifted her right arm and yanked the invisible cord.

That meant time was out now, and that he would have to prove her lie.

She did not believe there was a chance in hell he could. So she went to the refrigerator and poured herself another glass of wine. She went into the washroom again, let the water run cold, and again splashed water over her face.

One of the little guest towels said *His*. The other, *Hers*.

The daughter they had been discussing had given these towels to them when she was eight year's old. They were the tackiest things Vivian Samantha Darling-Pabst could think of in the whole of this world.

The son of a bitch had put them out today deliberately.

She returned to the room to find him standing by the phone. He was holding it out to her.

I have on the line, he said, one Seymour Alexander Glass.

She responded crossly.

Why in God's name would I want to speak to someone I don't even know, and especially when I am deeply engaged in our game?

Mr. Glass, he said, will confirm your lie.

Then she got it. The son of a bitch knew of their daughter's affair, and had the very party on the line.

But she would not under any circumstances talk to her daughter's lover.

She signed the cross of Jesus on her chest, as was required, and three times said, *I concede my sin for the love of the Holy Realm,* as was also required.

He politely said goodbye to Mr. Glass, then docked her scoresheet a million points.

Then he of course had to sweep across the floor, gloating like a rooster. A *cock-a-doodle-doo* here, a *cock-a-doodle-doo* there.

As if the son of a bitch was still not down forty-eight million.

After this they agreed to go their separate ways for one hour, at which point they would reconvene the game.

She took a shower.

She neither knew nor cared what he did.

She lay naked on her back on the wide bed, drumming her fingers against the mattress, for a good many minutes.

Seymour Alexander Glass, she thought. So that is the name of this hotshot secret lover my daughter, until this morning, pretended did not exist.

Existed for how long? Before my daughter's separation from her husband, no doubt of that.

Christina Dolores Heiss, she told the ceiling, you are a floozy.

The man drove a junky car, did not carry the groceries, had not got out to open her daughter's door, wore rumpled clothes, and, moreover, had on his face an ugly moustache. She knew what that meant.

Bad teeth.

So not only was her daughter a floozie, but also a floozy without taste.

She then left the bed; at the dressing table, she plugged in the hair dryer, the curling iron, and ran a comb through her wet hair. She drank her wine.

And where, she asked herself, while this daughter was buying groceries and kissing this lover in his junky car, had she dumped the child?

Good question, Vivian Samantha Darling-Pabst, she told herself.

Then she left the dressing table to close the drapes because the sun was too hot, but, more importantly, because Thomas James Pabst, that son of a bitch, came by the window pushing a wheelbarrow filled with sand.

The son of a bitch had dropped his load long enough to grin and throw the little wave.

When had the son of a bitch got his sand and what did he intend doing with it were her two questions.

She then dressed and spent the final twenty minutes blow-drying her hair and making up her face.

It seemed to her that her husband's game tactic was an extremely dirty one, past all shores of forgiveness.

She caught her eyes in the mirror and said to the eyes, "Score one for the son of a bitch." She was almost smiling.

His cockiness would now be his downfall and she would win back her points with a snap of her fingers.

Before leaving the room she smeared paste over each of the doorknobs.

Give the son of a bitch, she thought, a taste of his own medicine.

Entering the game room at the precise moment required, sitting down in her game chair and yanking the invisible cord, she was surprised to find he had not yet put in an appearance.

The clock ticked around.

This was gross infringement. Each second he was late would cost him one thousand.

She refilled her wine glass from the fridge bottle and looked first at the door with its ripped screen, then out over the lawn. He wasn't to be seen. He had constructed out beneath the red maple what looked to her eyes very much like a kid's sandbox. The red wheelbarrow sat by the sandbox and in the sandpile he had stuck a child's yellow plastic shovel.

The son of a bitch had lost his mind.

Now here he came.

He was entering the house via the garage and the son of a bitch was whistling.

She looked again at the ripped screen and said to herself, Let the son of a bitch whistle when he fixes my screen.

He entered, smiling.

She had to profess it, she was astonished. He had dressed himself up in a tuxedo that she had not seen in ten years. He had splashed himself with a strange scent. He had even combed his hair, which was something he never did without her holding a pistol to his brow. The son of a bitch had even snipped from the garden a carnation for his lapel.

It occurred to her to ask, What is the occasion? She didn't. She knew he would say that he was smelling victory and the removal of himself from beneath her thumb.

He was celebrating. He might even be cocky enough to say that after this game today she would be *his* slave.

Not bloody likely. He was still down thirty years steady labor, and the clock ticking.

The son of a bitch was now popping a champagne bottle.

She had refilled her wine, tossed back a healthy swig, and filled her glass again, before she noticed more fried tortilla chips on the table, a red rose, and a bowl of black olives.

The rose was in water.

The son of a bitch had been busy.

Care for a dribble? he asked.

She said no. No, she said, I have told you a thousand times that champagne gives me the hiccups.

He filled her glass, regardless. Before she had sat down and crossed her knees, her champagne glass was empty and he was refilling.

Bottoms up, he said.

Then he took his position on the sofa, yanked the invisible cord beside his head, and the game resumed.

Be so kind, she said, as to dock yourself three-hundred thousand points for Gross Infringement.

That much? he said.

But he so docked himself.

The son of a bitch had a big smile on his face. If that smile got any bigger he would be liable for another huge docking.

Ready? he said.

Ready.

His 'ready' was mere courtesy. She would have his butt docked for Extreme Courtesy if he did it again.

You have said your daughter, Christina Dolores Heiss, twice today called and each time you slammed the door in her face; is it not true, however, that after your first slamming of the door in her face this same daughter kicked in the screen, made wilful entry into this house, and stood in face-to-face confrontation with you in this very room where we are now speaking?

Vivian Darling-Pabst heard this question through with mounting horror. The son of a bitch had done his homework and now, within seconds of the game's renewal, had her pinned again.

Christina Dolores Heiss The Floozy must have got into her hot little Pinto the minute she was kicked out of here and burned rubber getting over to the tennis courts to relate to him every little detail that had transpired between mother and daughter.

She reached for the bottle, but he was too quick. He gave a quick yank to his invisible cord, and scooped up the bottle.

Allow me, he said.

She was seething. My little rat tattle-tale daughter, she was thinking.

She searched his tuxedo for flaws, looked to see were his shoes polished, were matching cuff links in place, his bow tie acceptable. The son of a bitch had even cleaned his nails.

The only trouble she could find, she decided, was with his nasty face.

Yes, she said, flinging an arm about in a cavalier manner. Yes, it is as you say, we stood face to face in this room this morning.

And what was your daughter's purpose in insisting upon this confrontation?

My daughter Christina Dolores Heiss insisted on telling me, us, although you were not at home, having gone to your precious tennis, that she was going through with the divorce of her husband of one year, and taking up life with a different party whom she said she loved.

Loved? She employed that word?

No. 'Madly adored' were her precise words.

Kindly dock yourself five hundred smackers.

She did so.

Plus five hundred more smackers for the intended abuse behind your phrase 'precious tennis.'

She did so.

Then she said, Kindly deduct, kind sir, one thousand smackers from your score for referring to 'precious tennis' as a 'phrase' when clearly it isn't.

He did so.

He then returned to the interrogation.

Did Christina Dolores Heiss in this first confrontation not mention a child?

Vivian Darling-Pabst yanked at her invisible cord, immediately catapulted herself from the chair, shot a furious look at the clock, and plunged into the kitchen.

A game's ultimate bonus score was determined strictly by the clock. The victor received one million bonus points for each minute played. They had been playing for thirty-two minutes. If the son of a bitch soared to victory at this juncture she would be behind the eightball by thirty-two million.

In the kitchen she filled her wine glass with what it was intended to hold, slammed the bottle back into the refrigerator, and returned to her hot seat. She would not drink any more of this fiend's champagne, which only made her hiccup. The son of a bitch knew that or he would not have popped the bottle in the first place.

The carnation in his lapel, that was another of his little mockeries, like the towels and the red rose.

She yanked at the cord again, signalling renewed action. There was no way in the world the son of a bitch was going to wriggle free of his servitude.

Yes, she said, Christina Dolores Heiss mentioned a child.

In what connection did she mention this child?

The child, she at first said, was her own affair.

Yes?

— And none of my business.

Yes?

Nor anyone's business except her own and the husband she was divorcing.

Yes?

Kindly dock yourself twenty-five thousand points for stringing together three 'yes' questions in a row.

That much?

Twenty-five thousand points is the agreed-upon penalty for that infringement.

After consulting the game penalty chart he so docked himself. Then he again bore in upon her.

Did this daughter Christina Heiss not say you had made it your business?

She did.

Was this when you first slapped her face?

No, it was not when I first slapped her face.

When did she claim you had made it your business?

She claimed *we* had made it my business when —

He interrupted.

Kindly dock yourself five-hundred points, he said, for introducing an unidentifiable *we.*

You *asshole!* I will not!

Kindly dock yourself an additional one million penalty for using an Outlaw, or Strictly Forbidden, Word.

You are an asshole.

Shall we take this argument to The Bench, or will you without further adieu accept a penalty that has now reached six million five hundred?

She contemplated her wine. Then she drank her wine. Then she looked at the champagne bottle, he looked at the bottle, then filled her empty glass. Then she emptied that glass.

Her one leg, crossed over the knee, swept up and down furiously.

I pray thee, kind sir, I do, kind sir, accept thy kind offer and mark, sweet sir, that I am in thy debt for thy wondrous leniency.

All in the accepted form.

She then docked her account six million, five-hundred points.

It had been almost worth it.

At any rate she had removed his crass smile. The son of a bitch still carried a debt-load in excess of forty-two million.

He breezed back into the Interrogator's role:

When did the daughter currently known to you as Christina Dolores Heiss claim to you that you had made her child your business?

She claimed I and my life's partner Thomas James Pabst had made it *our* business dating from the earliest stages of her pregnancy when we —

Kindly dock yourself one million points.

Not without reason I won't!

The Interrogator has not asked you about the role played in this drama by Thomas James Pabst. Until the Interrogator does, any role played by Thomas James Pabst is irrelevant to the inquiry. Kindly dock yourself said figure or instigate an appeal to The Bench.

You fucker! she said.

She thought she had said this under her breath.

Apparently she had not because he was instantly on his feet, jabbing a rabid finger into her face.

I impeach thee and cry foul! he shouted. *I impeach thee and cry foul!*

The son of a bitch had just earned himself another eleven million points.

Then the son of a bitch got another question in before she could think to yank her cord.

Did this same Christina Deborah Heiss not say that you had made the child your business during the stages of her early pregnancy when you said to her that not only could you not see how she could bear to have a child by her husband but also that you failed to see how she could have consented to share his bed in the first place?

She did not dare look at him for fear she would throw the guacamole dish in his face.

So she pinned her knees together, dipped one of his chips into the guacamole, and chewed this until the clock's second hand had reached the final seconds.

Yes, she said. But —

The Interrogator has asked for no 'buts'. Kindly dock yourself one hundred.

She did so.

Was not the accusation made by this same Christina Dolores Heiss that despite your deepest desire for a first and only grandchild you urged upon her your case that the pregnancy be aborted because of your consummate hatred of the man she had married, one Roscoe K for Kelly Heiss?

That might have been her interpretation.

Her interpretation at the time?

Yes.

Did you not say *at the time,* quote, and, more specif-ically, at the time Christina Heiss announced her pregnancy in this very room, quote: 'I would sooner be shot than carry that pig's child?'

Maybe.

Maybe, or do I hear a categorical yes?

Yes.

Kindly dock yourself five hundred.

She did so.

She very much wanted to yank her Time Out cord, but she wanted a drink more, so she emptied her glass, refilled it with champagne, and emptied the glass again.

The champagne was now tepid; she wished she could hit him with a ten million point penalty for serving tepid, undrinkable, cheapskate champagne of the sort one would not wash a dish with.

Not that she had washed one since they had inaugurated these guacamole games twenty years ago.

Now, he said, to turn to matters even more into the historical, what historically have been the reasons cited by your daughter for her separation from and eventual divorcing of this said husband, Roscoe Kelly Heiss?

His redundancy was dubious. She considered issuing a *lame question* challenge. But if the challenge was decided in her favor it only meant a measly one hundred points.

Your daughter, she said, *historically* has said she did not love her estranged husband. She has said she never loved him. She has said she had only married Roscoe Kelly Heiss so she would no longer be compelled to live in this house with us.

At this, he gave the merest touch of the glass to his lips. One eyebrow went up.

He thought he was being cute.

With *us?* he said.

A goddamn bricklayer, yeah! she thought.

With *me,* goddamn you! Is that what you want to hear?

My worthy opponent will kindly dock herself five million points for the third lie deliberately told in this game, with an added ten million penalty for scurrilous language.

Son of a bitch, she thought.

And yet one more million, he said, to be docked from my honorable opponent's account for asking a question when she is not in the Interrogator's role.

The bastard had now cut her lead by two thirds.

Is it not true that today when your daughter repeated the charge that she married Roscoe Kelly Heiss only so as to enable her to quit this house did you or did you not slap her face?

It was a lie and a provocation and yes I slapped her face.

The first time?

Yes, I later slapped her face a second time.

Although after this first slap she embraced you and cried and tearfully begged you to forgive her for uttering such a falsehood in explanation of her marriage to Mr. Heiss?

The radio was playing. I did not hear the exact words of her apology.

Although you understood the nature of her behavior to be one of apology you threw the radio to the floor where it broke into a thousand pieces, you flung your arm at the broken screen door and ordered her to leave your house, did you not?

I may have done. I was not taking note of my every little decision.

He hesitated for a fraction of a second before deciding to let that reply stand.

You did not say, 'You bitch, leave my house?'

Possibly.

You are not sure?

Exactly. I am not sure.

You may have merely thought it?

The province of my thought is outside the scope of this game. Kindly dock yourself ten thousand points.

I will not dock myself ten thousand points.

She decided not to push it.

But she did say:

Kindly dock yourself one thousand points for saying I broke the radio into a thousand pieces when you could not possibly have counted those pieces.

I will not, he said. To break a thing into a thousand pieces is common phraseology, and I will not. For that matter, your request comes too late in the exchange and I must therefore ask you to dock yourself one thousand.

I will not, she said.

Then I must requisition The Bench for a decision.

So she relented and chalked up another thousand against her account.

The champagne was tepid, her glass was empty, the guacamole surface was glazed, and suddenly she had a splitting headache.

The son of a bitch now leaned not an inch away from her knees. If a single finger so much as brushed a knee she would wham him good.

Who else was witness to this scene?

No one.

Was there not a man in your driveway seated in a red car holding a baby?

If I had known a strange man sat in my driveway, holding or not holding a baby, I would have called the police.

You did not, then, go to your shattered doorway, and tell this man that if he did not come and take your daughter out of your sight you would no longer be responsible for what you said or did, and furthermore, that he was, quote, 'a deplorable piece of shit' for running around with a married woman?

She counted to ten. To twenty. She longed to buy extra minutes from the bank, to drum her feet six times, concede the game, and have this torture be over. But she would not give him the pleasure.

Instead, she drummed her feet three times, signalling repentance, while reciting in a high voice, *Oh, kindest of good knights, I have assailed thee with my lies which encamp upon the wind like a putrid odor, and I wallow unto your mercies and plead contrition from my cup that runneth over.*

That way she escaped from her lies with a penalty of a mere ten million.

Then she yanked furiously at her Time Out cord and hastened from the room.

The fucker. The game was now practically even.

*I*n the bedroom Vivian Darling-Pabst flung herself upon the mattress and lay like a corpse for thirty minutes.

After that time she removed her wet dress, her shoes, and let twenty minute's cold shower-water cascade over her head and shoulders.

Did he imagine she was finished? If he so imagined, then God help the son of a bitch.

Not a way in hell she was going to spend the rest of her life polishing his doorknobs.

There *were* extenuating circumstances. He was craftily posing questions in a form that did not allow for the exposure of extenuating circumstances. She was assuredly not faultless when it came to the present difficulties with her daughter but that bitch, and she often was a bitch, had engineered most of them.

Get her in The Guacamole Game and within five seconds she would be confessing to a thousand sins and crying, *Mama, Mama, skin of my skin and flesh of my flesh, I am a hopeless twerp, Oh pray do forgive me and allow me devoted entry into your heart!*

Six months probation kneeling by the doorknobs and possibly she might.

*V*ivian Samantha Darling-Pabst resurfaced after one hour, wearing warrior gear: barefoot, no stockings, no panties, a gun-metal wrap-around skirt that rode ten-inches above her knees, a transparent gun-metal blouse buttoned once at the waist, no brassiere, her hair piled on top of her head and a great, black hat with brim wide as a sombrero.

Around her throat a silver Mexican necklace, ornaments the size of door knobs.

Jingly earrings that reached her shoulder blades.

A bottle of nail polish called Negra Modelo.

She was going to eat the son of a bitch alive.

Whereas, he — well, where was he?

He was out in the garden, still in the tuxedo, alongside buckets of paint. He had painted the sand-box boards a vile green; he had painted in white clouds. Now he was painting yellow play-buckets onto those sides and tubby snowmen wearing black hats.

The son of a bitch had looped ropes over a tree limb, apparently meaning to make a cute baby swing.

The son of a bitch seemed blissfully unaware that this property had a co-owner.

She looked at the clock. The clock, mounted on the wall by the broken door, had been specially purchased in support of the game. Its second hand was significantly larger than its others.

The son of a bitch was already three minutes late. Five and the penalty would double.

She considered locking the doors.

She emptied the last dribbles from the wine bottle in the fridge into her glass, then uncorked another. Her headache was gone. She felt herself a new woman. She would scuttle his butt good.

Here the son of a bitch came.

She took her chair.

Pretty, he said, coming in, casting a glance over her attire. Damned sexy. Great hat.

The son of a bitch had fried up more tortillas and put them in the oven to keep warm. He put these on the table. He unwrapped the guacamole, dipped in a handful of chips, and stuffed his mouth. The son of a bitch even took the time to pass the two bowls to her.

She munched. Drank.

She saw his start of surprise as he looked her in the face. She had globbed a gallon of mascara around her eyes, so much that when she blinked she felt the weight. She had painted her lips scarlet. The wide black hat brim bumped something every time her head moved.

Unless he had done so on the sly, he had yet to look at the clock.

Then he replenished the olive bowl, poured himself champagne which now reposed in a bucket of ice.

He sat down, pulled his invisible cord. Six minutes late. Without a word to her he docked his account 720,000 points.

This rattled her.

Is it true or false, he said, that one month ago in consequence of a serious rupture between you and this daughter, you vowed never again to speak to her?

True.

Or allow her entry into this house?

The son of a bitch was waiting for her *'but'*. She bit her tongue and held it back.

True.

But today she twice gained entry, once by breaking down that screen door which now hangs by the one hinge, resulting in her slapped face, and returning in one hour in the company of what two parties?

Roscoe Kelly Dickhead Heiss and her baby.

Kindly deduct —

She deducted one thousand from her account for use of the word Dickhead.

The name, please, of this baby.

Vivie.

'Vivie' will not suffice. Answer fully or dock yourself.

Vivian Grace Heiss.

Taking her name in part from one Vivian Samantha Darling-Pabst?

True.

The age, please of Vivian Grace 'Vivie' Heiss?

Three months, some days, and a few hours.

Occupation?

Was she going to let him get away with this?

Baby, she said.

He took the time to pull his cord and laugh. Then, just as she was herself about to laugh — at her own wit, not his — he pulled the cord again, returning them to the game.

God, she thought, you are insufferable.

She emptied her glass; he refilled it with champagne.

She leaned back in her chair, splaying her knees wide. Let the son of a bitch, she thought, think a while on *that*.

Once, they had played the guacamole game in the nude. It had not been a good idea.

A minute passed. He had not asked the required question.

She uncapped the Negra Modelo and began painting her toenails, propping a foot onto the table edge.

Another minute passed.

The son of a bitch just sat there, looking from her toenails to her legs, to her breasts, to her face, then starting all over again. His lips tight, nodding his head.

The son of a bitch apparently intended to let her paint an entire foot. Or both of them.

She gave a quick shiver to her torso, unable to resist a smile: the son of a bitch jumped.

Still he sat there. It hadn't even occurred to him to yank his Time Out cord. Five minutes had now passed.

It was not until she paused in her nail-polishing to empty her drink and signal for another, that he stood, yanked his cord, and said, Am I going to have to take you to The Bench on the issue of Player Comportment or will you kindly desist?

She yanked her cord. They were now both in Time Out positions.

The Bench, she said, has consistently displayed a tolerant attitude on matters of non-verbal Player Comportment.

She extended her leg. He blew upon her Negra Modelo toes. She had to refill her own glass.

True, he said. But The Bench *is* intolerant of activities which undermine the respect and dignity of its chambers.

She fluttered an airy hand. Then take me before The Bench. Or kindly dock yourself 720,000 points for Interrogative Malfeasance, plus five million for Obstruction of Game.

He sat back down. You are not going to win, he said. I am going to pin you to the wall.

She laughed. Not in this lifetime, she said.

He docked himself the points and they resumed the game.

I now return, he said, to the other party present at your second confrontation today with your daughter Christina Dolores Heiss, the aforesaid Roscoe Kelly Heiss, who made what appeal to you?

The prick going by that name asked me again to forgive him.

He asked forgiveness for what action?

The prick asked me to forgive him for sticking his tongue in my ear at a party in this house three months and twenty-eight days ago. The stupid prick said —

Kindly dock yourself thirty thousand for use of the words *prick* and *stupid prick,* which are appellations not established outside the view of you and your daughter, together with an additional penalty for employing the phrase *going by that name,* since no one disputes Roscoe K. Heiss is his legal name.

I do thee challenge, she said in the accepted mode, inasmuch as you have yourself referred to him as a prick on numerous occasions.

I do thee challenge your challenge, he said, inasmuch as my defining him as a prick was done in common discourse outside the realm of this competition, which discourse in no way, shape, or form establishes he is a legitimate prick.

I do thee, stalwart foe, counter-challenge your counter-challenge out of the commonly-accepted view that as all men have pricks they might be so described as being pricks.

They were then obliged to pull their invisible cords, thus to momentarily withdraw from the heat of battle while they carried their arguments to The Bench. Arguments weighed by The Bench required considerable integrity on the part of the opponents. Otherwise, the game sank into chaos.

He argued before The Bench that the only honorable decision The Bench could render was one based on that definition of prick which existed in any standard dictionary.

She argued that the very fault with her opponent's argument was in calling for a "standard" dictionary, since The Bench obviously must be aware that the parlance of the word prick throughout prevailing contemporary society was one in transition, and it clearly was a duty of The Bench to bring vision to its decision making; and that, furthermore, evidence could be brought to bear that would strongly bear out the contention before the floor that Mr. Heiss was in fact widely regarded in his local community as an outstanding example of a prick.

The Bench called for a one-minute recess.

It urged the parties to work out between themselves a compromise.

They decided to withdraw their challenges and counter-challenges.

However, she was still levied a quarter million penalty for initiating a challenge that had consumed so much of The Bench's time, without winning any validation.

They returned to the fray.

We have, one, he said, the uncontested fact that on or about three months and twenty-eight days ago at a party in this house to celebrate the pending birth of Vivian Darling-Pabst's first grandchild Roscoe Kelly Heiss did stick his tongue in the latter's ear.

Ear! He was all over my face!

Interruption noted. Two, we have the uncontested fact that the aforesaid Heiss has abjectly and repeatedly apologized for this —

It is not a fact, she said. I do contest it.

For this act, offering the simple explanation that —

I do not for one minute accept his stupid explanation! It is an insult to my intelligence.

— explanation that the act took place in a darkened pantry, that it was a case of mistaken identity, that —

Fuck him! Fuck you too.

— that inasmuch as the daughter and mother were wearing identical perfumes, that inasmuch as they are of nearly identical appearance, that he, Roscoe K. Heiss —

That stupid Roscoe Heiss, she said, put his *tongue in my ear*, licked all over my face, and I don't care what the son of a bitch says, this was not a case of mistaken fucking identity. I am twenty years older, she was nine months pregnant, and if you or anyone else think it was mistaken identity, then I want a goddamn divorce!

Her hat had fallen into the guacamole. She had spilled her drink onto the floor. She was up on her toes, shoving the table back, waving the champagne bottle.

Did he not speak your daughter's name? Was Roscoe K. Heiss not saying in that dark pantry, 'Darling, please don't divorce me? Darling Christina, please give me another chance!'

How do I know what the prick was saying? He had his tongue in my ear! He was licking my face!

She yelled this at him, swinging the bottle, chips sailing across the room.

He was ticking off her penalties: one million for the first interruption, double that for the second, then tripling, quadrupling — a total penalty of sixty-three million for the interruptions alone. Plus a million each for the five Strictly Forbidden words, and a whopping twenty million, the game's single largest penalty, for bringing into the game proceedings any mention of divorce.

In one swoop she had dropped eighty-eight million points.

She yanked her cord, swatted at his head, and stomped away from the field of battle.

Where in god's name, she heard him ask, did you get those trashy clothes?

They were left here, she said, by your floozy daughter.

Smoldering. The very idea! That all this while the son of a bitch had been *siding* with that womanizing prick Roscoe Heiss. That he *accepted* the puny, insulting, wildly improbable excuse of that prick.

A divorce? Damn right, she wanted a divorce.

All her equity, gone like that! A life-time of polishing door knobs! Well, Jesus Christ!

In the long tub she closed her eyes, felt the mercy of bubbles, the warm spin of water, the scented oils. Her drink, straight gin now, goddammit. She plugged her head with the Sony earphones. Drown me in Wagner, she thought. His outrage, Wagner's, the one being ever on the planet whose fire, wrath, venom matched her own.

The trouble with the game was that too much advantage lay with the Interrogator.

When matters were tranquil again she would propose that the rules be revised so that one could buy the Interrogator's role for, say, five million.

It might be that he would accept an impromptu, one-time-only alteration in the present game.

He was the world's biggest fool, and might go for it. For as little, say, as one million.

Then cream his butt.

Something had got into the son of a bitch. He was playing for keeps today.

Normally he was a softie.

If he had not been such a softie they would not have produced such wilful, stubbornly opinionated, obstructionist daughters.

The son of a bitch had not even yet got around to the *other* one.

But the *other* one was strictly in her corner. The other one was steadfastly loyal to Mom, *whatever* the issue. Mom was pretty sure of that.

Whereas Christina since a child had let herself be her father's doormat.

If he brought in the other one, she would murder his butt.

In any case, she would annihilate him once it came her turn to be the Interrogator. No mercy. She would strip him of his very skin, nail his bare ass to the lamppost. Long had she been too easy on him, allowing him to wriggle out of this and that exchange out of pity for a fellow human being whom the fates had deprived of the virtues. Like intelligence, diligent application, focus.

Nail his butt for a trillion, a zillion. Never mind neither would live that long.

It can be my legacy to Vivie, she thought.

With these deliberations concluded, she pitched in more oils, revved up the whirlpool, propped her feet against the tub rim — sank up to her nose.

In the meantime, sap the rage, honey. Regroup.

Wagner, she thought.

So absolutely fucking appropriate.

What was the son of a bitch doing now?

Later, looking to find where she had deposited the gin bottle, spotting him prancing across the lawn like a witless schoolboy, she asked herself that. There he went in his fancy tuxedo, carrying the red tool box, a roll of new screen wire.

Christina had given him that toolbox two Christmases ago, before Roscoe K. Heiss had come along. Inside the tool box had been one red brick. That brick, Daddy, she had said, can be the first brick laid when you build me my first house. It had been cute, then. Everyone palsy-walsy.

She had *heard* Roscoe Heiss mouthing Christina's name, but this was *after* he had stuck his tongue into her ear. Somehow *that* had made it worse; it was a life-saving act that she had been in the pantry because Christina was a softie like her father and if Christina had been in there she would have melted on the spot and very likely still be with the prick. The new thing in Cristina's life might drive a junkie car, wear rumpled clothing, sport a silly moustache and be in fact a deplorable piece of shit but *anyone* on god's earth was an improvement over Roscoe K. Heiss whose sole goal in life, insofar as she could tell, was to drive a red T-Bird and screw every woman alive.

Mary Heiss his mother for godsake was an unpardonable crime against nature, as were all the Heiss's.

Now here came the son of a bitch across her lawn again, this time transporting a wheelbarrow load of ready-mix cement, shovel riding the top. Did the son of a bitch have in mind digging a kid's wading pool? So it appeared, because there he was in front of the window with an idiot smile, blowing kisses, pantomiming digging, pantomiming swimming strokes — exhibiting his last hold on sanity.

She flung the curtains shut.

He had always been a crazy son of a bitch; now he was surely certifiable.

Before she sighted him she had spread out over the bed all of Christina's baby pictures. She had been there in the bed's middle, weeping over every one of them, including those so washed out no one any longer was identifiable.

He was sitting back on the sofa now, legs crossed, his arms spread out on the sofa's back, admiring his door when she came in.

The door had been restored, the tools put away.

A hole had been dug close by the maple tree. Perhaps the hole was not intended for a pool. Perhaps he meant burying someone there.

He had taken off his tuxedo coat. He is wearing the wide red suspenders that their other daughter gave him on his last birthday. She had also given him red socks, but today he is not wearing the red socks.

"You look stunning," he said.

She was in fact dressed to the nines. Spiked heels, panty-hose, black strapless evening gown, hair twisted to the side and held there by three silver combs. Lipstick, cheek-enhancements, thin silver necklace, earrings resembling minnows.

It could be that the son of a bitch was going to propose taking her out to dinner.

If so, he might have mentioned it before she consumed a pound of guacamole.

The trouble in that regard was that the son of a bitch could consume ten pounds and because he was a tennis star when not hefting heavy bricks in his new role as one with the people he could eat ten pounds of guacamole with an entire suckling pig as chaser, and still not gain an ounce.

She splashed ice, a drop of tonic into her gin. She looked at the clock. One minute to go until the final round.

She sat in her chair, her knees together.

She looked at his red suspenders.

She sipped gin. He poured his champagne glass full.

Stunning, you said? Thank you. She swept out her arms in a magnanimous gesture.

Okay, you son of a bitch, she said, read out the score.

His face took on a pained expression. You have accumulated a penalty of one hundred and thirty two million and change. I have penalties of six million and change. Deducting my previous debt, you are left with a debt-load of just under seventy-six million.

She shifted her eyes to the repaired door.

Yes, he said, the door. I have added one thousand points to your total, for the door. I hope you do not feel that figure extravagant.

She tapped a foot.

I wish to buy the Interrogative roll, she said. I am prepared to offer one million.

He gaped. Then he snapped his red suspenders. Then he laughed.

One million? he said. I would not sell it for fifty million.

She looked hard at him, then said, If you think I am sleeping in the bed with you tonight you have lost your mind.

She yanked her invisible cord; a moment later he yanked his. The game resumed.

True or false, he said. Your daughter Christina Dolores Heiss does not nurse her baby?

His opening gambit surprised her. But she knew where the son of a bitch was going with it.

True.

And has, aside from three brief days following delivery, never nursed this child?

True.

Are you or are you not an ardent believer in the breast-feeding practice?

I nursed mine, if that's what you mean.

Answer the question.

Yes. Although 'ardent' is hardly —

You viewed your daughter's statement that she was incapable of continued nursing of her new-born infant as an outright corruption of the truth, did you not?

I may have said something like that.

'May have' or did?

Yes. All right, I did.

Never once considering that this was outright interference to which your daughter might object?

Surely I had a right to express a concern about my only grandchild's welfare?

But she objected to your interference, did she not?

Yes.

Which introduced another rupture in your relationship, did it not?

Yes.

And when that daughter said to you that nursing was painful to her, that she produced insufficient milk to nourish the child, you continued to wage your campaign, yes or no?

It might be stated that way.

Yes or no, or kindly dock yourself.

Yes.

Did you not say to her that if she had not filled her mouth with candy bars, with junk foods, she might have been in a position to lactate properly?

I did not.

This is a caution. You did not?

No. I told her a tofu diet, which was the diet she followed during her pregnancy, was the fault.

Which she took as yet another indication of your unending criticism of her life-style, yes or no?

You try carrying a baby to term while feeding her nothing but tofu!

I beg your pardon?

Withdrawn, oh kind sir, I appeal to thy Lordship's wondrous mercy and do withdraw the heinous statement.

Not quite the prescribed form but close enough.

Tofu or otherwise, he said, did or did not your daughter give birth to a healthy nine-pound eight-ounce infant?

Yes.

And bottle-fed or otherwise is not this child today a beautiful child enjoying the best of health?

Yes.

Yet you have continued to harp upon this issue of breast-feeding and did so again today when your daughter twice called at this house, yes or no?

The child was hungry. Your daughter was at my stove warming a bottle in my skillet and I very innocently reminded her how easy it was to open a blouse.

Yes or no, or default on the question.

Yes.

Even with your daughter's doctor's repeated assurances that your daughter can *not* breast-feed due to any number of complications, you have so harped, yes or no?

Ding Yi Foo is an *herbal* doctor. He makes her eat *bark!*

But he is her doctor. Kindly dock yourself ten thousand.

She did so.

She wiped a hand across her brow. She was soaking wet. The wetness was on her brow and on her neck and under her arms she could feel herself dripping.

While at the same time today making the accusation that she refused to suckle her baby out of fear that it would diminish her beauty and lessen her appeal to the, quote, 'deplorable piece of shit waiting for you out in his junkie car,' yes or no?

I have no memory of speaking such words.

No memory?

None.

Did your daughter at any point say to you, quote, 'Mom, would you like to hold the baby?'

Yes.

Did you hold the baby?

Yes.

Did you then bottle-feed the baby?

Yes.

Did you rock the baby?

Yes.

Did you sing to the baby?

Yes.

Did your daughter sing to the baby?

Yes.

The baby then fell asleep?

Yes.

Did you and your daughter then hug and kiss?

Yes.

Did you not vow eternal love?

Yes.

So we had here a moment that might be defined as one of quiet reconciliation?

Yes.